Get Real, Chloe Torres

CRYSTAL MALDONADO

HOLIDAY HOUSE · NEW YORK

To my fellow fangirls,
who love with their whole heart

• ❋ •

Copyright © 2025 by Crystal Maldonado
All Rights Reserved
HOLIDAY HOUSE is registered in the U.S. Patent and Trademark Office.
Printed and bound in March 2025 at Sheridan, Chelsea, MI, USA.
www.holidayhouse.com
First Edition
1 3 5 7 9 10 8 6 4 2

Library of Congress Cataloging-in-Publication Data is available.

ISBN: 978-0-8234-5237-8 (hardcover)

EU Authorized Representative: HackettFlynn Ltd.,
36 Cloch Choirneal, Balrothery, Co.
Dublin, K32 C942, Ireland.
EU@walkerpublishinggroup.com

Chapter One

I have had a lot of humiliating things happen to me in my almost eighteen years on this planet.

When I was eight, my dad insisted on holding my hand as he walked me into class on my first day of third grade. For the entire year, everyone called me Baby Chloe.

In middle school, I literally fainted when my teacher pulled out the frogs we were supposed to dissect in class. Legend has it I even hit my head on a stool on the way to the floor. Cool.

And once (. . . recently) I went into a beauty store with my cousin-bestie, Diego, and thought the foam bubble bath sampler they had was edible, so I fully *took a bite* in front of the sales associate.

But there has yet to be humiliation like the type I'm suffering from today.

Because today, on this humid summer day, I am sweating buckets in a wig and poofy, plum-colored ball gown.

I am dressed as a fairy-tale princess.

In front of my longtime crush.

And her entire family. As they celebrate her little cousin's birthday.

Wepa!

It's the exact opposite of how I wanted to spend the weekend before my *own* birthday.

To be fair, I'm getting paid to be here—I've been working for the last year at If the Shoe Fits, a company that sends princesses to birthday parties and corporate retreats—but that doesn't tame the mortification I feel. Not even a little.

When I arrived and realized whose house it was, I briefly considered running, heels and all. That would clearly be less awkward than reuniting with Sienna and the entire Aguilar family as the hired help, right? I could call my boss and tell her I came down with food poisoning and I had to bail, and then—

"Chloe?"

Sienna's voice instantly froze my racing thoughts.

It was as light and kind as I remembered, even though we hadn't spoken since the summer before freshman year. Her green eyes gazed at me from underneath ginger curtain bangs, and I was sent right back to the swoony girl I was in middle school.

Back then, it was me and Sienna and Ramona, and we were *inseparable*.

A perpetual late bloomer, I admittedly didn't have many friends when I started at Elmwood Middle School. Thankfully, Ramona and I were seated next to each other in homeroom. I was instantly taken with how cool and mature she seemed, in her head-to-toe black clothes and dark purple lipstick. She had the kind of corkscrew curls that would make any girl jealous—especially me, who tended to have frizzy waves more than anything else. To outsiders, she might have looked intimidating, and she absolutely was. But when I spotted an Intonation sticker on her notebook, almost hidden among the sea of other band and political stickers, I knew I had an in.

Even though cheesy pop bands didn't *seem* like the kind of thing Ramona would love, she was drawn to any act of rebellion. Liking something mainstream as a girl who was anything but was the best kind of contradiction to her. We became fast friends, even though we weren't that alike. Though we both enjoyed art and Intonation, if I was a bright, sunny day, she was a storm cloud. Yet we worked. I loved annoying her with my positivity, and she loved rolling her eyes at me. We bonded quickly over only having one parent, too—I had my dad, she had her mom.

It wasn't long before we added Sienna into the mix. Middle-school Sienna was all long, lanky limbs and bright red hair, and she had what some might call an *overt* obsession with Intonation. As in, she couldn't talk about much else except the band. She even showed up to school one day in an Intonation shirt. When someone made fun of her, Ramona swooped in and claimed Sienna as ours, and that was that.

Intonation provided the much-needed gateway for the three of us to form real, legitimate bonds. In between our obsession with the band, we had sleepovers and manicures, makeovers and movie nights. We even daydreamed about having our own girl group—who would someday open for Intonation on tour, *obviously*—called Deadly Flora. My girl-group alter ego was called Oleander, Sienna was Hydrangea, and Ramona was Nightshade—and yes, we had choreographed dance moves and a couple of our own songs. It was silly and it was the best.

My dad would jokingly call us La Tripleta (after the Puerto Rican twist on a Cubano sandwich) because he felt like we were three parts of a whole. Sometimes it really felt that way. Where there was one of us, there were the other two. We embraced it, sharing everything from lipsticks to secrets to crushes.

It just so happened that my crush was Sienna.

I still remember the moment my heart decided all it wanted was to be hers. We went on a field trip to the local science museum, and, in the gift shop, Sienna discovered a single teddy bear among the sea of plushies whose ears had been sewn on backward. She felt so sorry for it that she bought it and promised to give it a good home forever—even though some of our classmates snickered seeing her, at twelve, carrying a bear onto the bus.

I, however, was totally smitten. How could I not be, when she was so openhearted and secure in herself? And when the freckles on her nose were so adorable?

I started thinking of Sienna as this perfect being I was lucky to be near, which I know now is probably not very healthy. But I couldn't help it. I wanted to be with her, yes, but I wanted to be *close* to her more, so I kept my crush to myself and leaned into the pining, telling myself I was okay just being friends.

And I was. Because Sienna and Ramona were my *best friends*. They showed me the magic of girl friendships and all the unfettered joy that came with them. Sure, we fought, but mostly over little things. Our biggest fights came only when it felt like two of us were leaving the other one out.

Our trio was everything to me. We were three girls who navigated the world together and could talk as seriously about periods and zits as hypotheticals like *What if Intonation showed up at the school dance to perform and instantly fell in love with us?*

I still don't think there's anything more powerful than girl friendships. Ours meant the world to me, which is probably why I felt like I was mourning a death when it suddenly ended.

I hadn't seen it coming. Sienna dropped the bomb one afternoon that she wouldn't be joining Ramona and me at Elmwood High. Instead, her parents had enrolled her at an academically elite private charter school on the other side of town. She said she needed to focus on fitting in and studying, and it felt like her way of saying goodbye.

It was devastating news that I could barely handle.

Ramona and I stopped talking to Sienna—which felt shamefully easy without school to bring us together each day—and the two of us grew closer.

Suddenly I could see what I hadn't before. While I'd been crushing on Sienna, Ramona had developed feelings for *me*. And that felt good, especially after Sienna had chosen another school over us—over me.

Then, well...I don't know. I started realizing how much Ramona really liked me. I freaked out, and I ghosted her, which made everything so much worse.

The final nail in the coffin came with the announcement that Intonation had broken up.

By then, the summer was over, all three of us had stopped speaking, and our yearslong friendship felt like little more than a memory—a meteor that burned bright before disappearing into the sky.

I never expected that four years later I'd be standing in front of Sienna again.

Yet the Sienna who answered the door didn't look so different from the Sienna I knew. Same freckle under her right eye. Same pouty lips, which she'd always dramatically stick out when she wanted us to give in to some demand. Same dangly earrings she'd declared her "signature" back in eighth grade. Same clear sense of style, a mix of boho and casual that meant gauzy dresses and flowy midi skirts.

But her red hair was more strawberry blond, pulled back into a messy ponytail with wispy bangs perfectly framing her heart-shaped face. Her lips were coated in a shimmery lip gloss that meant I was instantly and definitely staring at her mouth. She was beautiful. My heartbeat quickened, as if that old crush of mine wasn't gone so much as lying in wait. "Chloe?" she repeated.

"Sienna, I think you mean *Princess Julieta,*" a voice said gently, coaxing me out of the reverie I'd slipped into. I looked over and saw the birthday girl's mom eyeing me in a way that begged, *Please please please don't ruin this magic for my kid!*

I plastered on the bright smile I've perfected over my months portraying Princess Julieta—a copyright-free princess who smiles serenely and chirps when she talks—and crouched down so I was eye level with the small girl who materialized in front of me.

"Hi! I'm Princess Julieta, and I'm so happy to be here today to celebrate your birthday, Ana!" I chirrup, ignoring the fact that merely *seeing* Sienna has shoved my heart up into my throat. "I hear you're turning five years old."

Ana looks up at me with big eyes, awestruck. And that helps bring me firmly back to reality. *I'm not here to ogle a former friend; I'm here to make a little girl's dream come true.*

That's what I really love about being part of If the Shoe Fits—helping

5

little girls feel like magic is real, even if it's only for an afternoon. It's also not lost on me that If the Shoe Fits lets a fat girl like me portray princesses for these babies, who, I think, benefit from seeing bodies of all sizes being celebrated. That means a lot.

I reach into the sparkly handbag Princess Julieta carries with her (mostly so I can store party favors and emergency ChapStick), and pull out a plastic tiara decorated in rhinestones. I hold it out to Ana with a smile. "This is for you."

Glee overtakes her entire face, and she lets out a delighted squeal, and I think, *Maybe I can make it through this party.*

Even if that means humiliating myself in front of my first love.

Chapter Two

After leading the birthday girl and her friends through an enthusiastic sing-along of royalty-free princess songs because If the Shoe Fits is *not* looking to get sued, answering incessant questions about what it's like to be a princess, posing for photos, and lots and lots of dancing with Ana, I'm spent.

Thankfully, Ana's mom announces it's time for food and presents—my usual cue to split. I make a big show of saying goodbye to the guests, paying special attention to Ana, before making a break for it.

As I reach for the doorknob, a voice from behind me asks, "Chloe Torres? Leaving before cake?" I recognize Sienna's playful tone before I even turn. She's smiling when I do, so I smile back. "The Chloe I knew would *never*."

"It's just that we're technically not supposed to accept food," I say with an apologetic shrug. "But I promise: under normal circumstances, I let my sweet tooth dictate my every move."

At this, Sienna lets out a laugh, and my shoulders instantly relax. It feels better than I imagined to hear that sound after so long.

"Your sweet tooth sounds a little bossy," Sienna observes, and then I laugh too.

"You should see her around a pint of Ben & Jerry's."

She gives me an amused look. "If you really think you shouldn't stick around, that's cool, but I promise no one will ever know you snuck a piece. The party's in the dining room, but the cake's in the kitchen. It's chocolate!"

I arch an eyebrow at her. "With chocolate frosting?"

She motions toward the kitchen. "Come see."

And then I'm following her—this girl who used to be one of my best friends, this girl who took up so much space in my heart, this girl I yearned for—through her aunt and uncle's house, as if no time has passed, as if I'm not dressed up like a knockoff fairy-tale princess, as if this is all totally and completely normal.

I find myself nervously toying with one of the gems on my sparkly bag, and from behind Sienna, I ask, "Are you *sure* no one will mind?" Sienna whips around unexpectedly and I nearly crash right into her. "Oh! Sorry."

"No worries. And I *promise* my aunt Sonia won't care. There's enough to feed an army, yet you saw yourself—there are only six kids here!" She shakes her head, her dangly gold earrings clinking as she does. "She bought this super-fancy cake decorated with fondant and characters and whatever, so that's what she'll bring out to Ana when it's time for candles. But she got an entire sheet cake too, with just, like, regular frosting. *That's* the one for eating."

"Supersmart. Most of the parties I go to opt for the fancy picture-perfect cakes covered in fondant, and then they choke them down, even though *nobody* likes fondant."

Sienna wrinkles her—tiny, perfect—nose. "Totally. And the place where she got the sheet cake is amazing. It's this little bakery I'm obsessed with. I swear, one bite of their double chocolate will change your life."

My stomach growls at the mere thought, and I glance down sheepishly. "Guess I am a little hungry."

Trailing after her, I find myself in a kitchen outfitted with kitschy pastel-colored appliances and a black-and-white tiled floor. On the island are more than a dozen princess-themed plates, which each hold a plastic fork and a decadent-looking slice of chocolate cake covered in what looks like a rich ganache.

Sienna swipes two servings and hands one to me.

Unsure of what else to do, I hold up my plate to hers. "Cheers?"

She giggles and pretends to clink her plate against mine.

I take a bite. Instantly, my mouth bursts with rich flavor from the most divine double chocolate cake I've ever tasted.

"Holy shit, this is so good," I murmur.

Sienna's eyes go big. "Right?! I told you: Life. Changing."

She's not wrong. Or maybe I'm just really hungry. Either way, the dessert is a sliver of heaven, and I'm going to savor it because clearly I am hallucinating that I'm in Sienna Aguilar's aunt's house enjoying cake right now. Maybe I passed out in the summer heat? That'd be very on-brand for me.

Suddenly, the two of us are standing and munching in silence.

My gaze darts around the room, desperate for something— anything—to reignite the conversation.

"Is that a philodendron Birkin?" I ask, pointing my fork toward the leafy, pin-striped plant on the windowsill. Sienna glances at it, but by the way her brows furrow, I can tell she has no idea what I'm talking about. "The plant."

"Oh, um. Maybe?" She gives me an apologetic shrug. "I'm not sure. I don't know much about plants."

"I've recently become obsessed with this idea that I should become one of those cottagecore bisexuals who is really good with growing things, you know? I don't know why. I've barely been able to keep a pet rock alive, let alone anything green. Still, my ADHD pushed me down a total rabbit hole one day, and I found myself researching all kinds of plants, and I got really stuck on knowing everything about window plants—well, actually, the philodendron Birkin technically doesn't do well in direct sunlight, which I learned the hard way when I put mine in my window and singed all its leaves off—but I found myself thinking I could *totally* have a green thumb despite having zero evidence of..." My voice starts to trail as I realize that Sienna's squinting at me and smiling in a way that I can only describe as pained. I clear my throat. "But, um, anyway...cool plant is all I meant."

God, Chloe. Cool plant? Can you be normal for, like, a second?

"Yeah, for sure." Sienna nods and puts her plate down, having only taken a bite or two. "It's definitely a cool plant."

My cheeks flush, and suddenly the room feels small and my wig feels itchy and I don't want cake anymore.

I clear my throat, gently setting my plate beside hers. "Well, I really should get going."

Sienna blinks at me, once, twice, then offers a lopsided smile. "Oh. Okay."

"Thanks for the cake." I dig into my bag and search for my keys, holding them up triumphantly once I find them. "Good seeing you."

"Let me walk you out," Sienna offers.

"Thanks, but I got it!" I say, marching down the hall and quickly realizing I absolutely don't got it. Did this house triple in size in the last five minutes?

"It's a left, Chloe!"

I turn on my heel and march confidently in the other direction. "I was just testing you!" I call, and then I rush out the front door and sprint to the safety of my car.

Chapter Three

"*I'm sorry, but you went* on a tangent to your cute former bestie-slash-unrequited love about…plants?" My cousin Diego wrinkles his nose in disgust. "Why didn't you just tell Sienna you're planning on remaining single for eternity and call it a day?"

Normally, I love Diego's flair for the dramatic, but right now, I kind of want to strangle him. Because after filling him in on my embarrassing run-in with Sienna, I could use a little support that I *didn't* ruin absolutely everything after I went and did that thing where I can't stop talking.

Sometimes my brain seems to have a mind of its own. Even though I talk fast, like lightning, I swear it's only a fraction of how quickly the thoughts are pinging around my head. I spent my life wondering why I had days where I couldn't focus on a single thought, while on others I'd throw my whole heart and soul so deeply into an art project that I'd forget basic functions, like eating and sleeping. Until my therapist gently suggested I might have ADHD.

Which, duh.

Once I got the diagnosis, suddenly everything made sense.

I had a *reason* for why my spatial awareness was complete trash and I constantly had bruises blooming on random parts of my body. I *knew* why my room was a cluttered graveyard of all the discarded supplies I'd needed for hobbies, projects, and genius new ideas I'd been convinced were going to be my life's passion. All the random sticky notes I plastered everywhere finally had meaning, and I could now explain to my dad why I often wrote notes to myself directly on my hand like my own washable tattoos. It made sense why I would perpetually lose my keys or have five half-emptied cups in my room and on my desk and maybe even under my bed, somehow, at any given moment; why I'm terrible at following directions; why my short-term memory is mostly shot.

Some people call ADHD a superpower, and I do get that. I can crush a watercolor painting or write a ten-page essay over the span of several hours if I commit hard enough. I can juggle roughly a bajillion tasks at once. I have lots of talents, because I take on and commit to so many interests, even if it's only for a small blip of time.

But also: my brain regularly feels like it's full of bees.

So you can understand how, in a fit of nerves, I might blurt out some random facts about windowsill plants.

"I panicked! Our conversation had died and the plant was the first thing I saw and I got excited because it was something I could actually talk about and…I don't know! It felt like a safe topic," I say defensively. "What would *you* have talked about with her?"

Diego rolls onto his stomach on my bed and looks up at me, batting his long eyelashes. "If I unexpectedly found myself in the same room as a former crush, and I was dressed up like a sad, off-brand princess—"

"Hey!"

"Then I would embrace it for all it's worth. I would've been like, *Oh, hey, Sienna. Can I take you for a ride on my horse and carriage?*"

I make a face. "That was pathetic."

"I'm just warming up!" Diego says defensively. "Okay, okay. How about: *I'll show you my palace if you show me yours.*"

"Diego!"

"Or! *How about you and I get out of here and make sure this fairy tale has a happy ending?*" He wiggles his eyebrows up and down for dramatic effect. I reach for a pillow and throw it at him, hard. "Ow!"

"*Gross.*"

Diego sits up in my bed, nestling the pillow I threw at him in his lap. "Why were you so tongue-tied around her anyway? It's not like you care what she thinks anymore. You're over that. Been over that." When I don't say anything right away, Diego leans toward me. "You *are* over that, aren't you?"

"I mean...I think so?"

"Chloe Marie Torres! It has been literal years!"

"And I was over her—I was!" I insist. Then I sigh. "But seeing her again maybe dredged up some old feelings? She's so pretty."

"And somehow *I'm* pathetic? Right."

"Oh, whatever. At least I made two hundred dollars for the party. What did *you* do today?"

Diego crosses his arms. "*I* was busy planning *your* weekend. You're welcome, brat."

I make a kissy face at him. "Love you, boo-boo."

This back-and-forth makes up a big part of my relationship with Diego. Not only did we grow up together, but something about us just *clicks*, as both cousins and best friends. I love his huge personality, quick wit, and vibrancy. He lights up every room he's in and commands everyone's attention without even trying.

Just one year older than me, Diego is *constantly* reminding me of how much wiser and more mature he is. Yet he gets me in a way few others don't. After Mami left when I was only four, his family took me and Papi in and made sure we didn't get swept under by our grief. Now I consider Tío Gabriel and Titi Rosa and their kids—their oldest, Yarielis, who's off at college; Diego, on a gap year; and his two younger siblings, Ricky and Naya, who are eight and six—partly mine. I'd like to think they feel the same.

Diego was there when I had to be sent to therapy after Mami, when I broke my arm in the fourth grade, when my friendship with Sienna and Ramona shattered to pieces. And he has been there for all the really fun moments too: when I became obsessed with Intonation ("Your taste is literal trash," he told me), when I got my driver's license ("Finally, I get a chauffeur"), when I had pieces in my first art show ("Why aren't you charging one million dollars per piece, stupid?"), when I got accepted into RISD ("I knew some poor college would feel bad enough to accept you").

I would do anything for him, and I know the feeling is mutual.

Picking up the thread of our conversation, Diego says, "So, here's what I ended up planning. Tomorrow, we get up, get ready, and I'll drive us to Boston so you can go absolutely batshit over that exhibit you won't stop talking about."

"*Chromatic*?! Oh my gosh, you're going to love it! It's this immersive exhibit that looks like you're stepping into a kaleidoscope and—"

Diego holds up his hand to stop me. "You're spoiling my reveal."

"Okay, fine, I get it. Please continue."

"Thank you. From there, we hit up the Isabella Stewart Gardner Museum, the Museum of Fine Arts, and finally the Harvard Art Museums, where I can hopefully make out with a rich professor. I've basically plotted out a bar hop for you except it's with art museums because you're such a huge nerd. You're welcome."

I'm so excited I let out a little squeal. "I can't believe you planned the whole day for me. It's like you enjoy me as a human?"

Diego looks offended. "Don't be disgusting. Now, can we focus here? We're supposed to be getting ready."

"We can't start getting ready until after my dad leaves," I remind him. "Unless you're ready to introduce him to your alter ego?"

Diego and I have evening plans at Speakeasy, the café-slash-queer-space-of-choice in the next town over. He tells his parents he's using this time between high school and college to figure out what he really wants to do in life. They insist that's not enough and that he cannot, under any circumstances, "just sit around all day memorizing TikTok dances," so he also works at the family restaurant, El Chinchorro Boricua.

At night, though, Diego has started quietly experimenting with drag. Though our bodies aren't at all similar—Diego is tall and slim, while I'm short and fat—I have an eclectic collection of over-the-top, quirky jewelry, vibrant lipsticks, and eye shadows the colors of gemstones, all of which Diego has borrowed hungrily. He's even performed at a few amateur nights, easily winning over the crowd with his lip-syncing prowess and humor. He's *phenomenal,* and I wish he didn't feel like he had to hide this part of himself. But at least he shares it with me, and I'm happy to support him however I can.

Tonight, he'll be part of the annual Speakeasy three-part drag competition series. Round one takes place this week, round two is next Saturday, and then the top two winners from each round will compete in the finals. There, a winner will be crowned and added to the Speakeasy official performance roster. It's a big deal. And if Diego doesn't win, I'm coming for blood.

At least we'll have some privacy tonight. Papi and my stepmom, Karina, are leaving for an overnight stay in the Berkshires. Diego can get ready for the show in peace, and I can breathe a little easier knowing I won't accidentally overshare something with the wrong person. Then, tomorrow, we're spending the day in Boston so I can visit as many art museums as I want. It's the perfect way to celebrate a birthday.

We even invited some of our friends to come to Speakeasy, at Diego's insistence, because "only pitiful people spend birthdays alone": Whit Rivera and her boyfriend, Zay Ortiz, who I met earlier this year when we worked on the homecoming dance together; Benito, the guy Diego is talking to; and a few of our mutual friends (who, fine, are *mostly* Diego's friends, but whatever).

"Shit, I forgot your dad was still here. When is he leaving?"

I check my phone. "Any minute now."

And just like that, there are three soft knocks on my door, followed by two taps—the special knock my dad has used with me since I was a little girl.

"Come in," I call to him through the door.

It slowly opens and my dad peeks his head in. A tall man of average build, Papi has dark, wiry hair that's graying at the ends and a beard he keeps neat and trimmed. His bronze-colored skin matches mine, but where I have glasses, he wears contact lenses. As a kid, I was convinced Papi was the strongest and funniest and best dad in the whole world.

Now that I'm older, I know it's true.

"Diego! I didn't even know you were here," Papi says.

"Well, I *am* famous for my quiet, unobtrusive nature," Diego jokes, pretending to flip long hair over his shoulder.

"Ah, yes, two words I have never once associated with you." Papi gives Diego a wry smile, and I can't help but laugh. "I just wanted to say goodbye before Karina and I head out."

I don't point out to Papi that he's already said goodbye to me, like, four times, two of which happened in the last hour. "You guys are going to have the best time."

"Yes, but I hate the idea of leaving you alone." He frowns.

"I most definitely won't be alone. Diego and I have big plans to watch reality television and order a gross amount of pizza." It's not technically a lie. We'll probably do that at some point. "Plus, he's taking me to see that new *Chromatic* exhibit tomorrow."

"I'll take excellent care of her, Tío," Diego assures him. "You know I will!"

I roll my eyes at my cousin. "I'm going to be eighteen on Monday. I *think* I'll be okay."

Papi puts his hands up in defeat. "I know, I know. I worry too much."

"You do. We'll be fine, Papi." I give him a reassuring smile.

He smiles back at me, decidedly un-assured, but at least he's trying. "Be good, nena."

"I always am," I say, wrapping Papi in a big hug. "And speaking of how I'm always so good—wouldn't now be an excellent time to tell me you've changed your mind about me going to see Intonation?"

I've been begging for months to go to Intonation's reunion show in Vegas, and it's been a no every time. He tends to see me as a kid still, and I hate to admit that I've mostly let him, which does me no favors.

Papi pulls back from the hug and shakes his head. "It's still a no, mija. You can barely keep track of your house keys!"

"They only ended up in the fridge last week because I was in a hurry and needed to grab a yogurt on the way to my job, where I'm responsible for *children*," I remind him.

He shakes his head. "I'm just not comfortable with you going to Las Vegas alone."

"But Papi, you can trust me. You *know* you can trust me."

He sighs. "Just—let's not. Okay? Not right now. We'll talk again after your birthday."

I force a smile and nod. "Okay. Now go enjoy the Berkshires with Karina."

Papi kisses the top of my head. "I love you. Be safe and have fun in Boston."

"I will," I promise.

(And I promise I'll have fun at the secret drag show with Diego, too.)

Chapter Four

"*Well?*" *Diego asks, twirling around.*

A million thoughts pop into my brain as I take in his transformed appearance. An hour ago, he was your average Puerto Rican gay kid from suburbia. Now, as a drag queen named Coqui Monster, Diego has painted his skin a glittery green; he's wearing a little lime dress and white over-the-knee laced-up platforms; exaggerated painted-on eyebrows; a gorgeous brown, curly-haired wig that looks big enough to hold the world's secrets; and his signature contact lenses, which make his eyes resemble those of a coqui—the tiny little frog that sings all over Puerto Rico.

"I'm going for 'sexy amphibian,'" he explains.

"I'm obsessed. It's maybe your best look yet?" At that, Diego beams. "And how about me? Is this okay?" I'm done up as an exaggerated version of myself: vibrant eye shadow, bright lipstick, and glitter all over. My chin-length black-and-lavender hair is tied into space buns, and I'm wearing sparkly cat-eye glasses. For the outfit, I've chosen a holographic skater skirt with suspenders over a rhinestone-covered mesh top, and I've swapped my usual hoop nose ring for a crystal stud.

Diego studies me. "You look like you got caught in an earthquake in the glitter section of a craft store."

"That's exactly what I was aiming for!"

"We look super hot." He shimmies his shoulders in delight. "Let's roll."

In my car, Diego takes control of aux because he insists it helps him get into character. After he scrolls through Spotify, searching among his many curated playlists to find the perfect one for the drive, he turns to me and arches a brow. "So, what is it that made you hot for Sienna again, anyway?"

"I'm *not* hot for Sienna."

I can feel his side-eye without even looking over. "Girl."

"Okay, fine, I'll admit I've been thinking about her a lot." I sigh. "She's *pretty*."

"You already gave that as a reason, shallow-ass. And anyway, I'll be the judge of that. What's her handle?"

"I'm not sure," I say, a total lie, as if I haven't crept on her profile when I absolutely have. He purses his lips, letting me know he's onto me, and I cave. "Fine."

I give him Sienna's handle and he pulls up her profile. "Oh! She's *cute*. For a white girl, I mean."

"She's Argentinian."

"White Latinas exist." Diego scrolls through her photos. "But yeah, she's gorgeous. A little basic, though. Is she even gay?"

"Basic? Are you serious?" I ask, narrowing my eyes. "And yeah, she's pan."

"Darling." He scrolls some more. "So, what else do you like about her?"

"Oh, I don't know. She's really sweet?"

"Okaaay? And?" Diego is clearly not loving the answers I'm giving.

I sigh. "Okay, fine. I don't even know why I'm thinking of her so much. Obviously I would check her socials every now and then, just to see what she was up to. But it's like seeing her again in person made my brain explode. I keep wondering if she's anything like the soft, caring girl I used to be friends with. And, like, what might've happened if she hadn't switched schools? I mean, she was my first serious crush. That feels special somehow, you know?"

Diego clucks his tongue knowingly. *"Ohhh."*

"What?" I ask.

"Nothing."

I grip the steering wheel tighter. "No, say it."

Diego toys with the hem of his skirt. "Well, to me—and I say this respectfully because I love you—it sounds as if you might like the *idea* of Sienna more than you actually like present-day, real Sienna."

"What does that even mean?"

"Again, respectfully? You have a tendency to...shall we say, live in the past more than others?"

"*Excuse* me?" I ask.

"Haven't you been listening to Intonation a lot more lately? And didn't I catch you the other day crying over photos of yourself from your kindergarten graduation?"

I scowl at him. "I was adorable, okay? So those were happy tears. I was proud of kindergarten me who didn't know she had ADHD and still persevered through learning her ABCs! Besides, what's wrong with being nostalgic? Or with Intonation? Their music holds up, you know!"

Diego rolls his eyes. "Okay, I've got more. You've been comfortable with your dad being overprotective of you lately, when you used to tell me it drove you batshit."

"Because I'm *Baby*," I pout. "I need to be taken care of!"

"Plus, you've avoiding *all* the milestones that come with graduation, like that'll make it so you don't have to move on! You went to school on Senior Skip Day—"

"I had a huge art project I needed to finish up."

"You skipped *prom*—"

"I had no one to go with," I remind him.

"Your papi and I had to drag you to graduation!"

"Graduation is overrated."

He holds his hands up in the air. "You're impossible. All I'm saying is it almost feels like you don't *want* to move on to this next chapter of your life."

I scoff. "Diego!"

"What? I'm just being honest with you!" he protests. Then he bats his exaggerated eyelashes. "Isn't that why you love me?"

"Supposedly."

What he's said weighs on me, even as the playlist shifts to an upbeat song and Diego excitedly pulls on my arm and squeals, "I live for this one!" I give him an amused smile as he starts to put on a miniperformance in the passenger seat of my Jeep, but the moment he looks out the window, I find myself drifting away.

Is Diego right that I'm holding on to the past more than other people?

That I'm nostalgic in a bad way?

That I've been skipping the milestones that celebrate the end of this chapter? That I'm avoiding what comes next?

I guess. Maybe. Yeah.

Growing up has always been one of those things I never thought would happen to me. I hoped I'd get to stay a kid forever, and not have to worry about all the boring, mundane stuff that comes with being an adult, like mowing the lawn and switching to toothpaste for sensitive teeth.

So many adults I've met seem to lose their whimsy, their playfulness, and forget what it means to be imaginative and impulsive and fun. Though Papi and Karina seem to have struck at least some kind of balance, I know for a fact Papi isn't nearly as lively as he used to be when he was young. Papi told me once he used to be in a band. An actual band! Meanwhile, Karina spent her free time in law school on the roller derby team. Neither of them does those things anymore.

And Titi Rosa's nursing job leaves her so stressed and bone-tired. In fact, I can't think of any hobbies Titi Rosa has that don't involve keeping her four kids alive and well. Even Tío Gabriel is so focused on the restaurant and being the family's Mr. Fix-It—he's always working on cars or replacing appliances.

Growing up seems to mean losing the parts of myself that have made me who I am. I don't want to get a job that keeps me so busy I only have four hours to myself at night—most of which I'll probably spend dreading the next day at work. It's inhumane and capitalistic and horrible and I hate it. But I know I won't have a choice.

Given all that, why is wanting to stay in this part of my life a little bit longer so bad?

"Hellooooo?" Suddenly Diego is waving his hand in front of my face. "You in there?"

I blink, realizing I've totally spaced out. "Sorry! What?"

"You missed the turn, babe." He points behind us. "You good?"

"Whoops! I was just thinking about Sienna," I lie.

"Get that li'l white girl outta your head and get me to my performance." He flips his curls over his shoulder. "My fans are waiting."

Chapter Five

Speakeasy is part coffee shop, part LGBTQIA+-friendly space that hosts pop-up bookstores, weekly drag shows, art installations, open mics, yoga, and occasionally pet adoption events (come for the latte, stay for the puppies).

At night, it morphs into an eighteen-and-over event space and unofficially becomes the place where queer high school seniors hang out the instant they're of age. Diego started practically living here the second he turned eighteen, and, thanks to a very convincing fake ID, I've been tagging along since. I can't believe that after tonight, I won't need the fake ID anymore. I suddenly feel nostalgic for even *that*.

Maybe I do have a problem.

Inside, Speakeasy is a mix of vibrant-colored art and decor, disco balls, and a bright pink stage. Dance music pours from the speakers, and Diego—Coqui—is immediately greeted by everyone. We make our way through the already crowded space toward the table that sits closest to the right side of the stage, where we see our friends: Whit, Zay, Benito, Miracle, Nic, and Jordan.

"*Okay,* Coqui!" Nic screams when they spot Diego.

Diego twirls around and gives them his best over-the-shoulder look, biting the fake nail on his index finger. He mimics the sound the coqui makes. "*Co-kee, co-kee.*"

"You look so good!" Benito stands to pull Diego into a hug, and

I know under my cousin's green face paint he must be blushing. "I'm in awe."

"As you should be," Diego teases.

"Chloe!" Whit breaks into a huge grin, her dimples deepening as she rises to her feet and holds open her arms for a hug. "Happy birthday, love!"

I reach for her and we share a warm embrace. "Thank you!"

"You look incredible," she gushes. "Like a glitter goddess."

"So do you!" I motion toward the table. "You all do!"

Diego clears his throat dramatically. "And me, Whit?"

"Is that the famous Coqui Monster?!" She pretends to scream. "Ohmygod, I love you so much!"

"Oh, I know." Diego grins. "I've gotta go prepare. Wish me luck." We do, and he blows us all kisses as he makes his way backstage.

While Jordan, Nic, and Miracle are nestled in a booth, I slide into the open chair next to Zay. Booths are the known enemy of fat folks everywhere.

Nic claps. "We brought you something, Chloe!" It's a pink bakery box that reads PETEY'S SWEETIES—that's a queer-owned bakery in town that makes the most divine treats. "Happy birthday! I totally had to smuggle this in."

"Oh my gosh! You didn't have to. But I love that you did. Thank you so much!" I open the box to reveal a s'mores cupcake: graham cracker cake and chocolate buttercream frosting with a toasted marshmallow on top.

"It's basically summer in cupcake form," Miracle explains. "There's even marshmallow filling inside!"

I gaze at the delicious-looking cupcake before me. "You are beautiful," I whisper with feeling.

"Sooo, birthday girl, how ya been?" Zay asks, leaning in so I can hear him over the music that's already blasting. "We haven't seen you in a bit!"

"I know, I know! I've been really busy working this summer."

He nods. "I feel that. Where?"

I laugh a little. "Well…I'm sort of a princess for hire."

Whit scoots closer to us. "I'm sorry, but did I just hear you say you're working as a literal *princess*? Like at kid parties?!" She digs into her purse and pulls out a notebook and a pen. "Adding that to the summer to-do list."

Zay laughs, watching her closely as she writes down *SEE CHLOE AS PRINCESS* on the corner of a page already overflowing with ink.

"What is this to-do list?" Miracle asks, taking a sip from her Shirley Temple.

"I've been keeping this list of all the things I want to do with Zay before the summer ends. You know, like, go on a roller coaster and visit the Isabella Stewart Gardner Museum in Boston."

"Hey, Diego and I are supposed to go there tomorrow! It's going to be amazing," I say.

Nic waves their hands excitedly. "Oooh, is that the place that's like a Venetian palace?"

Whit lets out a dreamy sigh, then turns to Zay and puts her hand on his chest. "When I die, I want to be buried in that beautiful museum's central courtyard."

"Grim, yet also oddly specific," I note with a laugh. "Have you been able to cross anything off the list so far?"

Zay shakes his head, laughing that deep laugh of his. "It's as if you don't even know this girl at all. *Of course* almost everything has been completed." He puts his hand on top of hers and squeezes. "But honestly, it's been nice. She makes sure every day is an adventure, and that we're getting to make the most of every single second before we leave for college."

A flush colors Whit's face. "Aww! Babe!"

"Wait. Aren't you both going to UMass?" Jordan asks. "It's not like you're going to be separated."

Whit laughs. "Yeah, but we just really love each other, and this gives us an extra reason to hang out and do fun stuff together."

She and Zay kiss, in that way couples kiss when they're so grossly in love you want to barf but also immediately have exactly what they have.

Nic pretends to gag, which elicits a round of laughter.

"I'm going to order a drink," I announce, getting to my feet. "Make sure no one touches the cupcake."

"We'll protect it with our lives," Zay promises.

I fix my skirt, then head over to the coffee bar, which serves both alcoholic and nonalcoholic drinks. I order an iced coffee in hopes it might help me stay awake longer, even though it never has before. (Shout-out to you, ADHD brain.) Diego often calls me an old lady trapped in a teen's body because of how early I go to bed, as if being an old lady isn't my life goal.

While I wait, I idly scan the room. My stomach drops when I spot a familiar face in the crowd.

Please, Lord, don't let that be Ramona Cruz.

Only it very clearly is: all 5'7" of her, with tight black curls, black lipstick, and a permanent scowl. My former best friend. The third person in our previous girl squad.

And shit, she looks hot. When did she get so hot? Has she always been this good-looking? She stands with her arms crossed, and I notice both of them are covered in tattoos.

God, she still looks so cool and confident, and it makes my hands sweat. Then my heart aches because it's been so long.

What the hell, universe?

I duck behind the counter to hide. One impromptu run-in with a former bestie was enough for one lifetime, let alone one day.

"Iced coffee for Chloe?" a voice calls.

I reach a hand up to the counter and, without looking, feel around for my drink. The person behind the counter with a buzzed head peers down at me.

"Are you Chloe?" they ask.

"That's me," I squeak.

"You good, Chloe? Hiding behind the counter is a little concerning. Do I need to call security?"

"I'm good," I whisper. "I'm only hiding because the earth refuses to open up and swallow me whole."

They hand me my coffee. "Been there, babe. Here's your drink."

I take it and sneak-run back to my table. Thankfully, as I slide into my seat—and before anyone can ask why I was scuttling like a little goblin—everything darkens, hiding me from view.

Overhead, local drag superstar Greta Herwig's voice announces, "*It's time, bitches!*"

I pretend I didn't just see Ramona Cruz. I pretend I didn't see Sienna Aguilar earlier either. I pretend the universe isn't out to get me. I pretend that this *definitely* isn't a sign that turning eighteen is going to be horrible.

Tonight, I'm focused on supporting Coqui Monster. Nothing else.

Chapter Six

Is there anything worse than feeling like you just fell asleep and having your phone ring?

Yes. It's feeling like you just fell asleep, having your phone ring, realizing it's six in the morning but you have to answer the call because it's your aunt, and then hearing her on the other end tell you she needs you to watch her adorable yet extremely energetic kids because she got called into the hospital for an emergency shift.

"I'm sorry, nena, but they're short-staffed, and I need to go. I've been calling Diego for twenty minutes and he hasn't answered," she explains. "Where the hell is he?"

"He's still sleeping," I admit.

"Wake him up." Then she starts to yell so loud I need to pull the phone away from my ear. "DIEGO! GET YOUR ASS UP—NOW!"

"Okay, okay!" I say over her yelling. "Titi, I've got it! We're leaving right now."

"Please hurry." Then she adds, "But don't speed."

Titi hangs up, and I look over at Diego, who is snoring loudly. After he demolished last night's drag competition and secured a spot in the next round, he *might* have stolen one of the neon-orange 21+ Speakeasy wristbands so he could have a celebratory drink (or two or three).

We didn't get home until two in the morning, so we've barely gotten four hours of sleep. I'm exhausted. But Diego is basically a corpse.

I try tugging on his arm. "Diego, wake up."

He doesn't move. I try again, more forcefully, and Diego groans and swats at me.

"Go away," he growls.

"Come on, Diego. Your mom called and she needs us to watch Ricky and Naya. We have to go *now*."

When he doesn't budge, I have to physically pull him out of bed.

He has green paint and glitter smeared all over his face and arms, and he barely even opens his eyes as I frog-march him to the car. (No pun intended.)

"Take these," I say, shoving a pack of makeup remover wipes, a bottle of water, and a packet of aspirin into his hand. "You're a mess."

"But a hot one. I'm so hot," he says through a yawn.

I pat him on the shoulder. "If you say so."

I drive us across town at a respectable speed (the last thing I need is a ticket) and sprint into the house so Titi Rosa can catch her shift. When I get inside, she greets me with a kiss on the cheek. "Where's Diego?"

"He's coming. We stayed up too late, so he's really tired."

Titi narrows her eyes at me. "Mmm."

Diego stumbles inside, rubbing his eyes. Though he's managed to clean most of the leftover makeup, he's still peppered with glitter and wearing the neon-orange 21+ bracelet.

Titi grabs his wrist to take a closer look. "What's this?"

Diego stiffens when he realizes what his mom's looking at. "It's nothing, Mami, just a joke that—"

She glares at him. "So *this* is why you look like shit this morning. You better get it together. We'll talk later."

The tips of Diego's ears go red and he gazes down at his feet. "Yes, Mami."

"Ricky and Naya will be up soon." Titi turns to me, lips pursed. "*You* don't smell like alcohol the way my darling son does, so is it safe to assume you're fine to watch them? Because if I need to call Gabriel to come home from the restaurant, I will, but he will not be happy."

"No, that's okay—I've got it, Titi. I promise. They're in good hands."

Her face softens a little. "I know you had birthday plans for today. But thank you, Chloe. I owe you." She turns to Diego. "And you. Take a shower. You smell like tequila and trouble."

"O-*kay*, Mami," Diego says with a sigh. With that, she leaves for work, and he groans. "I'm fucked."

"It'll be fine. But maybe you should take that shower. Your skin has a concerning green hue and I'm not sure if it's from the makeup or the hangover."

He gives me a sarcastic smile. "Why not both?"

Diego heads to the bathroom to get cleaned up, and I get started making some coffee for the two of us. Naya and Ricky bound down the stairs before it even finishes brewing. They're loud and full of an absurd amount of energy for barely seven in the morning.

But I promised Titi I'd handle this, so I will, ruined birthday plans be damned.

* * *

It's a long day. Ricky and Naya argue about just about everything: what to eat for breakfast, what to do after breakfast, what to do after the after-breakfast activity, and on and on and on.

We end up at the children's museum. Diego and I split up, one kid each: Ricky desperately wants to play on the gigantic indoor jungle gym, while Naya wants the arts and crafts room. I'm in my element as we work on butterfly-shaped suncatchers made out of construction and contact paper. Naya tells me about the drama happening at summer camp while we work, and I find myself riveted. Apparently one of the campers has been bribing other campers with candy so they'll be her friend! I am easily swayed by sweets, so this would absolutely work on me, but I remind Naya this is *not* something she should emulate. She rolls her eyes.

Unfortunately for me, Naya gives up on her suncatcher well before I'm done with mine, so I try to hastily finish them both before she completely loses her patience. I get exactly sixty seconds before she starts whining.

"I'm bored. Can we pleeeease go play restaurant?" she begs.

I can't even be upset at this. My ADHD brain means I understand completely how hard it can be to stay focused. But art is the one thing I'm really, really good at focusing on, and if I lose out on a whole day of art museums, I at least want to take a butterfly suncatcher home so I can hang it in my window.

"Just let me finish cutting this out, okay? I'm almost done." She lets out a long sigh, so I reach for some markers and a piece of scrap paper. "Bet you can't cover this entire paper with color before I finish."

Naya's brown eyes gleam at the challenge. "You're going down."

She starts to scribble on the paper like a fiend, and the idea buys me enough time to finish up. A few moments later, she slams her marker down on the table and shouts, "Done!"

"Oh, darn. You beat me," I say just as I finish cutting the final wing of Naya's butterfly. I hold hers and mine up for her to see. Her butterfly's wings are filled with an assortment of small scraps of rainbow tissue paper, while mine uses pastel colors. "But these came out pretty good, right?"

"I love them!" Naya pauses a beat. "*Now* can we go play restaurant?"

We do, meeting up with the boys. Several rounds of pretend restaurant later, Diego and I call it. We take Ricky and Naya to get some lunch and then head back to Diego's house.

"How are you feeling?" I ask once we're inside and Ricky and Naya are settled on their tablets. (I need a break, okay? And a nap, too, while we're at it. I have no idea how parents do this all day every day!)

"Well, my headache has worn off, so maybe we hit up Speakeasy again for round two?" Diego jokes.

I grimace. "Let's see how that talk with your mom goes before we do anything like that."

"Ugh, don't remind me." Diego lowers his voice and hisses, "As if she didn't drink when she was nineteen!"

"Can you be grounded even though you're, like, old?" I ask.

Diego gasps. "I am not *old*, you wretched hag!"

I burst out laughing. "I mean, aren't you, though?"

"If you hadn't saved my ass this morning by hearing Mami's call, I would disown you," he says. "And no, I don't get grounded anymore. My parents talk to me like adults. Because we are."

Right. Diego is an adult, and tomorrow, legally, I am, too. So why don't I *feel* like one? Instead, I usually feel like the twelve-year-old version of me—just with glasses and a slightly taller body. That can't possibly be how every adult feels. How would anything ever get done?

The front door opens and in comes Titi Rosa. She looks tired.

"Hi, Mami. Let me take that." Diego rises from the couch to grab her bag and hang it on the coatrack for her.

She arches an eyebrow at him, but a smile spreads across her face. "Sucking up, are you?"

He shakes his head and laughs. "Just trying to make amends. These little hellions! I don't know how you and Papi do it." He drops his voice to a whisper. "I spent one morning looking after these kids and I've decided I'm never having any."

"Ay! That's your brother and sister you're talking about," Titi says, but she's laughing.

Diego shrugs. "I said what I said."

"Don't listen to him. They were great," I assure her. "And we got you some lunch. It's in the fridge in case you're hungry."

"I'm starving, actually. Thank you. Come, tell me about the day while I eat." Titi motions for us to follow her into the kitchen. On the way, she kisses Naya and Ricky hello and pauses to admire the sun-catchers Naya and I made.

Diego and I settle at the kitchen table as Titi takes the chicken Caesar wrap from the fridge and joins us at the table. "So, they were fine?"

"They really were. We took them to the children's museum and we had fun," I say.

"Speak for yourself," Diego sniffs. Titi swats at his arm playfully. "Kidding, of course. They were good. Completely exhausting and sometimes shrill, but good."

She laughs. "That's what you get. I've parented with a hangover before and it isn't very fun."

The tips of Diego's ears flush red again. "I'm sorry, Mami. I didn't go too wild, I swear."

"He didn't," I assure her. "And there was so much to celebrate, I was really worried he might for a second."

Diego shoots me daggers from across the table.

Titi puts down her wrap and looks at me curiously. "You mean, beyond your birthday? Well, don't be shy—share the good news."

I look over at Diego, mortified, and launch into a lie. "Yes, our friend Jordan just got a really great job and we were celebrating."

"Oh, really?" Titi turns to Diego.

They stare at each other for a moment until Diego breaks. "Fine. Maybe...maybe I've been doing a little drag here and there."

Titi Rosa's face lights up. "What? And you kept it a secret? You know how much I love *RuPaul's Drag Race*!"

(I bite my tongue so I don't interject with an "um, actually" lecture about how drag extends beyond *RuPaul's Drag Race* because now isn't the time and yay! Titi Rosa is handling this well!)

Diego looks at her, surprised. "Wait. You're not mad that I'm a drag queen?"

"Why the hell would I be mad about that?" she asks. "If anything, I'm just mad you didn't tell me. I could've been helping you with your makeup this whole time!"

"Wait, really?" Diego grins at her. "Okay, then, you'll be excited to know last night was the start of the Speakeasy drag competition, and I made it through to the next round!"

Titi squeals and throws her arms around Diego in a hug. "That's my baby. Now, tell me *everything*."

We fill her in as she eats the rest of her lunch, and I can't help but smile at how warmly Diego's drag has been embraced by Titi. If our Boston trip had to get ruined in order for him to be reminded of just how much his mom loves him, then that's perfectly fine by me.

Chapter Seven

The next morning, like clockwork, Papi does his special knock and bursts through my bedroom door wearing a cheesy birthday hat. It's 7:41 a.m., the exact time I was born.

I sit up in bed and put on my glasses as he bellows "Happy Birthday" loud enough to wake our ancestors. He finishes the song by putting a birthday hat on me, too, and then taking two noisemakers from his pocket and handing one to me. We both blow into them at the same time, causing the colorful paper to unfurl and a loud whistle to ring out. This has been our tradition for as long as I can remember, and it never fails to make us laugh, silly as it is.

"Thank you, Papi." I grin at him.

He puts his hand over his heart. "I'm just relieved you're not too old for that yet."

I shake my head. "Never. I hope you do it until I'm ninety-nine."

He leans down to kiss my forehead. "You got it, mi amor. Happy birthday. How do you feel?"

I wrinkle my nose at him. "The same."

"You look older. Wiser, even. Are you suddenly dreaming of doing your taxes?"

"Come to think of it, I've been contemplating investments for my 401(k)."

"Now that's my girl," Papi teases. "You can never start investing too early."

With an exaggerated groan, I flop back on my bed and bury myself under the blankets. As a director of tax services for a huge corporation—or maybe it's executive director, or chief executive? I can never remember—Papi is forever giving me financial advice. He means well, but jeez.

"Okay, okay. Point taken." He tugs at my comforter until just my eyes are peeking out. "Hey, I heard about your trip getting canceled yesterday. I'm sorry, nena. I know you were really looking forward to it."

"Oh, that's all right," I say, sitting up. "Naya and Ricky were fine. I did accidentally spill the beans that Diego's a drag queen, though. But Titi Rosa seemed pretty delighted."

Papi laughs. "Yes, she told me. She also told me you really came through for her, so thank you. At least we'll be able to celebrate you at dinner tonight. I should be home around seven."

"That sounds great. Dinner starts at seven thirty *sharp*," I remind him. "Don't be late."

He frowns, knowing he has a tendency to get caught up at work. "I won't."

"Good. Now go make the big bucks," I tease.

He laughs. "You know, you're getting bossy in your old age."

"Just trying to embrace it."

* * *

I go back to bed for a little while. It's my birthday, and I'm not trying to wake up before four digits.

When I eventually make my way downstairs, I'm surprised by what I see. Though Papi went to work hours ago, he's covered the living room in birthday decorations celebrating some of the many things I've loved through the years. There's a gigantic *cartoon* banner that reads HAPPY BIRTHDAY; some *toy* figurines on the coffee table from shows I've loved throughout my childhood; and even a unicorn piñata.

On the table are a gift bag, a card, and a note that says *OPEN ME*. I rip it open. The bag contains sidewalk chalk, bubbles, a jump rope, candy, and a few other tchotchkes that would make any kid green with envy.

Inside the card, in Papi's messy handwriting, a message reads:

We can't celebrate what's to come without paying tribute to what used to be! You'll always be my little girl, but we're so proud of the young lady you've become. Since we can't celebrate until dinner, here are some fun reminders of child-hood. Enjoy, mija!

love,
Papi & Karina

Tears spring to my eyes. I'm often a sentimental mess, but this really does feel like such a kind and thoughtful gift, a recognition of who I was, and also an acknowledgment that I really am growing up. I love it and hate it at the same time.

Papi and I have always been close, especially since my mom left when I was four. It should've broken us both, but Papi did everything in his power to ensure that it didn't, showering me with more love, understanding, and pride than I could've imagined. (Ongoing therapy for us both helped too.)

He never missed any of my school plays or art shows, proudly displayed my paintings and sculptures throughout the house no matter how out of place they looked, humored me during my Intonation phase, and never even got annoyed when I turned their music up way too loud while doing homework.

More than anything, he made sure to show up for me every day, regardless of his own stuff. He has been the steadiest part of my life, and maybe that's partly why the idea of growing up and moving on stings.

But even if I don't feel ready to move on, it doesn't matter—my world is changing, and it has been for a while.

First, there was Karina, the woman who went from Papi's colleague to my new stepmother over the span of four years. How could I be anything but happy for my dad? She brought light to his eyes again. I've grown to love Karina, and to appreciate her for the glow she gave our lives, even if it was a difficult adjustment and meant lots of change: to the house, to our routine, to the size of our family.

Second, my acceptance into RISD. I've kept telling myself that this is *so far away*, I have time, I'll feel ready once school starts, but now I'm mere weeks from leaving for Providence and there's still a pit in my stomach whenever I think of it.

The final "lasts" of high school somehow snuck up on me. Classes. Graduation. Then my last summer break before college. And now my birthday, which has forever signaled the end of summer and the start of something new.

It's so much.

"Good morning, querida," Karina says as she pads into the kitchen and gives me a kiss on the cheek. She sweeps her long black hair up into a messy bun. "Happy birthday!"

I smile at her. "Thank you! Did you help with all this?"

She shakes her head. "That was *all* your father. You know how syrupy he gets about birthdays."

"You forgot 'over-the-top' and 'extra.' "

"Yeah, but that's just his general state of existence," Karina says with a laugh. "Coffee?"

I wrinkle my nose as she reaches for the decaf can of Café Bustelo. "I think I'll pass."

"Don't blame you. I wouldn't be drinking this stuff unless I had to." She sighs, then reaches a hand down to rub her round belly, which is growing every week. "You hear that? You can come out anytime. Mami would like to go back to drinking regular coffee!"

That, of course, is the final reminder that absolutely nothing about my life will be the same after this summer.

Though I'm pleased that Karina and Papi will be having a baby, and feeling reasonably positive about becoming a big sister, I can't help but worry it'll be hard to watch from my dorm room as they suddenly become the family I always hoped for.

I need some fresh air.

Chapter Eight

"**Okay, but why does it** look like a penis?"

"It does not!" I scramble to my feet to inspect the chalk drawing I've just completed in my driveway. A slice of ripe orange on the left... a vibrant green kiwi on the right...each surrounded by tropical leaves and white blossoms, with a banana in the center.

It totally looks like a penis.

But I'm not about to tell Diego that. "You see phallic symbols in everything."

He shrugs. "It's a gift."

We're making use of the chalk Papi gave me. Though acrylics and watercolor are my favorite mediums, I like experimenting with different ways of creating—even if it's simply sidewalk chalk.

Art has a way of calming my otherwise chaotic brain. I often get lost in whatever I'm making. But I'm distracted today. In fact, most of the stuff I've created lately has been kind of terrible. It's like, as soon as I found out I'd be going to this prestigious art school, the creativity was zapped right out of me. I keep wondering: What if turning my passion into my job is actually a terrible idea? I don't want capitalism to kill my creativity, and I need art the same way I need air or water, so losing it isn't an option.

I'm hoping I can find a way back to it before I leave for school, because there'd be no greater humiliation than arriving at art school as an artist who can't make art.

I frown as I look down at what I've drawn. "Ugh, whatever." I take what's left of my seltzer and pour it over the chalk.

"A little dramatic, don't you think?" Diego teases, and I stick out my tongue. "So. You haven't been asking me about my love life lately, and I'm offended."

"That's never stopped you from oversharing before."

Diego gives me a thoughtful look. "Hmm, that's true. I don't know what's gotten into me. Anyway. Benito and I are officially going on a date!"

My eyes go big. "Wait, when did this happen?!"

"After we hooked up last night," he says, a coy smile on his face.

"I thought you weren't looking for anything serious?"

"I'm not. But Benny's cute and I want to see where this goes." When I start to smile, Diego gives me a death stare. "Don't jinx it. Now, have you texted Sienna yet or what?"

"Why would I have texted Sienna?"

"Because fate put you together again! And you were all googly eyes for her!" Diego shrugs. "You might as well try and get some before summer's over and you go your separate ways for good."

"God, you make it sound so grim."

"I mean, is it not the truth? Do you really think Sienna is going to hang around this town after college?" Diego pokes me in the side. "*You'll* be back, for sure. But she won't."

"And what's so wrong with coming back?"

"I'm kidding! Come back or stay in Rhode Island—do whatever makes you happy. It's fine. I'd actually be perfectly happy if you moved home after college." While I'm away at school, Diego will be here helping out at his family's restaurant as he figures out what comes next for him.

"Why would you want that? You're always talking about how you can't wait for us to leave this place."

"Yeah, but, like, *together*." He frowns. "In fact, drop out. You're abandoning me. Why can't you just stick around and suffer with me so I'm not all alone?"

I laugh and start idly making some chalk flowers. "You have legions of friends *and* fans in town. You don't need me here with you."

"But you're my best friend. Mi prima. That's another level of friendship, you know? Now you're going off to raggedy-ass Rhode Island without me and it's annoying."

I put my hand on my heart. "Aww, Diego. You care. That might be one of the sweetest things you've ever said. You're going to miss me!"

Diego scowls at me. "I did *not* say that."

"For what it's worth, you're my best friend too."

"You're delusional," he says, looking down at his phone. Then he glances back up at me. "And if you keep talking like that, I won't drive you to Boston today so you can see your stupid exhibit. It's almost nine already."

"Wait. You really want to go?"

"Not if you keep talking about your feelings. Now, are we going or what? We have to leave ASAP if you want to make it back in time for your birthday dinner." Diego rises to his feet and points a finger at me. "And don't you dare say thank you or I'm changing my mind."

I grin at him. "I wouldn't dream of it."

* * *

Obviously I wouldn't say this to Diego, but I had a really great time in Boston. We made it to the Chromatic exhibit, and it was even more mesmerizing in person than I imagined. We got sushi and shopped (Diego bought himself a dusty-pink robe with feather trim as a reward for his success, while I ended up with a pair of supercute duck earrings), and then we got back in the car and took the Pike home.

We make it back to my house by seven, and soon after, I find myself surrounded by my family: Diego, Papi, Karina, Tío Gabriel, Titi Rosa, and the kids. Titi Rosa was really pushing for me to have a huge, over-the-top party, but since we do that for literally every other familial celebration, I thought something quiet and small might actually be nice.

Tío Gabriel has prepared all my favorite foods for our meal: tostones, pasteles, roasted pork, and rice, and I thank the melanin gods and goddesses for gifting us such delicious Puerto Rican food as part of our culture. As far as birthdays go, it's pretty much all a girl could ask for.

Then there are the gifts.

From Tío Gabriel and Titi Rosa, I get a beautiful gold necklace engraved with my name.

Ricky and Naya each give me handcrafted cards. I try not to take offense that Naya drew me as wide as the house I'm standing beside, but at least she nails my nose ring and gives me superlong eyelashes.

From Diego, I get a traveling watercolor kit "because you wouldn't shut up about it."

Then, from Karina and Papi, I get an envelope.

"Open it!" Karina squeals. "We think you're going to love it."

Everyone goes quiet as I pull out a long, rectangular piece of paper. It's shaped like a vintage concert ticket and looks homemade. Suddenly I'm understanding why my dad was asking me all kinds of questions about how to use Canva.

The ticket reads:

Ultimate Entertainment Presents **INTONATION: ONE NIGHT IN VEGAS** **Planet Hollywood, Las Vegas, NV** **Sat., Aug. 17, 2024, 8 p.m.** **SEC: On the Rise, SEATS: 1–3** **Proof that: Papi and Karina are the best**

Immediately, my hands start to shake. "Wait. Did you get...?"

"Tickets to see your boys!" Karina points at the paper in my hand. "Three of them! For you and whoever you'd like to bring with you. They apparently don't make printed tickets anymore, so your dad got creative and made a ticket of his own."

He beams at me proudly, and I just blink, not quite processing this gift. "But you said—"

Papi holds up a hand and interrupts. "I know what I said, mija. And I was wrong. A certain someone"—he glances over at Karina—"helped me understand I have no business telling my now eighteen-year-old daughter she can't travel to see her favorite band for their reunion show. We got the tickets weeks ago, but you stepping up for your aunt yesterday, even when you had special plans of your own, really showed us this was the right decision. You said this concert will be once-in-a-lifetime, right?"

My heart can't stop beating wildly. I adjust my glasses and look from the paper in my hands to my dad to Karina.

It's finally happening. I'm going to see Intonation.

"Oh my God," I breathe. I leap from my seat and swoop in to give Karina a gigantic hug. *"You are a literal angel!"*

"Hey! I'm the one who found the tickets!" Papi teases. "And I made sure to get you the good seats."

I rush over to crush him in a bear hug too. "Thank you, thank you, thank you! I honestly would've taken anything! I'm just so happy I'm going!"

He scoffs. "So I could've gone with nosebleeds instead of those seats on the stage?"

"THESE ARE THE SEATS ON THE STAGE?!" My voice is louder than I intend but I can't help it!

"Bitch!" Diego snatches the paper—which is totally getting crushed in my hands with all the excited flailing—away from me to get a closer look. "These are going for, like, *thousands* of dollars!"

"Language, Diego! We have impressionable ears here." Titi Rosa laughs and puts her hands over Naya's ears. "Not that they can hear after Chloe's shouting."

"Does that mean Chloe is going to sing onstage?" Naya asks her mom. "Like Beyoncé?"

"She's not going to sing onstage, dummy," Ricky argues. "She's going to *sit* onstage to watch Innovation or whatever."

"Don't call your sister a dummy," Tío Gabriel warns. "And I think the group is called Indication. Right?"

I ignore all the wrong names and grab the ticket back from Diego, scanning it as quickly as possible. How is this real? My eyes barely register any of the letters or words until I reread *SEC: On the Rise, SEATS: 1–3*.

The On the Rise section features seats on. The. Literal. Stage.

My body is coursing with so much adrenaline that I might literally pass out. I'm going to see Intonation! In Las Vegas! For their one-night-only charity concert!

"Thankyouthankyouthankyouthankyouthankyou!" My words tumble out like they're one, and I pepper Papi's and Karina's cheeks with kisses.

"Well, we're happy you're happy," Karina says, grinning.

"Who will you take? Maybe that other friend of yours who likes Intonation. Whitney?" Papi suggests.

"And me, obviously!" Diego says.

"I love you, but you don't even *like* Intonation," I argue.

"So? For tickets like these, I'll bust out choreography." He starts to mime a heart thumping out of his chest, one the band's most famous moves.

"You have *work*," Tío Gabriel reminds him.

Diego huffs, plopping back into his chair and crossing his arms. "Fine."

"I think Whit might already have tickets..." I say, biting my lip. "But let me think about it. I'm so excited my brain has gone completely blank, but I'll definitely put these to good use."

Papi smiles. "I know you will, nena. We'll figure out the details later. But soon, okay? I need to book your flight and hotel."

I lock eyes with Karina. "I can't believe you convinced him. I owe you my life."

Karina grins. "You deserve this."

"This is getting boring," Ricky whines. "Can we have some cake now?"

Titi Rosa ruffles his hair. "That's for the birthday girl to decide."

"I never say no to cake!"

Chapter Nine

Whit: Wait. You got tickets ONSTAGE?

    Whit: Girl.

    Whit: Girl.

    Whit: GIRL!!!!!!

    Whit: You're making me want to ditch my abuela and sister so so so so bad rn!!!!!

    Me: im sorry! i knew it was a long shot but i had to offer!!!

    Whit: I'm so honored you did, and so sorry I have to turn it down 😔 I can't abandon them. Plus, we have floor seats, so it should be okay. I mean, it's not ON THE STAGE. But still!

    Me: oooh, are they not doing general admission for this show?

    Whit: No, thank GOD because Abuela can't stand for that long. But she should be okay with the floor seats. I'll just get stabby with anyone who stands in front of her

    Me: if you change your mind, i gotchu boo

    Whit: You're the best 🖤

I tuck my phone away and sigh. It seems silly that I somehow have stage tickets for Intonation but no one to go with. Whit and Diego are out of the running, so who *am* I going to take with me? Has my life gotten so pathetic I can't even find two friends to go with me to a concert, in Vegas, for *free*?

If this was four years ago, the answer would've been a no-brainer.

Ramona, Sienna, and I would have gone, obviously—or simply passed away from the shock of it all. But I can't picture the two of them wanting to get back together for some kind of forced friend reunion.

Unless...?

I bolt upright in bed.

Because *wait.*

It's late, but I throw on all the lights in my room and start digging through the piles of random papers, notebooks, art supplies, old textbooks, and everything in between in hopes I might find what I'm looking for.

I get distracted a bunch. There's an old (awful!) portrait I drew of Intonation, old school papers I've saved for no real reason, sketches. I even find a fact sheet I wrote out for each of the band members:

Lucas Thomas:
"The Nice One/Leader," 6'1", British, Black, hazel eyes, favorite color is blue

Rider Morales:
"The Tattooed Bad Boy," 5'9", American, Puerto Rican, brown eyes, favorite color is green

Henry Roberts:
"The Religious One/Baby," 5'7", American, white, brown eyes, favorite color is orange

Alexander Sun:
"The Prankster," 5'11", American, Korean, brown eyes, favorite color is red

William "Liam" Hayes:
"The Nerdy Gamer," 5'10", American, white, baby-blue eyes, favorite color is gray

I laugh out loud at the hearts I've drawn around Liam's name, and the idea that I felt it was necessary to record these facts somewhere.

A while later, in the depths of my closet, I finally stumble upon a bedazzled box I stored old trinkets in. I rip the top off and there, beneath an old Pandora charm bracelet and a lucky penny, is the list I've been looking for.

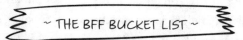

~ THE BFF BUCKET LIST ~

Chloe Torres, Sienna Aguilar, and Ramona Cruz aka La Tripleta aka Deadly Flora have made a pact to complete The Best Friend Forever Bucket List before college. Together, we vow to:

1) See a firefly
2) Eat ice cream for dinner
3) Be in three places at once
4) Go camping
5) Get drunk together
6) Skinny-dip
7) Stay up all night and watch the sunrise
8) Make out with someone
9) Take a road trip
10) See Intonation together LIVE wearing feather boas like from the "Late Nights" music video and maybe have them each fall in love with us* +

* Get a grip, guys – Ramona
+ It could happen! – Chloe

Please sign below to make this pact legally binding.

Chloe Torres

Sienna Aguilar

Ramona Cruz

It's been years since I've laid eyes on this list, and I burst out laughing when I read the intro and some of the things the middle-school version of us felt were musts. (Skinny-dip? Really? Calm down, girls.) Also the fact that we were convinced signing the paper made the list legally binding is sending me. Clearly none of us was destined to become a lawyer.

Still…seeing the familiar handwriting on this page takes me back. We all took turns making suggestions on what to add, but the last two—*take a road trip* and *see Intonation live*—were the only ones that felt like absolute musts. We really thought we'd be able to knock everything off this list before the end of that summer before high school, even though we couldn't even drive.

Obviously, the list got forgotten somewhere between Sienna's new school and Intonation breaking up.

Yet one reunion show, two random run-ins, and three tickets later, this list suddenly seems like the most important thing in my life.

The only question is whether I can get Ramona and Sienna to feel the same.

* * *

By morning, I've created a rough outline of what a road trip from our small Massachusetts town to Las Vegas might look like, with rest stops, overnight stays, and all.

Have I slept? No.

But could this be the most brilliant idea my hyperfocused ADHD brain has ever come up with? Obviously.

Papi is less than thrilled when I share my idea with him. I didn't even know the frown lines on his face could get as deep as they do as he looks over what I've put together.

"No. Absolutely not. This was not at all what I had in mind for your trip to Las Vegas." He pushes my laptop back to me. "You're not taking a road trip across the country!"

"But Papi, you agreed this concert was once-in-a-lifetime. I have it all planned out, if you'll just listen." I glance at Karina for help, pointing toward the route on the map. "See? These are the hotels where we'll stay. And this is the exact route we'll follow—no diversions. I mean, unless someone really has to pee. But we'll make sure to turn on our location tracking on our phones so you can see where we are at all times. I can call you every hour, if you want!"

"And who's paying for this? Hmm? I said I would cover the flight and one overnight stay for you and two friends. Not whatever this is." He waves a hand dismissively.

"I know, and I wouldn't dare ask you to pay for all of this, I swear! You and Karina have already been so generous. *Beyond* generous, really. I'm so grateful for everything you've done for me." I pause. "It's just that...as you know, Diego can't come with me to this concert, and neither can Whit. The cross section of friends and Intonation fans in my life is pretty small, except for my old friends Ramona and Sienna."

"Oh, I remember them! They were so sweet. Is that who you'd like to take?" Karina asks.

"Yes! You remember how close we were, right?" I look at Papi. "You used to call us La Tripleta because we were always together! Wasn't that cute?"

Papi crosses his arms, which isn't a no. I take it as a sign to go on.

"You know how obsessed we used to be with Intonation. We taught ourselves all the moves to their music videos!"

Karina leans back in her chair and giggles. "That's right! That *was* cute. And they put on that show for us after one of our dates. Remember that, Ito?" She pats him on the chest, and I smile at her nickname for him. Though his name is Carlos, she affectionately called him Carlito, which eventually became Ito.

I continue. "So, okay, you're probably thinking: *Great. Fly out with Ramona and Sienna and call it a day,* right?"

He grunts; his frown lines are immovable. "Oh, yes. That's exactly what I'm thinking."

"And I would, except...the three of us made this list of things we hoped to accomplish during our senior year of high school. Seeing Intonation in concert was one of them. Unfortunately, they broke up, so we were never able to see them live. But you!" I walk around the countertop and pat Papi's and Karina's hands dramatically with my own.

"You and Karina—giving, kind, caring, considerate, amazing humans that you are—have made it so that it's now possible for the three of us to achieve that."

"You still haven't explained. Why a road trip?" Papi presses.

"The road trip was on that list we made too! So, you see, we could go after both of these dreams we had at the same time." I don't dare pull out the tattered piece of paper from the pocket of my overalls. Not when the list also says things like *Skinny-dip* and *Make out with someone*. Papi is cool, but not *that* cool. "Even more than that, I think this trip would give the three of us a chance to become friends again—or at the very least to get closure on why our friendship ended. If we fly, it'll be like I'm going to this concert with strangers. And you don't want that, do you?"

Papi scoffs. "So being stuck in a car with strangers is better? This is not making your case any stronger!"

Karina shoots me a look, then jumps in to save me from myself. "I think what Chloe means is that she's hoping this is about more than just a concert. It could be an opportunity to rekindle a friendship that meant something, right before they all go their separate ways for school. You can understand that, can't you, Ito?" He softens the slightest bit, so she presses on. "So much is changing for Chloe. You told me part of what you hoped for with this trip was that it would encourage her to take chances."

I don't know why, but the idea of even my dad thinking I don't take enough risks in my life gives me pause. Maybe Diego really was right. I am holding myself back. I might need this trip now more than ever.

Papi shakes his head. "A road trip where three young girls are traveling to Las Vegas alone is not what I had in mind. I meant she could try a new type of sushi or something! Not this."

"May I also remind you that you were at Woodstock '99 and you turned out just fine?"

Papi shoots daggers at her with his eyes. "That was a different time!"

"Ito, you said you wanted this to be a chance for *independence*. For her *and* for you," Karina says softly.

Honestly, past Papi is right. We have long been stuck in this dynamic where I'm his forever little girl. But I'm realizing that maybe that hasn't been doing either one of us any good.

He sighs. It's a long, defeated sigh, and the corner of my lip twitches. He's faltering. This could really happen.

"Go back to the payment thing. Explain?" Papi asks.

I do my best to conceal the ball of hope growing in my chest. "I'm so glad you asked. I've been saving up all year—with the barista job during the school year, and then this summer princess job—and, with the super-rough calculations I did last night, I could definitely cover the hotel and gas costs myself."

"Are you sure about that?" He arches a skeptical brow. "What about food?"

Shit. Right. I hadn't factored that in. But I could put it on a credit card and work it off! "Well…"

"And emergencies? What if you get a flat tire? How about parking at the venue? Souvenirs? I know you love souvenirs and there's no way you won't be buying some." Papi scans the route I've mapped out. "And what kind of hotels are these, anyway?"

"Well, they're not the fanciest, and I think there's one that's more of a motel—"

"Absolutely not! Ay, Dios mio." He starts pacing. "This is huge, you know that?"

"I do know that," I confirm.

"You're asking for the moon here!" He runs a hand through his hair the way he does when he's stressed. "There's so much we have to consider with a trip like this. Starting with where to find enough bubble wrap to cover you from head to toe."

I start to smile.

Papi turns to me and points a finger accusingly. "This cannot be something that is ill-planned. We will sit down, *together*, and we will work out all the details. I will pay, not you, because you need to save your money for unexpected expenses that may arise. And you will let me choose the hotels. They will be well-lit and near safe, easy-to-get-to towns."

I nod quickly. "Absolutely."

But he's not done. "You'll get a rental car instead of taking your own. You will be there for the full inspection. You will pack an emergency bag of essentials. You will be in touch every single day. And I mean that! You will make these girls get permission from their parents before they leave."

"Of course," I say.

"And you will *absolutely* turn on your location tracker."

There is a pause.

In a quiet voice, I ask, "Does this mean I can go?"

"You need to let me start researching these hotels first. If I can figure that out, then..." He shakes his head, as if he doesn't want to say the next word. "Fine."

I squeal. "Papi, you won't regret this!"

"I better not!" He looks over at Karina. "She really said, 'some are motels.' Like she's some kind of vagrant. My daughter! Ay!"

I pull him and Karina into a hug. "I'm the luckiest girl in the world."

"Yes, you are," Karina teases. "Bring us back something good, will you? Oooh, maybe a little"—she mimes smoking a joint—"for your father? He needs it."

"Ha ha. Very funny," Papi says dryly. But the corner of his mouth is turned up into the slightest of smiles.

Chapter Ten

Papi and I talked (and maybe argued a little) for a long time about the details of the trip, including how long it should be. While I wanted to cover as much ground as quickly as possible, he said I needed to take it slow and build time into the trip for potential changes.

I mean, technically, the drive can be done in about forty consecutive hours, but that doesn't account for *anything* else, so I figured three days would be plenty if we all took turns driving. But Papi argued I wasn't accounting for meals and rest, and he didn't want anyone else driving the car. Given that he's footing the bill for everything, he ultimately won, and we landed with a seven-day plan to get there, plus an eighth day to fly back.

Which means, in order to get to the concert by August 17...

"I'll need to leave in just *four days*," I explain to Diego, swirling my straw in my mango tea. We're at the local boba place and I'm forcing him to listen to my every feeling about this plan. "How the hell am I going to convince Sienna and Ramona to go on a road trip with me by then?"

"You're fucked," Diego says with a shrug. "Told you you should take me instead."

"You have to work at the restaurant!"

"And *that's* supposed to stop me from traveling across the country to be onstage during a sold-out show?" His face lights up with an idea.

"Ooh, imagine if I showed up in full drag? I'd get so much attention. I could steal your boyfriend! Which one did you like again?"

"That would be Liam, and I have moved well beyond the stage in my life where I want him to fall in love with me."

"Are you sure? Because it wasn't that long ago that you went on a date with that guy just because he looked like Liam."

"I told you never to repeat that story again!"

With a laugh, Diego offers an insincere "Sorry!"

I glare at him. "*Anyway.* If you really want to go, we'll figure it out."

"No, no. I'm just messing with you," Diego says with a grin. "Plus, if I go, how will I win the Speakeasy drag competition?"

I slap my hand to my forehead. "Oh my gosh. I can't believe I've been so caught up in my own shit that I forgot about your competition! I'm such an idiot." I pull out my phone. "That's it. I'm going to text Whit and give her my tickets."

Diego snatches my phone from my hand. "Absolutely the fuck not! You're going."

I reach to take my phone back, but Diego presses his palm to my forehead to keep me at arm's length.

"I'm not going to miss your show!" I argue.

"Yes, you are. This concert is way more important! You love that stupid boy band. And there will be plenty more opportunities to see me win drag competitions." He arches an eyebrow at me. "Unless you don't think I have what it takes?"

"Of course you have what it takes," I argue. "That's why I want to be there!"

"If you believe in me, then you know I can win this show and plenty of others. So you'll go to this concert. I'll have Benito take a video and it'll be like you were right there with me."

I slump back in my seat, letting Diego finally rest his arm. He shakes his head. "Thank goodness. My arm was starting to shake. Your head is freakishly strong, you know that?"

"Are you sure you won't hate me forever if I miss your event? I know it's important to you."

"It is important to me, but it's also important to me that you actually do something for yourself. Go on this goddamn adventure and live a little! Maybe you'll finally make some friends that aren't me."

"Funny," I say wryly.

"Seriously, though. I know I'm giving you shit and all, but I think you owe it to yourself not just to reconnect with these friends you loved for so long, but to prove to yourself that you can stand on your own two feet. Even if nothing comes of the friendship, you need this."

When Diego sees my expression go soft, he grimaces. But I smile at him anyway. Because he gets it—he gets why this spontaneous, over-the-top idea suddenly feels like something I *have* to do.

"Thanks, Diego."

"Ugh, whatever." Diego swishes his drink around and the ice rattles together. "So, what're you going to do, then? To get Sienna and Ramona on board? The clock is ticking!"

I reach for my phone and type in the name of our old group chat: Deadly Flora. Though the group name pops up, no messages show. It's been too long.

"Maybe I text them?" I suggest.

Diego nearly chokes on his drink. "A group text? With people you haven't texted in literal years? Okay, serial killer."

"Oh, whatever! Like you have a better idea."

Diego sits back in his chair and taps his fingernails on the table between us as he thinks. "Honestly...I think you need to explain yourself in person. It's the only way this plan doesn't make you sound like you've lost your mind. Over text, it's like, 'Oh, hey, people I haven't hung out with for years. Want to be trapped with me in the car for a week to go to one of the most coveted concerts of the decade? I swear I'm not a murderer, haha!' Which is exactly what a murderer would say. But in person, you can do your little doe-eyed bird thing and make it sound quirky and fun and they'll totally cave."

I arch an eyebrow at him. "Little doe-eyed bird thing?"

"Oh, don't start. You know you do a little doe-eyed bird thing where you, like, bat your eyelashes and make your eyes real big and get everyone around you to want to care for you because you're just so adorable."

"I do not!" I protest.

"Really? How about that time you got caught vandalizing?" Diego clasps his hands together and props them under his chin, making his eyes round. " 'Oh, please, Officer, I had no idea painting murals on public property wasn't allowed! I swear! I'll volunteer with little old ladies at the senior center if you let me go!' And it worked, too!"

"That was *one* time! And I did volunteer at the senior center! I made great friends with Ethel. We're still pen pals!"

Diego laughs. "Whatever, girl. Use your twee little fruit-print outfits, pastel-colored hair, and underpaid-art-teacher-vibe for all it's worth."

I cross my arms in a huff. "I am not adorable."

"Whatever you gotta tell yourself."

I steer the conversation back to the original topic. "If I can't text Ramona and Sienna, how am I supposed to meet up with them in person?"

"That's where I come in. We'll look at their social accounts and figure out where you might casually run into them."

"Isn't that stalking?"

"Not if you're good at it. And what's a little light internet stalking between old friends?" Diego motions for me to hand over my phone. "C'mon. Gimme."

I unlock the phone and reluctantly slide it to him. But what choice do I have? This is the only plan I've got.

It doesn't take long before Diego slides my phone back to me. "Sienna works as a lifeguard at the Elmwood Country Club. Ramona was a little harder to track down, but her tagged photos were a gold mine. She's working as an apprentice over at Permanent Record, that tattoo shop downtown. Don't they have a shop in Boston, too? They're a big deal. Kind of badass she scored an apprenticeship there."

I stare at him. "How did you figure all that out so fast?"

"I told you. I'm good at what I do." He blows on his fingernails as if they've just been freshly manicured. "So, then, let's hit up Sienna tomorrow afternoon. You can do the whole doe-eyed bird thing. Then we'll head to Permanent Record. Ramona might not be there, but we can ask around."

"You say it like it's so easy."

"All you need to do is remind them what made the three of you so close." Then Diego peers at my still-half-full cup of boba. "You gonna finish that?"

* * *

To successfully remind Sienna and Ramona of what made the three of us so close, I have to start with myself first. So that night, I turn on Intonation's debut album, dig through some old photos, and become a tween again.

It's wild how quickly I'm flooded with memories.

Like the time the three of us went to Six Flags and vowed to ride as many roller coasters as possible. Only it rained, so we were soaking wet minutes into our visit. Still, since we practically had the park to ourselves, we rode the coasters over and over. We went home with hoarse throats and huge smiles that day.

Or when we went to our first middle school dance and spent a good portion of the night trying to rescue a family of bunnies we found outside in the courtyard. (Ramona is a secret softie for animals.)

Or the mortifying time we performed as Deadly Flora in the school talent show. We knew nothing about actually performing. Ramona took on the drums, Sienna opted for guitar, and I sang. We were so focused on getting the right look down that we hardly practiced and failed spectacularly. But we still have the photos to show how cute we looked!

There were not-so-great moments, too.

In seventh grade, Sienna accidentally overheard her parents talking and found out her dad was actually her stepdad, and her bio dad lived somewhere across the country. The truth wrecked her. Ramona and I were there as she sobbed in the aftermath, and we were there as we reassured her that the person who'd raised her was every *bit* her father, if she wanted him to be. The three of us even started the Deadbeat Parents Club. We made buttons.

When I started having a hard time in some of my classes, Sienna and Ramona were there to help me figure out why my brain always felt so frustratingly jumbled. They'd be with me when I sat down to do my math homework, and they wouldn't leave my side until I was done, even if it took hours. They even helped me talk to my dad about it, and—when I got my ADHD diagnosis and subsequent medication not long after—they celebrated the wins that came along with figuring out the best ways to accommodate my needs.

And Ramona lost it when she found out her older brother, Manny, had enrolled in the army. It was like one day he was there, considering community college options, and the next he was shipped off for basic training. They were so close that the unexpected shift felt like a death in the family, especially for her mom, who had been raising Manny, Ramona, and their three little siblings all on her own.

We were there when Ramona was the first of us to come out as queer, we were there when Karina came into my dad's life and I felt totally unsettled by the change, we were there when Sienna was crumbling under the pressure from her parents to be the perfect student. We were there for each other in the big and the small ways that matter.

And now it's up to me to show my friends why what we had doesn't have to remain a thing of the past.

Chapter Eleven

I have no idea how Diego and I are meant to gain entry into Elmwood Country Club, where Sienna works, knowing neither of us is a member. They restrict day passes to people twenty-one and older, and I can't really afford to waste any money, anyway, so that's out.

But Diego assures me he has a plan, and I should wear a white collared shirt and black pants. The best I can do is a white button-up and some leggings, but I figure it'll do, though my lavender hair makes me stick out like a sore thumb. I choose plain black frames from my collection of prescription glasses to help me blend in that way. He says nothing when I pick him up, so I assume I've passed whatever test this is.

"I've snuck up onto their beach so many times it's like second nature to me now." He waggles his eyebrows at me. "We're going to use our brownness to our advantage and pretend to be the help."

The way he says this makes me laugh. "Using racism for good. That's new, but I kind of like it?"

"If racism is going to exist anyway, we might as well try to benefit from it." He shrugs and flicks his sunglasses down over his eyes. "Come on."

I follow Diego as he confidently strides toward the country club. Even from the parking lot, I can see that the staff members are all wearing white collared shirts emblazoned with what I assume is the club logo over crisp black pants. That this place forces the staff to wear black pants in the dead heat of the summer makes me feel less bad about sneaking in.

We step onto the open patio, the only place where the building isn't gated. Country-pop music is playing from the speakers above. It's just after noon, but everyone here seems sloshed, so it isn't hard to blend in with the servers. Diego grabs a black serving tray with some abandoned drinks on it for good measure.

"Naughty, naughty!" a chipper voice with an Australian accent says. "Sneaking in again, are you?"

Diego spins on his heel and bats his eyelashes at a slim girl with wavy brown-and-blond hair. "You know you love me, Margot."

Margot pulls him in for a side hug. "Trying to score some free drinks again?"

He shakes his head. "No. I'm on a mission today. Well, my cousin is." Diego nods his chin at me. "This is Chloe."

I offer a small wave. "Nice to meet you. Thanks for not ratting us out."

Margot smirks. "Who says I won't?"

"She's joking," Diego assures me. "Chloe's trying to track down Sienna Aguilar—is she at the lake?"

"Oooh, yeah. Should be over on the east side, if I'm not mistaken." She points behind us. "That way."

"Think you got this?" Diego asks, tilting his head to the side.

I give him a firm nod. "I'm good. Be back soon."

Heart pounding in my ears, I make my way toward the beach, dodging one particularly drunk older gentleman who snaps his fingers at me and demands a refill. It's easy to spot the lifeguard stand, and I march over with as much confidence as I can, gripping my tote bag for reassurance that it's got all I need.

"Hey!" I shield my eyes from the sun and call up to Sienna once I'm within earshot.

Sienna turns and squints down at me from the towering lifeguard chair she's perched upon. "Chloe? Or is that Princess Julieta?"

"Just Chloe today, sorry to disappoint."

"No disappointment at all. What're you doing here?"

"Oh, you know. Testing my luck by sneaking into country clubs in the middle of the day. The usual."

Sienna smiles. "Ah, of course."

"In seriousness, I'm—well, I'm here to ask you something. It's a little weird."

"I'm okay with weird." She pulls out her phone and checks something, then begins to climb down from the chair. "And your timing is perfect. I'm about to go on my break, and I'm dying for something to drink. C'mon."

We walk back toward the country clubhouse together, Sienna taking the lead with some small talk, and end up in a staff break room. She fills up her water bottle and takes a long drink. "So? You promised something weird."

My hands suddenly start to sweat. Am I really about to do this?

"Okay, so. I'm not sure if you'll remember this, but when we were kids, you, Ramona, and I made a list of things we wanted to accomplish before we left for college."

Sienna's face lights up. "Our bucket list! Oh, gosh. I haven't thought about that in forever."

"Neither had I, until the other night. I was looking through some of my things and I actually found it." I dig into my tote bag and pull out a copy of the list, handing it to Sienna.

"No way," she breathes, taking the piece of paper. Her eyes scan it, an amused look on her face. "God, I remember taking ourselves *so* seriously when it came to what made it on the list. This is hysterical! And also sweet."

"I thought so too. And, well…for my birthday, my dad actually surprised me with tickets to see Intonation."

Her mouth falls open. "Wait. The Vegas charity show?!"

"The one and only. The thing is, he gave me three tickets, and I was trying to figure out who to take. I know this is really unexpected"—I take in a breath, and the next words come out in a rush—"but I just kept coming back to you and Ramona. I know it's been *so long,* but I was thinking it could be fun if we went together. And if we're going to throw caution to the wind and all, we could turn it into a road trip? Which was also on the bucket list. Like, we would basically use this summer before we all leave for school to actually try and make our younger selves proud. It's totally outlandish, I know! And I would completely understand if you said no. But it would mean a lot to me if you'd consider it. Selfishly, I don't want to go to the show alone, and I also want to prove to my papi that I can handle a big trip like this, you know? Be independent! Make decisions! Travel! It might be a nice final hurrah and—oh!" I dig my hand into my tote again and pull out an envelope. Inside is a handwritten note, a photo of us as Deadly Flora during that wretched talent show, a copy of our bucket list, and an itinerary. "I know I'm rambling, and I anticipated I would, so this explains everything in much clearer detail than I'm doing right now."

Sienna reaches for the note, stunned. "Oh my gosh."

"Before you say yes or no, just read the note, okay? And think about it. And okay, I'm going to run away now because I feel very awkward. Also, sorry to bother you at work. Bye!"

I turn on my heel and practically sprint toward the patio in search of Diego. He and Margot are still chatting, so I grab Diego's arm, wave a hasty goodbye to Margot, and pull him all the way to the car.

"Jeez, where's the fire?" Diego asks, rubbing his arm where I yanked him. "Margot was filling me in on some of the country club drama!"

"Sorry, but I started to lose my nerve the more I talked, and I just needed to go," I admit. "I did it, though! I asked Sienna! I gave her the note."

Diego reaches over and grips my shoulder. "You did it."

"And now I want to barf," I whine.

He tsks at me. "Barf later. We have another stop to make."

* * *

Maybe I should be less nervous to approach Ramona now that I've gotten the first ask out of the way, but I'm shaking like a leaf.

I couldn't even work up the courage to say hello the other night at Speakeasy.

How am I going to do *this*?

"Ooh, should I get a tattoo?" Diego asks as he mulls over some of the flash tattoos displayed on the wall of Permanent Record. "Look how cute this one is! Why do I kind of want it on my lower back?" He points at a hibiscus flower, which, yes, is very much cute, but that's not the point.

"We're not here so you can get a tattoo," I hiss.

"Oh, you're no fun," he says with a sigh. Then he leans over the counter. "Hi! We're here for Ramona?"

The person behind the counter smiles. "Great! I'm Lucy. Do you have an appointment?"

"We do. For three o'clock. We're getting matching tattoos." The way the lies come right off Diego's tongue is almost enviable.

Lucy checks the computer, then frowns. "Hmm, I'm not seeing anything here..."

"Really? That's so weird because I actually made the appointment with Ramona herself." Diego mirrors Lucy's frown, pulling out his phone to check for a confirmation we absolutely never got. "Ugh, I'm having trouble getting internet in here. Would you be able to check with Ramona?"

"Yeah, for sure. Wait right here, please," Lucy says, before disappearing upstairs.

"Why did you do that?" I whisper.

Diego waves a hand at me. "Let's see if it works before you get all grumpy."

A few minutes later, Lucy comes to the top of the stairs, Ramona in tow. My breath catches in my throat at the sight of her. Her curly hair is knotted in a half bun on top of her head, and her dark eyes are lined in black. Her tattooed arms are crossed over the crop-top tee she's wearing on top of ripped black jeans and combat boots. She looks... *good*. I swallow.

I'm so mesmerized by seeing her in the daylight rather than hidden in the darkness of Speakeasy that I barely register the scowl on her face.

"Can I help you?" she asks, stomping down the stairs. Her raspy voice feels as familiar as it always did, even if the question is clearly pointed.

"Chloe has something she wants to talk to you about." Diego shoves me forward. "Go on, Chloe. And sorry, Lucy. We don't actually have an appointment."

She gives him a thin-lipped smile. "I see that."

I shoot Diego my most poisonous glare for not thinking this through. But there's no going back now. So I turn to Ramona and put on a bright smile, though my insides are quivering. "Hi— Hey. Long time no see. Um. Do you have a minute?"

She blinks at us, and the air in the room feels... *heavy*.

Diego clears his throat. "Lucy, can we talk about some of these flash tattoos?"

Lucy looks over at Ramona. "You good?" Ramona gives her a slight nod, and Lucy turns back to Diego. "Come on into the office." She guides Diego into a small room, leaving me and Ramona alone.

"I'll make it quick, then. Here." I grab the note and list from my tote and hand them to her. "This is probably the strangest request you'll ever get, but I hope you'll consider it and not, like, burn the letter before reading."

Ramona doesn't reach for the note. "You know I don't like surprises, and now you're springing two on me?"

"I'm sorry." I bite my lip. "I didn't know where to start."

"Maybe you could've started by saying hello when you saw me last weekend rather than hiding and pretending I wasn't there?"

I cringe—literally cringe—at the thought of Ramona watching me hide behind the bar at Speakeasy. "You *saw* me?"

"Stealth has never really been your strong suit," she says dryly.

"Right. I definitely should've said hello. I saw you and totally panicked. I'm sorry. And I'm sorry for coming to you out of the blue at work like this. I'm sure you feel totally blindsided."

"Yeah," Ramona replies in a clipped voice. "It's not great."

God, this could not be going any worse. There is no way Ramona's ever going to agree to this. I'm still holding out the note like some kind of idiot! Stuffing it in my mouth and eating it feels less shameful than continuing to offer it to her, as if hope didn't die, right here, in this tattoo shop.

Admittedly, this is part of what I've always loved about Ramona. She's tough as hell. It's great until it's aimed at you. Then it's terrifying. Like right now.

"Do you need a favor or something?" Ramona asks.

"What? No!"

She snatches the note, dangling it in front of me. "So this won't say anything about how you've found your life's passion and you're making a bunch of money working from home and you need me to join the downline for your MLM?"

"Ew, gross. No. Absolutely not. Cross my heart."

Ramona starts to open the envelope so she can read the letter. I stop her. "Not here! Please."

"Why not?"

"Because you're making me really nervous and I'd rather not be here when you read that over."

She rolls her eyes. "Oh my God, relax."

"I can't! Not when you're looking at me like that."

Ramona plasters a fake smile on her face. "Better?"

"Actually, yes." I stand up straighter to try to regain some of the confidence I've lost through this interaction. "All I'm trying to do is ask if you want to go see Intonation with me. You know—relive our glory days as obsessed fans who wanted to marry them?"

Ramona narrows her eyes at me. "You remember that I'm gay, right?"

My cheeks flush a little, but I recover. "Yeah, well, is there anything gayer than three queer former besties showing up to a boy band concert?"

"Does this mean she's coming too?" Ramona doesn't say Sienna's name, but she doesn't have to.

"Yes," I say, then amend. "Maybe. I hope. I was hoping you'd both say yes. I just got three tickets to their reunion show."

"For your birthday." It's more of a statement than a question, and I'm surprised she remembers my birthday. Then again, I remember hers and Sienna's, too.

I nod. "Yeah. For my birthday."

Ramona looks down at the envelope in her hands. Then back up at me. "I can't just up and leave, you know. I have a job. People depend on me."

She says it as if I couldn't possibly understand, and it makes anger flare defensively in my chest. Either I've gotten softer, or she's gotten sharper.

"I never said it would be easy for you to get the time off work. That's why I am simply *asking*. And I acknowledge that this is a lot. *I* am a lot. I get it. So read the note or don't. I only wanted to invite you because it would mean a lot to me—and I think it could mean a lot to you, too, if you'd stop pretending to be tough for, like, two seconds and actually let it."

I turn and signal to Diego that we're done, then walk out of the tattoo shop without waiting for him.

I hope it looks way more badass than I feel. At least it's over, though. I put myself out there. I asked. I tried.

I only hope Ramona and Sienna can remember how occasionally endearing my over-the-top, impulsive ideas can be…and that they say yes.

Chapter Twelve

Waiting to hear from Sienna and Ramona is actual torture. It's been two days since I talked to them, and I haven't heard a word from either of them. I'm supposed to leave *tomorrow*.

The only thing that provides even a mild distraction is that I have another party to attend as Princess Julieta—my last for the summer. But in between singing and entertaining the kids, I find my mind drifting to this harebrained scheme of mine.

What was I thinking?! Why did I think this was a good idea? A sea of shame washes over my whole body every time I think of this road trip I dreamed up. I wish I had left the idea in the recesses of my mind rather than impulsively trying to make it happen.

Papi must be able to read the misery all over my face the moment I get home, because he swoops into overprotective dad mode. "What's going on? Are you okay?"

I pull off my princess wig and free my hair from its French braid, massaging my scalp. "I'm fine, just in my own special purgatory waiting to hear whether Sienna and Ramona will go on this road trip with me. And feeling especially pathetic that I have no other friends I can ask. And that I resorted to this absolutely wild plan in the first place."

"I never should've gotten the three tickets. It's too much pressure," Papi says, shaking his head.

"Ito," Karina warns from the kitchen. "Let the girl sulk! There's still time for everything to work out."

"Okay, okay. You're right," Papi calls to her. To me, he says, "But if they say no, though, what's plan B?"

"There is no plan B," I admit. "I mean, I'll still go. But going alone feels pathetic."

"We'll go with you," Papi offers. "Finally put those years of you forcing us to listen to them over and over and over to good use."

Karina comes into the living room rubbing her belly. "That's a nice thought, but I'm well past the point of being allowed to fly."

Papi frowns. "As soon as I said it, I knew it wasn't a good idea. I don't want you to be that far away from the doctors."

I plop onto the couch. "I'll figure something out."

His forehead furrows. "Do you want a different gift, mija? I can sell these tickets if they're making you this miserable."

"No! I want to go. I really, really want to go," I assure him. "But I also really, really want Sienna and Ramona to come."

Papi pats me on the shoulder. "They will, mi amor. They will."

But how can he know that?

Neither Sienna nor Ramona has texted me since I've spoken to them. It feels like the ultimate confirmation that this ask is far too big.

I think the worst part is the shame. My most impulsive ideas have a fifty-fifty chance of leaving me feeling this way, but this feels worse than normal.

"How about you start packing?" Karina suggests. "At least that's something you can control."

I nod. "That's a good idea. Okay. I'll do that."

In my room, I start the impossible task of packing bags for a hypothetical trip that may not happen. Then, restless with anxiety, I restart the Deadly Flora group chat.

Me: hey! i haven't heard from you guys about the trip. i know it's a lot, so i totally understand if you'd rather not go. but please do let me know if it's a no. if you're still considering, then let me know that, too. either way, i'll plan to be at open sesame bagels tomorrow morning at 7 with a car packed and ready to go. i hope you'll both be there, too 🖤

After I send the message, I immediately silence notifications. The anxiety is just too big to swallow.

The text from Sienna comes later that night.

Sienna: I'm in!!!

Sienna: I'm sorry it took me so long to confirm. I had to rearrange some things and make sure my mom could properly take care of my cat without overfeeding him. 🐈 But I'll be there!

And I breathe a sigh of relief. At least I'm not making this trip alone.

Me: i'm so happy to hear that, sienna!! ★ yaaaay. see you tomorrow!

I let Papi know, which switches him into overdrive triple-checking all our reservations, confirmations, and everything in between.

• ✦ •

Then, in a blink, it's the morning of the trip.

If anyone has ever wondered where my doing-the-most gene comes from, they should meet Papi. In addition to all that he has already done for my birthday, he went out of his way to rent a newer version of my dandelion-yellow Jeep so I'll be as comfortable as possible driving cross-country. He also packed bags of snacks and drinks and an "emergency car kit" that includes a compressor (as if I know how to use that), flashlights, blankets, a first aid kit, a glass breaker, a seatbelt cutter, and extra phone chargers.

"Are you sure you have everything you need?" Papi looks frantic as he surveys the items stuffed into the back of the Jeep. "I feel like we're forgetting something."

"If we add anything else to the car, there won't be room for Chloe and her friends," Karina teases. "I think she's good, mi amor."

"Oh! The pastelillos!" And Papi rushes toward the house.

Karina and I burst into laughter. "Think he'll be okay while I'm gone?"

"He may go bald from the stress, but this is a good challenge for him. A *necessary* one. You know I'll take good care of him."

"Oh, I don't doubt that. Remind him that once I'm back, we have the whole week on the Cape before I leave for school."

"Of course I will."

I point at Karina and smile. "As for you, I hope you take it easy, rest as much as you can, let Papi treat you like the queen that you are, and don't go into labor without me!" I put my hands on either side of her belly, lowering my voice to a whisper. "You hear that, baby? Wait for me before you make your debut."

She pulls me into a hug. "I'm going to miss your sunshine over this next week. You take good care of yourself, okay?" Karina rubs my back soothingly, then pulls away. "And most importantly, have the time of your life!"

"I will, promise."

Karina glances at the house and back at me. "Don't tell your papi I said this, but it's okay if you're a little reckless. Not with the car or anything, but I just mean—you know. Live a little. Take some risks. Make good mistakes."

I smile. "I can do that. Love you, Karina."

Though we don't often say this to each other, I want her to know it's true before I leave on this trip. It feels important. As she hears the words, her eyes glisten with tears.

"I love you too, kid." She kisses me on the cheek. "I'm going to go check on your father."

Karina pads into the house and I slip into the Jeep to do my own last-minute once-over without distractions. Along with my clothes and essentials, I have a brand-new refill of my ADHD prescription, a book (*For Brown Girls with Sharp Edges and Tender Hearts* by Prisca Dorcas Mojica Rodríguez), my tote and all the essentials, a few games like Uno in case things get really bad, and my travel watercolor kit from Diego. My phone is loaded up with enough audiobooks and podcasts to last me the next year, and I've got some of Diego's Spotify playlists saved for emergencies.

When I look up, Diego's car is pulling into the driveway. He hops out still wearing his pajamas. "It's so early. See what I do for you? You better be grateful." He yawns.

I make an excessively sympathetic face. "Oh, you poor, suffering soul."

"I need my beauty sleep. This"—Diego motions toward his face and body—"doesn't just *happen,* you know."

"Oh, I know. I'm so grateful you sacrificed your rest to say goodbye to me!" I step out of the Jeep to face him.

"You better be. So, you and Sienna, huh?"

"Me and Sienna," I confirm.

"It'll definitely be a less terrifying trip without Ramona's scowl in the car with you," Diego admits. "Are you excited?"

I nod. "Actually, I am. I think this will be good."

"I mean, it's basically an all-inclusive vacation on Daddy's dime so you can see your favorite band of all time. I'd say you'll have a pretty dope time," Diego teases. I swat at him. "Seriously. Don't let Ramona being a brat ruin your trip. Enjoy it, or I'll fly out to Vegas just to screech at you!"

I hold a hand over my heart and nod like I'm getting all choked up. "You have such a way with words. I'm going to miss you bullying me."

"And I will miss being the one thing in your life that makes you cool, but it's only for a week, and then I'll resume my rightful place." Diego grabs me and pulls me into a hug. "Love you, stupid."

"Love you more, idiot."

Papi's laugh bellows from behind us. "I'll never understand the way you two talk to each other."

"It's how we bond, Tío," Diego says, pulling back from me. "Oooh, are those pastelillos?"

Papi pulls the Tupperware back and out of his reach. "For the trip!"

"Aww, c'mon. I'm up at the buttcrack of dawn to say farewell to your daughter. Can't you spare one?" He puckers out his lower lip. "Pleeeeease?"

With a sigh, Papi hands them over, and Diego happily makes one of the pastelillos his.

"Sooo good," Diego says, mouth full. "Okay, I'm out. Try not to miss me too much!" And with a wave, he climbs back into the car and takes off.

Leaving just Papi.

I knew saying goodbye to him would be a whole thing, but I don't exactly want to cry before the trip even begins. So my mouth takes off before my brain catches up.

"Now that I have the pastelillos, I really am good to go. I made Karina promise not to go into labor until I'm back, by the way. Make sure she doesn't do anything too strenuous? And I have a succulent plant on my windowsill that I haven't managed to kill yet—if you could water that once for me while I'm gone, that'd be amazing. I'll definitely call from every stop, so you don't have to worry about that, and—"

Papi puts his hands on either side of my shoulders. "I truly trust you, mija."

And with those five words, many of the worries that have been pinging around in my brain whoosh right out.

So, too, do the tears. I sniffle and collapse into my dad for a hug. He squeezes me tight.

"I promise I'll be safe."

"I know you will be," he says, stroking my hair.

"And it's only seven days." But I know that both of us are thinking about what comes after those seven days—when it won't just be a week, but a whole semester, until eventually...

"Sí. Seven days."

"Thank you, Papi. For everything."

I hear his breath hitch and I look up to see his eyes wet with tears too. Papi has always been in touch with his emotions, but seeing him all choked up because I'm leaving sends a wave of fresh apprehension through me. I know it's not because of *this*—it's because of what's to come—but that doesn't make it any easier.

"I love you, mija."

"I love you, too."

And with that, I climb into the car, secure the pastelillos in the passenger seat, and head toward my first stop.

Chapter Thirteen

I'm the first to arrive at Open Sesame Bagels. I order myself a breakfast sandwich and an iced lavender oat milk latte, plus the coffee orders I last remember Sienna and Ramona enjoying: iced chai for Sienna, iced black coffee for Ramona. Aren't brains weird? I can remember obscure things like coffee orders from years ago, but I literally cannot tell you what I ate for lunch yesterday.

I don't even know why I'm ordering for Ramona, as if she's coming. *But*...if anyone was just going to show up at the last minute, it'd be her. And maybe I'm still feeling a little hopeful she might.

When my order's ready, I take everything outside and grab a seat on the patio so I can watch for Sienna's arrival. It doesn't take long. She gets dropped off by her mom, and the nerves that shoot through my body make me immediately lose my appetite.

Sienna is wearing a pale green sundress and sunglasses. Her golden-red hair glistens under the sun like she's in her own personal shampoo commercial, and she's lugging two gigantic suitcases—with a purse and a sun hat strapped to one—behind her. She looks effortlessly beautiful, as always, and my throat instantly dries up. The flowy, tropical-leaf-printed jumpsuit I'm wearing feels like an earsplitting shout compared to the gentle whisper of her entire vibe.

"Morning!" Sienna waves.

I find my voice. "Hey! Let me help you with that." I meet her in the lot and grab one of her bags, leading her to my Jeep. We load her items into the car, Sienna stashing her sun hat in the front seat.

Her eyes scan the many things already piled inside. "Wow, this is already pretty full. Hopefully Ramona packs light."

"Yeah, if she comes," I say, forcing a light laugh.

"Still no text from her?" Sienna asks, and I shake my head. "Bummer. But we'll have fun anyway!"

"Yeah! Also, sorry my dad went a little wild with the packing. At least we know we'll have everything we need."

She smiles. "Is he still as overprotective as he used to be?"

"Maybe even more so now. He and my stepmom have a baby on the way, and it seems like that has kicked his paternal instincts into overdrive." I shut the trunk.

"Wow! I had no idea they were expecting," Sienna says. "Are you excited?"

"I am! They're having a girl, so that will be really fun."

Sienna drapes an arm over me. "Congratulations, big sis!"

Even though I had nothing to do with it, I still flush with pride. "Thanks! Oh, and hey—I got you a coffee at the table over there."

"That's so sweet! Thank you." We walk over to where I'd been sitting, and I hand her the drink. "It's an iced chai. I'm not sure if that's still what you drink, so I'm happy to replace it if there's something else you'd prefer?"

"An iced chai is perfect. I can't believe you remembered that." Sienna smiles. "Do we want to give Ramona a few minutes, just in case? I'd love to use the bathroom and grab something to eat. I'm starving."

"Sure. That works," I say, secretly glad I'm not the only one hoping Ramona might show.

Sienna tips her chin toward the bagel shop. "Great. I'll head inside. Text me if she shows up while I'm ordering and I can grab something for her, too."

"Sounds good."

As she disappears into the café, I sink back into my chair and let my shoulders relax. That wasn't nearly as awkward as I worried it would be. Even if this trip *is* just me and Sienna, it can still be amazing.

* * *

We wait for half an hour before we decide to call it. By then, the ice in Ramona's coffee has melted from the heat, but at least Sienna and I have both had a chance to eat our breakfast and settle into some sense of familiarity.

"Should we give her another minute?" Sienna asks as we climb into the Jeep.

"We've given her plenty of minutes," I say, my voice bitterer than I intend. "Dibs on her iced coffee?"

Sienna laughs. "It's all yours. As long as I get to pick what we listen to first."

I start the engine and Sienna works on connecting her phone to the car. Just as I begin to ease out of my parking spot, a motorcycle blares its horn, blasting past my car so fast I need to slam on my brakes.

I roll down my window, the Masshole in me fully taking charge. "Watch where you're going, jackass!"

"Ooh, spicy Chloe! I like it!" Sienna giggles. Then she suddenly touches my wrist. "Wait! I think that might be Ramona!" We both peer out the window to where the motorcycle halted.

Sure enough, it's her.

My stomach twists as I watch Ramona let go of the driver and climb off the back of the motorcycle. She pulls off her helmet, revealing her curls. I hate that I think she looks good: black tank top, combat boots, and ripped black shorts over fishnet tights. Totally impractical for summer. Totally Ramona.

Sienna hops out of the passenger seat. "Speak of the Devil."

"Sorry, am I late?" Ramona jokes. She slings a black duffel over her shoulders, then produces a coffee and a bag from Speakeasy. The absolute audacity! If she's late because she trekked to the *next town over* for food instead of grabbing something from the bagel place we're *literally at right now,* I'm going to kill her.

I throw open my door and step out of the car toward her. "Yes, you are. We were about to leave!"

"Made it just in time, then." She smirks. "I had a quick stop to make first. The coffee here is trash."

"Seriously? You're late because you think the coffee here is bad?" I huff. "Unbelievable."

Sienna reaches for Ramona's bag. "You want to copilot? Or would you prefer the back?"

"The back," Ramona says. "Thanks."

I put my hands on my hips. "You couldn't text that you were coming?"

Ramona reaches over and pinches my cheek. "You're so adorable when you're angry."

I pull my face away from her, ignoring the unexpected jolt I felt from her touch.

"Is that your girlfriend driving the motorcycle?" Sienna asks, waggling her eyebrows.

Another smirk from Ramona, but she says nothing and instead slips into the Jeep. "Should we get going? Seems like we're somehow already behind schedule."

"Oh, whatever," I grumble, plopping into the driver's seat. I adjust the rearview mirror. "And I had *already* ordered you a coffee, by the way. I'll drink this *trash* myself, I guess."

I look back at Ramona in the rearview mirror and we lock eyes, staring at each other. She looks away first, no apology. I say nothing either, just pull the Jeep out of the lot and hope I don't strangle her before we even cross the state line.

Chapter Fourteen

I wish I could say that as soon as Ramona, Sienna, and I are officially reunited, it's like no time has passed, and the conversation is so easy, and we can't stop laughing, and it's a dream.

But that would be a big honking lie.

Because the first few hours of the trip are actually pretty painful: quiet, slow, and light on small talk between songs on Sienna's playlist.

The good news is that I'm not nearly as nervous as I thought I'd be seated next to Sienna. Maybe the crush feelings I've been having weren't exactly that. The bad news is that I'm still SO IRRITATED at Ramona.

If we were on better terms, I'd want to keep arguing about how inconsiderate it was of her to never text me back. Instead, because this is supposed to be *fun*, we make polite conversation: about random pop culture things; Ramona's apprenticeship (she was able to take time off for this trip, though it had to be without pay); Sienna's desire to someday become a doctor (she got into Johns Hopkins and figures this is the perfect way to get her parents off her back); and my soon-to-be baby sister (and how I recently got to paint a colorful garden mural in her nursery).

It's not exactly groundbreaking friendship shit (although, in fairness, it's not quite nothing, either).

When we near Syracuse, about four hours into our trip, I suggest a pit stop so we can refuel and stretch our legs. I need a break.

Sienna volunteers to find us a cute place to eat, and Ramona mentions she's vegetarian. Once Sienna finds us a place with decent options for Ramona, I pop it into GPS and drive until we arrive in downtown Syracuse at a brick building with orange signs that read MODERN MALT.

"I picked this place because they have French toast covered in Fruity Pebbles, and I absolutely need that in my life right now." Sienna turns in her seat to Ramona. "They also have poutine. Remember when you went through that phase in, like, the seventh grade where you randomly ran around shouting 'poutine' at the top of your lungs just because you thought the word was hilarious?"

I stifle a giggle and glance in the mirror to see Ramona's cheeks turn pink.

"Unfortunately. I was going through my quirky girl phase," Ramona mumbles.

Sienna nods sagely. "It happens to us all."

We pile inside the restaurant, outfitted to look like a diner, and wait for a table.

"I have to run to the restroom." I point toward the sign. "Meet you at the table?"

In the bathroom, I pull out my phone and text Diego.

Me: okay, so, this is a disaster???

Diego: lol

Diego: girl it's been like 3 hours

Me: AND???

Me: FOUR HOURS STUCK IN A SILENT CAR

Me: BARELY TALKING

Me: AND SIENNA JUST PLAYS SAPPHIC SAD GIRL SONGS

Diego: k sounds like ur vibe tho?

Me: don't start!!!

Diego: ok ok. i mean u knew it was gonna be a little awkward

Diego: maybe u should address it?

Me: how???????????

Diego: can u chill on the question marks

Diego: just be like ok this is awkward and it will make everyone laugh

Me: as if it would be that easy!!!!!!

Diego: u use punctuation like ur punishing it

Diego: but do u have any better ideas

Diego: also are u texting while driving lol

Me: no, we stopped to get something to eat

Diego: ok good im not trying to have u die and then they turn these texts into a sad billboard

Diego: anyway

Diego: sit down w them and be like how can we make this fun for everyone

Me: okay, actually, i like that idea

Me: i have no idea why they even agreed to this in the first place, so it would be nice to know and talk beyond just, like, chitchat

Diego: ur welcome

Diego: now go away im at the movies w benny

Me: OOOH tell me everything later!!!!!

Diego: obviously

Diego: now bye

With a relieved sigh, I tuck my phone into my tote bag.

Okay. This is doable. Right?

I can practically feel Diego shoving me out of the bathroom with a *GIRL, GO,* so I finish up in the restroom, wash my hands, and find our table.

Sienna and Ramona are both poring over the menu as if it holds the nation's secrets. They're sitting on opposite sides of the table, a spot available on either side. Since Sienna has at least been making an effort, I choose to sit beside her. The side of Ramona's mouth twitches as I do, though she says nothing. But if she's going to be so petty as to get annoyed at which side of the table I sit on, then we're going to have bigger problems.

"How's everything look?" I ask, breaking the silence.

"Delicious. I was dead set on the French toast but now I'm second-guessing myself," Sienna says. "They have a chicken sandwich that sounds really good."

"How about you, Ramona?"

"There aren't a ton of vegetarian options," she replies in a clipped tone.

Sienna's shoulders sink. "I thought you said the menu looked okay to you? We could go somewhere else."

Ramona waves her hand dismissively. "No, no. I'll probably get the Look Ma! No Meat Omelette." She makes a pained expression as she speaks the name of the menu item aloud, like it's one of the worst things she's ever had to say. She's never been a fan of cutesy menus.

I bump Sienna's shoulder with mine. In return, Sienna smirks at me, but neither of us says anything, even though I know we're both thinking some version of: *Gahhhhh, Ramona, stop being so difficult!*

"Well, I think I'm going to have a burger," I say. "More importantly, though, I was hoping we could have a serious talk."

Sienna's green eyes turn to saucers. "Oh, no. Is it bad? Are you dying? I knew there had to be a bigger reason for this trip!"

"What?" I shake my head. "No! It's nothing like that. I mean, yes, I do want to talk about the trip, but that's not the reason for it. I'm not dying. It really was a birthday gift from my dad."

She breathes a sigh. "Oh, thank goodness."

"I mostly wanted to thank you both for agreeing to this. I know it was a huge—and let me reiterate, *very weird*—request," I begin. "I was thinking about it in the car, and I'm honestly not sure what I would've done if the shoe had been on the other foot. So...I was sort of wondering what inspired you to say yes, and maybe what you're hoping to get out of this? I mean, we have seven days. We should make the most of them, and I would really like it if all three of us could leave this trip feeling it was worthwhile, you know?"

"That's a great idea," Sienna says, nodding. "I was really skeptical at first because...well, we haven't really hung out in *years*. The offer, um, seemed really random and out of the blue. But then I read your note and you write exactly like you talk. It made me laugh. It reminded me so much of how following your conversation can be like going along for the ride to an unknown destination."

I laugh. "That's the kindest way anyone has ever explained my scatterbrained thoughts."

"It's true, though! Then looking at that dorky picture of us, plus the actual bucket list, brought back so many memories for me. I don't know. I guess I just thought it could be fun." She toys with her menu. "Plus…it'll be nice to be away from my mom and stepdad breathing down my neck all the time. I mean, don't get me wrong! They're fine. But a lot. They're so focused on my success that it feels suffocating. Seven days away from that sounds like heaven, honestly."

"That makes perfect sense to me. If this trip brings you nothing more than a little relief, then I'll be happy." I smile at her. "Thanks for sharing that."

"Of course. Like you said, we have seven days together. Might as well rip off the Band-Aid now, right?"

It's then that a server wearing a name tag that reads JON comes to our table, asking if we're ready to order. We take turns requesting our meals and drinks.

"And can we order a dish for the table?" I ask. "We'd love some poutine to share."

Jon collects our menus and whisks away to grab our drinks.

"You didn't have to do that," Ramona says.

I shrug. "What? It's vegetarian! And funny."

Sienna turns to me. "Okay, your turn. What made you invite us? I'm not sure I'd have had the courage, honestly."

"This is going to sound absurd, but it just sort of…made sense to me. I had run into you both by pure coincidence in the *same day*. Or, rather—I was the entertainment at Sienna's little cousin's birthday party…"

Ramona snorts just as Jon returns lightning fast with our drinks. "No shit?"

"Full princess dress, songs, and everything," I say, reaching for my ice water. "It left me feeling very humbled. And also a little nostalgic."

"Aww, I thought you did a great job as Princess Julieta!" Sienna giggles. "Ana hasn't stopped talking about how she had a real fairy-tale princess at her birthday."

"Well, that's pretty sweet. And then later that night, I went to Speakeasy with my cousin Diego—you guys remember him, right?—and I saw Ramona there," I explain.

"Not that you said hello," she reminds me. To Sienna, she adds, "Chloe ducked behind the bar to hide from me."

Sienna gasps. "You didn't!"

I fidget with the straw in my drink. "Oh, no, I fully did."

"Chloe!" Sienna thwacks my shoulder.

"Anyway! That was obviously odd. I'd gone so long without seeing or talking to either of you, then bam, I see you both the same day. So you were already front of mind. And then I got those tickets from Papi, and it made me think of our bucket list. I remembered being so sure that I'd cross everything off that list with you guys. So I got this wild idea in my brain that we should actually try to do it, and try to reconnect. Is that totally weird?"

"Not *totally*," Ramona concedes. "But definitely, like, up there." I take the balled-up paper from my straw and throw it at her. It gets caught in her curls. "Hey, now! We were all thinking it. Don't shoot the messenger."

"I can't help being a sentimental softie. I get it from my dad!" I clear my throat. "Plus, um. I've sort of been having a hard time with all these huge milestones—you know, my family will be expanding soon, I'll be moving away to college—and it's sort of a lot. This was my way of hanging on to the past for a little longer, I guess... but also proving to myself that I can do things without my family."

"I really relate to that," Sienna confesses. "I'll be thrilled to get some distance between me and my parents, but less thrilled to leave my friends behind. It'll be weird in the fall not being at the same school."

"Definitely," I agree. Then I tap the table in front of Ramona. "Okay, I spilled my guts. Now what made you decide to come?"

"Well, I almost didn't."

"Yet here you are," I deadpan. "What changed?"

"I don't have any cutesy or emotional story for you," Ramona admits, looking down at her hands. "But I was able to book a tattoo out in Las Vegas with this artist I really love. I've been following her work for about a year and she recently posted she'll be doing a few flash tats next week, so I grabbed a spot." She motions toward her upper thigh. "I'm going to get an iris here—since that's my mom's name—to celebrate her and all she's done for me."

There's a ringing in my ears.

I'm hit with the realization that her decision to come had absolutely nothing to do with me or Sienna.

Ramona wasn't moved by my note; she didn't look back on our friendship with fondness; and she sure as hell isn't hoping for any kind of reconciliation the way I have been. For her, this is entirely transactional. A free trip to Vegas with some random people. I don't know what to say.

Thankfully, Sienna speaks.

"What a beautiful idea for a tattoo," she says softly. "I bet your mom will love it."

Ramona chuckles, rubbing the back of her neck. "She'll hate that I'm getting another one. Hopefully she sees it's meant to show her I love her, though."

I try to push past my own hurt because I don't want to cry in a restaurant. Maybe it's not that what Ramona's doing is wrong; maybe *I* was the fool for tying so many emotions and expectations to this trip. Silly, sentimental, can't-move-on Chloe.

"I'm sure she will," I say, swallowing my feelings. "So, to be clear, you're not here because you had any desire whatsoever to go to the concert?"

Sienna tilts her head to the side, studying Ramona as we wait for an answer.

Ramona tucks a strand of hair behind her ear, looking a little sheepish. *Good.*

"I mean, I'll *go*, but it wasn't my top reason…" Sienna shoots me a sympathetic look, and I swallow hard, trying to hide the betrayal I'm feeling. When Ramona notes my face, she quickly adds, "I just didn't think you'd care!"

I give her a strained smile. "We don't."

Chapter Fifteen

God, I am livid. How can Ramona, in good conscience, show up for our road trip with her own agenda and not even *fake* caring about the concert? That was the whole point of this trip! I mean, I know it was me who built this up in my head, but the absolute nerve of that girl!

Who does she think she is? How does she not see how inconsiderate her plan is? My family is paying her way, but she has *zero* interest in the show or in this friendship or even in the road trip! It's so infuriatingly selfish that I have a hard time ignoring the hot ball of anger that's grown in my chest.

I even consider calling Papi to tell him I want to go home, but no. I deserve to go to this concert, and I need to stick this out and figure it out on my own.

I'm quiet with these thoughts through lunch, but the atmosphere when we get back into the car is tense.

Before I turn on the engine, in a quiet voice, I say, "I think it really sucks that you can't even pretend you want to be here with us, Ramona."

From the back seat, she says, "That's not what I said..."

It surprises me when Sienna speaks up. "Isn't it, though?"

Sienna and I lock eyes, and she gives me a look of solidarity. That, at the very least, settles my nerves a little. Okay. I'm not alone in this frustration. I take a deep breath and turn on the car.

Things are quiet. I don't even bother making the occasional cutesy observation of "Cow" or "Horse" along the way.

Beside me, Sienna uses the time from Syracuse to Buffalo to review the itinerary Papi and I put together. She takes it upon herself to start a shared collection of restaurants, attractions, and gas stations along the route and near our hotels.

"I wish we had time to stop at Niagara Falls," she says wistfully. "It's not too far from our hotel."

"Why can't we?" I ask. "We have plenty of buffer time built into this trip."

She toys with her hair, doing mental calculations. "Really? It feels too late to go today, and I'd rather not get us off course this early in the trip, you know? What if we get lost or something?"

"Are you doubting my ability to drive? Because you absolutely should be. I am terrible with direction." I hold up one hand and make an L with my thumb and forefinger. "I still do this to figure out left from right."

"Glad to know we're in good hands," Ramona mutters from the back seat.

I roll my eyes and ignore her. "So, no Niagara Falls?"

Sienna scrunches her nose. "I don't think so." She looks down at her phone. "On the bright side, this says we just take a right up here, drive about a mile, and then we're basically there. I'm excited. This is my first vacation without my family! It already feels so freeing."

"Really?" I ask. "How is it different?"

I don't admit that, despite this also being my first vacation without Papi, I'm finding it more overwhelming than freeing.

"Well, I mean...my parents are always *bickering* on vacation. They're terrible when they're out of their element, and they complain about literally everything." Sienna puts on a high-pitched voice, imitating her mom. " 'This place is so far from the hotel!' " Then her voice goes low like her dad's. " 'Why's this restaurant so expensive? Do they think they're a Michelin outfit?' It's so frustrating."

"That genuinely sounds miserable," I agree, feeling grateful that the most annoying thing Papi seems to do on vacation is come up with a dorky catchphrase and repeat it throughout the entire trip. When we visited Puerto Rico to see some of his and Titi Rosa's family, he kept jokingly going, "It's island time, baby!" Which was embarrassing but at least we could laugh about it.

Sienna nods. "Right? It's like, why bother going on a trip if you're not even going to pretend you want to be there?"

I look at Ramona in the rearview mirror and repeat what Sienna just said. "Yeah. Why *would* someone bother going on a trip if they're not even going to pretend they want to be there?"

She sinks low in her seat and puts her earbuds in, apparently done with listening to this conversation. Fine by me.

I ask Sienna to put on some music, and she chooses a 2010s playlist we can sing along to. The serotonin I feel when I hear the songs I loved growing up is enough to make me forget about Ramona's bullshit as we make our way to Buffalo.

Before long, we pull into our hotel parking lot.

"We made it," I say, more to myself than anyone. Because we did. We made it to our first stop and the world kept turning. Maybe I *can* do this.

The three of us gather our bags from the car and lug them inside. It's a modest chain hotel with ample lighting, just like Papi promised.

"Like I mentioned in that letter I wrote to you, we only have one room at each stop. I hope that's all right...he was worried if he split us up one of us would be kidnapped or something," I explain as we walk toward the desk to check in.

"Look, it's beyond generous that he's even covering all this. One room is more than fine," Sienna says.

Ramona clears her throat. "At home, I share a room with two of my four siblings. This will be paradise compared to that. Really."

I nod, appreciating that Ramona is making an attempt to be a little less unpleasant. "Okay. Great."

I check us in, then lead us up to the room. Inside, there are two queen-size beds and a couch that'll work as a pullout.

"I can take the pullout," I offer, even though I'm fairly certain a pullout bed will feel like literal death. But it doesn't seem polite to let either of the other girls sleep on it when it was my dad who booked the room.

"Don't be silly," Ramona says. "I'll take it."

Sienna shakes her head. "It's totally fine. I'm a heavy sleeper and I can take it."

I laugh a little. "Looks like we're stuck in a polite-off. I guess we can figure it out later. I mean, it's only"—I check my phone and grimace—"three thirty."

"Okay. But I really wouldn't mind," Ramona offers again. "Did we, um, have anything planned for the rest of the night, or…?"

"Nope," I admit. "Sienna?"

She pulls out her phone to scan the list she made. "I mean, there are a few places we could try. There's a historical museum?"

"I'm not sure my brain could handle reading a bunch of tiny placards with dates and facts right now. I'm sorry," I say.

"Honestly, great point." Sienna looks back at her list. "Okay, there's a botanical garden, but it looks like that closes at four. Let's see…Oh! There's something called the Wing Ride, where you go on a tour to discover the hidden history of chicken wings…but I wrote that one down more as a joke than anything, so…"

"I think we should go to Niagara Falls," Ramona suggests.

Sienna and I both look at her, surprised.

"We already decided we won't really have a lot of time there if we go tonight," Sienna reminds her.

"But you said you really wished you could go," Ramona says. "Shouldn't we at least try?"

I pull out my phone and search Niagara Falls. "It looks like the boats actually run until seven thirty in August…Oooh! And! At sunset, they have a light display that illuminates the entire waterfall."

"Really?" Sienna asks.

"Yeah! The website says the display will feature 'color palettes and movements inspired by nature, including the sunrise, aurora borealis, rainbow and sunset.' That sounds so pretty!" I turn my screen to show them both the photos.

"Wow, that looks incredible," Ramona admits.

"It really does," Sienna agrees.

I catch her gaze. "What do we think?" Whatever Sienna wants to do is what I want to do. I want her to know I have her back.

"Or we could stay here in the hotel and try not to die of boredom," Ramona says, trying to crack a joke. I don't laugh. Because I'm stubborn.

"We don't have to go," I assure Sienna.

But she breaks into a smile. "Let's do it."

I shimmy excitedly. "Yay!"

"Okay, let's take a few minutes to freshen up and then head out?" Sienna suggests.

"That sounds good," Ramona says. "This might be fun."

It's the nicest thing she's said thus far. I don't know if it's genuine, or just her feeling guilty for being such a buzzkill, but whatever. If a visit to Niagara Falls will help smooth things over, then I'm all in.

Chapter Sixteen

"*We ready?*" *Sienna asks.*

We're standing outside *Maid of the Mist*, the double-decker boat that takes tourists past the base of the American Falls and onto the basin of Horseshoe Falls.

I give her a firm nod. "Ready."

"Ditto," Ramona echoes.

The three of us trade our tickets for rain ponchos to wear during the ride (to protect our clothes from spray), then make our way onto the deck.

Though the drive into Niagara Falls was a little lackluster—lots of concrete and food trucks, and one tall glass building pretending to be the official welcome center draped in obnoxiously large red banners reading ATTRACTION and SHOPPING—Niagara Falls State Park is actually *beautiful*.

The scenery is so much more vivid than I imagined. On such a clear evening, it looks like someone pumped the saturation up all around us: the greenery is so emerald, and the water so cerulean, it's more like a painting than real life.

We climb to the *Maid of the Mist*'s upper deck and find a place to stand toward the front so we can see everything. Of the three of us, I'm the first to break out my new poncho. I slip it on over my outfit and hold out my arms. "How do I look?"

Sienna and Ramona exchange a look and then burst out laughing.

"Like a Smurf—but an adorable one," Sienna says, slipping hers on too. "At least we look like Smurfs together!"

We turn to Ramona expectantly, and she sneers. "I think I'll pass on the poncho."

I put my hands on my hips. "So you're going to let yourself get soaking wet?"

"I mean, it won't be that bad, will it?" Ramona asks.

"Oh, it's going to feel like showering with your clothes on," one of the male attendants quips. "But there's always one who tries to tough it out without the poncho. Congratulations! Sounds like today that might be you."

I bite my lip to keep from laughing as Ramona sighs and reluctantly tugs the crinkly poncho over her head.

"We need a picture!" I reach into my tote and pull out my phone. "C'mon."

"Oh, jeez," Ramona mutters, loud enough that I hear it.

But I'm not deterred. "Get used to it. I'm going to be forcing tons of group photos on this trip, and then I'll probably make a scrapbook, because that's the kind of person I am. Now, move closer!"

Sienna and Ramona do, and we all smile as I snap a picture. When I pull it up to review, my chest squeezes a little with joy. The three of us have another photo together, after all these years, and we actually look pretty happy in it. The cheesiness of it all is making me feel giddy.

"We did it," Sienna says, looking at the pic from over my shoulder. "We took our first dorky tourist picture of the trip! Can you send that to me?"

"And…me," Ramona adds.

"Thought you were too good for selfies?" I tease.

"Yeah, well, I looked really good in that one. Smurf poncho and all." She slips on her sunglasses, and I don't hide my smirk as I text the pic to our group chat.

By now, the boat has slowly started making its way toward the falls. I try to take everything in as we sail closer to the large white plume of mist.

Over the loudspeaker, the tour guide booms, "Cameras ready, folks, as we're nearing American Falls. There's not a bad view on the boat. Poncho hoods up, and enjoy!"

It's the last thing we're able to hear, because the sound of the falls up close is almost deafening. Once the boat parts the haze, we see it: the waterfalls, absolutely pouring down. The steady roar of water cascading into the river; the feel of cool droplets on my hot skin; the swish of the swirling rapids around the boat; the magical way the mist catches the summer sun, creating dazzling rainbows all around us—it all takes my breath away.

I'm enamored, and suddenly feeling very small and very grateful. I forget, even, to pull out my phone and snap a photo, so taken by what's in front of me.

"This is fucking incredible!" Sienna yells from beside me.

"Better than I imagined!" Ramona yells back.

Sienna gives her an enthusiastic nod. "I'm so glad you pushed for this! I didn't know how badly I wanted to be here until just now!"

"It's the perfect way to kick off this trip!" I scream.

We take it in, this beautiful and amazing and incredible sight, with smiles on our faces.

"Also, we look like Missy Elliott when she was wearing that garbage bag in her music video!" Ramona shouts. And she's totally right: the waterfall has generated so much wind that all our ponchos are inflated like balloons.

"Oh, yeah!" I shout, laughing. "We really do!"

Confusion falls over Sienna's face. "Who's Missy Elliott?"

I shake my head. "I'll show you later!"

But I don't have to because Ramona starts sing-shouting the song in question and absolutely . . . nailing it, somehow?

It takes me by such surprise I'm practically cackling because *finally,* she's loosened up a little and stopped worrying about trying so hard to look tough. Between that and the beauty around us and the sheer goofiness of this whole thing, I can't stop smiling.

Because this is the kind of stuff I was secretly imagining doing with

Sienna and Ramona when I was daydreaming about our hypothetical road trip. Road trips are *supposed* to be cheesy, and doing something super touristy like wearing a gigantic blue poncho to see one of Earth's wonders while your friend breaks into an unexpected Missy Elliott impression is somehow all I wanted.

The silliness I'm feeling must be contagious, because each time our tour guide spouts off a new fact, the three of us dramatically *ooh* and *aah* and scratch our chins like we're so impressed we can't stand it. We listen as they rattle off facts about Niagara Falls like:

Niagara Falls is actually the collective name for three different waterfalls!

The average depth of the water below Niagara Falls is 170 feet, meaning the gorge is as deep as it is high!

More than 600,000 gallons of water travel down the waterfalls every second!

And: fish actually travel over Niagara Falls, with around ninety percent of them surviving the plunge! (Not exactly odds I would take, but maybe fish, like me, are not so great with percentages.)

I *love* it.

The only downside is the mist keeps fogging my glasses, but I'll survive.

"All right," our tour guide announces after a bit, "we're coming up on our final waterfall: Horseshoe Falls, which accounts for about ninety percent of the water in the Niagara River and which is almost entirely located in Canada. Say hello to our Canadian friends, *eh*?" The guide does a terrible Canadian impression that makes us groan.

The boat moves closer to a huge, sprawling waterfall, a column of white vapor that seems to stretch all the way up to the sky. This time, I remember to take some photos and videos. Sienna is grinning like a little kid as the spray covers her face. When I turn to find Ramona, I see she's found a place to sit. Her eyes are closed.

I make my way over to check on her. "Hey. You okay?"

She offers a weak smile. "This is embarrassing, but the boat's starting to make me feel a little woozy."

"Oh, no! What do you need?"

Ramona shakes her head. "I honestly don't know. I've never been on a boat before."

My mind starts trying to cycle through anything I've read previously about cures for motion sickness. "Okay, so, I can never read in the car for this same reason, so I know looking at a screen will make it worse. Avoid your phone. And, um, I think drinking some water can help?"

"Can you grab my water bottle from my bag?" She points toward it. "I'm worried if I move I'll fall down or something."

"On it." I grab Ramona's bag and rifle through it until I come upon her water bottle, covered in stickers like DON'T TELL ME TO SMILE and MAY YOU HAVE THE CONFIDENCE OF A MEDIOCRE WHITE MAN. I pop open the top and hand it to her. She takes a long, grateful swig. "Better?"

She gives me a small nod.

"Hey, is everything cool?" Sienna asks, joining us.

"Ramona's feeling a little seasick."

"Oh, that sucks! Here, give me your arm." Sienna reaches for Ramona's arm, placing three fingers on the inside of her left wrist. She presses firmly and holds for a few seconds, then does the same thing on the other wrist. "Any better?"

Ramona takes a deep breath in through her nose. "Yeah, actually. That does help a little. You some kind of witch?"

Sienna laughs. "My abuela is super into alternative types of medicine, so I know all about these different acupressure points on your body that can help with certain things. The ones in your wrist can alleviate motion sickness. I'm glad it helped."

It's weird seeing Ramona be vulnerable like this, when earlier today I wanted nothing more than to yell at her. Suddenly, I feel much softer at the realization that she's not made of stone.

"What?" Ramona asks when she notices I'm looking at her.

"Nothing," I say, looking away from her and back at Sienna. "The boat ride's almost over, but any chance you're feeling up for taking a photo with all of us in front of the waterfall?"

"Oh, no, I've suddenly taken a turn for the worse," Ramona announces dramatically.

"You'll take another selfie with us and you'll like it." Sienna helps Ramona to her feet and we pose together. "Now, smile!"

Chapter Seventeen

After the boat ride, we give Ramona time to rest and recover before invading the souvenir shops. I pick out a mug for Karina and her beloved coffee; a Niagara Falls hoodie for Papi; a refrigerator magnet for Titi Rosa and Tío Gabriel; two stuffed moose for Naya and Ricky; a tiny Niagara Falls onesie for the baby (it's so small and cute!!!); and a postcard for myself. I get nothing for Diego because he finds souvenirs repulsive.

We get to watch the sunset over the falls, and that is even more stunning than you might imagine. Not even photos do it justice. Then night falls, the light show illuminates the water with color, and the three of us are quiet as we watch in awe.

When we get back to the hotel, Sienna announces she's going to hop in the shower, Ramona takes out a sketchbook, and I pull out the novel I brought. It feels like the vibe between the three of us has already shifted for the better, and I'm grateful. If we can maintain a cordial and friendly atmosphere for the rest of the trip, we might all actually have a nice time.

Before I can even finish reading the first page, Ramona breaks the silence in the room and blurts, "I'm sorry." I look over at her, surprised, and she continues. "I've been a jerk. About the trip."

My gaze falls to the book in my lap. "I mean…yeah. You have."

That makes us both laugh a little, cutting some of the tension.

"I know I should've texted you to tell you I was coming, but the truth is I was completely undecided until this morning," she explains, fiddling with the pages in her sketch pad. I can tell it's taking a lot for her to do this. "I woke up and panic-packed and called Sasha for a ride."

I clear my throat. "And Sasha is your...girlfriend?"

"God, no. No." She shakes her head. "We work together, and she almost killed me for waking her up so early."

"Serves you right," I say, a tiny smile tugging at the corner of my mouth. She smirks too.

It's not the apology I've been looking for, really—I was more both-ered by Ramona's reasoning for coming on the trip than anything else—but it's something.

"Now that we've cleared that up, should we do some shots?"

And I cough-laugh at the unexpected subject change. "I'm sorry, what?"

Ramona tosses her sketchbook to the side and rummages through her duffel bag. She pulls out a giant bottle of vodka. "I brought booze? Well, I made Manny get it for me. Still."

Sienna emerges from the bathroom with wet hair, eyebrows raised. "Did someone say booze?"

Ramona shows her the bottle she's holding. "Isn't *get drunk together* one of the items on the BFF Bucket List?"

Sienna claps her hands together excitedly. "It absolutely is!"

"Is this you admitting to us that you actually looked at the BFF Bucket List?" I prod.

"How do you know I didn't commit the entire thing to memory years ago?" Ramona asks, raising a shoulder into a shrug.

I point at her. "I knew it! You ol' softie!"

"Okay, enough talking. SHOTTTTTS!" Sienna whoops in a way I have never seen her do before, and I burst out laughing. "Put on some music, Chloe!"

I pull out my phone and select one of Diego's playlists as Ramona kicks off her Doc Martens and Sienna grabs three water cups from the bathroom.

"I don't know why, but I was not expecting that level of enthusiasm from you about vodka," I call after her.

Sienna returns, cups in hands. "Ahh, common misconception about the smart kids. Everyone thinks they're too goody-goody to get into much mischief, but holy shit. They *party*. Here." She shoves a cup into my hand.

Music blares from my phone as Ramona twists the cap off the vodka and pours a healthy shot for Sienna, then me, then herself.

"On three?" Sienna asks, a devilish grin on her face.

I hesitate. "Wait!"

Their eyes fall on me.

"You good?" Ramona asks.

"I am. It's just that—okay, I realize that admitting this out loud is incredibly embarrassing, but—I've never been drunk before?"

Ramona and Sienna exchange surprised looks. Then Sienna laughs. "You're joking...?"

I shake my head. "I mean, I've had *a* drink here and there, but that's been it. I've always been too nervous to go any further. Like, what if I'm a total weirdo when I'm drunk? What if I turn mean? What if I forget who I am, and I never remember again, and I spend my whole life trying to figure out what my name is?"

"It's alcohol, not amnesia," Sienna teases.

"We can pack it up and do something else," Ramona assures me. She reaches for the bottle, as if her mind is already made up, but I put my hand over hers to stop her.

"I never said that. I am nervous, though."

Ramona gives me a soft smile. "That's okay."

Sienna nods. "That's what we're here for. If you're going to do something for the first time, it should be with your friends, right?"

Hearing her say that calms me. Right. I'm with *friends* here.

I reach for the plastic cup that's been set out for me, then hold it up. "Okay. So. Cheers?"

They press their cups to mine and in unison say, "Cheers!"

Chapter Eighteen

The first shot feels like liquid fire as it slithers down my throat, and I fight the urge to spit the whole thing out.

"It gets better," Ramona promises. "Or maybe you eventually stop caring so much about the taste. Either way..."

"Oh, I have an idea! I'll be right back." Sienna grabs her purse and leaves the room without another word.

"Okay, then," I say with a giggle.

It's then I realize that Ramona and I are standing around, together, after the first real conversation we've had in a long time, and I suddenly feel a little shy. We stare at each other for a moment. My cheeks grow warm, and I wonder if it's the shot or something else. I quickly avert my gaze.

"I don't know about you, but part of me keeps having these out-of-body moments where I can't believe we're actually here," Ramona admits quietly. "With you, especially. I mean, we haven't really *talk*-talked since—"

"I think I'm starting to feel it already," I blurt, not wanting to rehash that right now. I can feel the avalanche of words tumbling out of me before I can stop them. "The alcohol, I mean. Can you feel it that fast? I haven't before, but I've only ever had mixed drinks or really bad beer, so I tend to nurse the drinks, which Diego always pokes fun at. He can really hold his liquor. He's also this amazing drag queen and, like, right before we left for this trip he won a competition for it and got the most wasted I've *ever* seen, actually. He was making out with this guy he's into, Benny, and people were cheering him on, and it was a total mess but super funny—"

The hotel room door swings back open, shutting me up. Thank goodness. Sienna emerges with two arms full of vending machine drinks: seltzer, cola, even some juice.

"These will definitely help," she announces, dropping the cans onto one of the beds. "Give me a few seconds to mix up some drinks for us and then I think we should play Never Have I Ever!"

"What's that?" I ask, and Sienna reaches over to boop me on the nose.

"You're cute," she coos. "For Never Have I Ever, we each take turns naming a thing we've never done. Then, if the other people *have* done that thing, they take a sip of their drink. But if no one has done whatever you just said, then *you* take a drink. It'll be a fun way to get to know each other again and figure out everything we missed. Now, Chloe, I'm guessing because of your sweet tooth something fruity would be good for you?" She holds up some cranberry juice. "Cranberry vodka is a *classic*."

I shrug. "That sounds good. You're the expert."

"And all too happy to play bartender."

Sienna gets us settled with our drinks. Ramona and I each grab a seat on a bed, while Sienna gets cozy in an oversize armchair. She clears her throat. "Since it was my idea to play this game, I'll go first. And we'll start easy. Never have I ever cut my own hair."

"Same. I wouldn't trust anyone but my tía with these curls."

"You guys have never cut your own hair before? I'm lucky if I go a whole week without doing that!" I take a timid sip of the drink Sienna's mixed me, pleasantly surprised that much of the bite from the shot has been hidden by the juice. "I get bored easily."

Ramona laughs at that. "Fair enough. You're up next, then."

"Okay. Um..." I think for a minute. "Never have I ever snooped through someone's phone?" Sienna glances at the floor and gnaws on the inside of her cheek. I point at her. "Okay, whose phone have you been invading?!"

"It was a long time ago! I was hanging out with this gorgeous dude who very stupidly did not have a code on his phone—"

Ramona makes a face. "What?"

"Exactly!" Sienna shouts. "It was like fate was tempting me. When he went to the bathroom, I poked around a little, which was for the best, really. His entire camera roll was pictures of cars. Total vibe killer." She holds up her drink and takes a sip. "Anyway, go for it, Ramona."

"Okay, let's see...Why is this so hard? Um...never have I ever... been on a reality television show?" Sienna and I both shake our heads. "Guess I'll drink. I *did* audition for one, though."

"Oh my God, which one?" I demand. "Tell us everything!"

"It was *The Price Is Right*," Ramona admits. "And the process is actually really boring. You literally apply online, but it turns out you have to physically be in the audience in order to even be considered."

Sienna tsks. "So your dreams were crushed."

"I'll never be the same again." Ramona sighs, taking a swig of her drink.

We go on like this, falling into a rhythm, and I learn:

I am the only one who has never played Spin the Bottle or gotten a tattoo. But I am the only one who *has* kissed someone I just met. (It was a really cute girl at a music festival, and we only had one day together, and I was living my rom-com fantasy.)

Sienna has consulted a psychic before, and also kissed more than one person in a twenty-four-hour period. She's never stolen anything, though.

Ramona has neither broken a promise nor sung karaoke, but she has given out a fake phone number.

We've all slid into someone's DMs before, and creeped on someone on social media. Sienna refills our cups, and I can't help but feel good about how quickly this game has reintroduced us to each other.

"Never have I ever been arrested!" Ramona declares, eyeing Sienna.

"Oh my gosh. You said that one on purpose!" Sienna shakes her head with a laugh, taking a sip. "Evil."

"Wait. What have you been arrested for?!"

Sienna shrugs. "I *may* have gotten caught sneaking into the abandoned mall."

"Pinecrest?" I ask. "You couldn't pay me to sneak into that place! Hasn't it been closed since the early two thousands or something? I feel like it must be haunted by the ghosts of, like, forgotten body glitter and old iPods."

"It was a dare!" Sienna insists.

I laugh, shaking my head. "When did this even happen?"

"It was last year. I only knew about it because my uncle was the officer on duty that night," Ramona explains. "He let her go with just a warning because he remembered her from when we were kids. You're welcome, by the way."

"I owe my clean record to you." Sienna blows her a dramatic kiss. "Oooh, okay! I have a good one. Never have I ever kissed a friend."

My gaze immediately catches Ramona's, and I look away as quickly as I can. My cheeks, which are already warm from the alcohol, burn.

Ramona rises to her feet. "I could actually use some air."

Sienna blinks, watching the hotel door shut abruptly behind Ramona. "What just happened?"

"Nothing. It was a fun game," I assure her. "It's late, though. I'm going to take a quick shower and get some rest."

Her brows furrow in total confusion, and I don't blame her. But I can't exactly explain—or maybe I just don't want to. Instead, I grab my bag and duck into the bathroom.

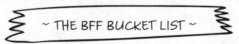

~ THE BFF BUCKET LIST ~

1) See a firefly
2) Eat ice cream for dinner
3) Be in three places at once

4) Go camping

5) ~~Get drunk together~~

6) Skinny-dip

7) Stay up all night and watch the sunrise

8) Make out with someone

9) ~~Take a road trip~~

10) See Intonation together LIVE wearing feather boas like from the "Late Nights" music video and maybe have them each fall in love with us

Chapter Nineteen

We oversleep. It's for the best, really, because the absolute chaos of scrambling to make it downstairs in one piece so we can check out without being charged a late fee is enough to distract us from how the night ended.

"This is going to throw our whole schedule off," Sienna whines, sliding into the front seat of the car beside me.

Ramona rubs at her tired eyes. "How do you rage so hard at night and then wake up ready to talk about schedules?"

"I contain multitudes."

"Can we at least get some coffee?" I ask, my voice coming out more gravelly than I expected. "I feel awful."

"Aww, baby's first hangover," Ramona teases from the back seat.

"Drive-through coffee only," Sienna says. "We don't have time to stop for any of that gourmet stuff. *Ramona*."

Ramona huffs. "Okay, fine!"

I pull into the first coffee place I see to get an assortment of iced coffees, waters, and toasted bagels, just enough to resurrect us from the brink of death. It works, which unfortunately allows my brain to think about everything from last night.

One hard truth we had to relearn? We all have weird sleep habits and needs. Like, Sienna can't sleep unless she has her sound machine turned on, and because she chose whale songs, we all started bickering. I insisted there was no way I could rest listening to what sounded like ghost mermaids haunting the ocean, while Sienna swore she'd read that whale sounds are proven to promote REM sleep, and Ramona complained she couldn't rest without total silence. The three of us eventually agreed to keep the sound machine on but switch to gentle rain sounds. Ramona agreed to borrow my noise-canceling headphones so she could sleep.

Then: I wanted to scroll on my phone for a little bit before I fell asleep, because the bickering wasn't exactly relaxing. But the light was distracting to both Sienna and Ramona, so I had to hide under my blankets with my phone. It made me feel like I was suffocating, and I had to decide if it was worth it. (It was.)

If that wasn't enough of a mess, my heart wouldn't stop racing all night. I hadn't let myself think about the kiss with Ramona in a long, long time.

And I definitely didn't want to think about it during this trip. Why couldn't I keep living in denial and pretending nothing ever happened?

The story I told myself for years about how and why our friend group broke up was mostly true: The summer before freshman year, Sienna really did change schools and made it clear she was moving on. Ramona and I iced her out and clung to each other in the aftermath. I realized Ramona had a crush on me. And I did freak out and ghost her, yes, but there were *things* in the middle I tried to forget.

The kiss happened at my house during a sleepover. I had just turned fourteen, same age as Ramona, and we had a really fun night. We watched a movie. We ordered takeout. We played *The Sims*. When it got late, we climbed into my bed and we listened to music and we talked, the way we always did.

Only, this time, Ramona's pinky touched mine, and I *felt* something. The tiniest flicker in my chest, a candle flame carefully lit for the very first time.

All it took was me lacing my pinky around hers.

She moved closer to me and, in the dark of my room, whispered my name. "Chloe."

The way she said it sent a shiver down my spine.

"Yes?" I asked, my heartbeat drumming in my ears.

"Can I kiss you?"

Her voice shook as she asked, and I was grateful it was dark so she couldn't see the nerves written all over my face.

"Yes," I whispered.

She kissed me.

Her lips were softer than anything I'd ever felt. She smelled like the flowery rose and coconut perfume I'd bought her for her birthday, and I committed the scent to memory. It was the gentlest and sweetest moment, despite only being a few seconds long. We said nothing more, but kept our pinkies linked as we fell asleep.

The next morning, I panicked. Ramona and I had kissed. Sienna was gone. And nothing at all felt the same.

I packed up my clothes and walked home without even saying goodbye.

After that, Ramona didn't text me. I didn't reach out either—too afraid to acknowledge what had happened, too worried about what it might mean, too fragile, too not-ready-yet, too cowardly, too young, too immature, too everything.

Now, it feels like so much time has passed that the kiss itself was a fever dream. It was easier to believe the narrative that we all drifted away naturally.

"Shit," I say suddenly, realizing that in the blur of yesterday, I forgot to check in at home. Though I texted Papi throughout the day with small updates, I never called like I was supposed to. Reluctantly, I unlock my phone and see I have a missed call from Papi and several unanswered texts. "I have to call my dad. I was supposed to do that last night."

I prop my phone on the dashboard, dialing home. I leave it on speaker so I can talk and drive at the same time.

"Mija! I thought you were dead!" Papi says on the other line. But his voice is more dramatic than angry, so I know that a night of sleep probably softened his frustration. Thankfully.

"In my defense, I texted you throughout the day *and* when we got back to the hotel last night!"

"And? You said you were going to *call* me every day!"

"I agreed to be in touch every day and I was!" I argue. "I'm so sorry I scared you. But does it make you feel better to know were having a good time?" (I leave out the part about the drinking.) "Don't you want me to have fun?"

"Ay, not when you have me thinking you've been kidnapped."

I smile at this. "I thought you were convinced I was dead?"

"*Don't* be cute," he warns.

"If I may interject—hi, Chloe's papi, this is Sienna—I promise you Chloe has been incredibly responsible." Sienna's voice has switched from its normal cadence to a high-pitched, overly polite customer service voice. I bet this is the voice she uses at the country club when she's talking to the patrons. "It's my fault she got distracted and didn't call. I asked if we could play a game and we all fell asleep." She's only telling half-truths, but she sounds convincing as hell. "It won't happen again."

Papi sighs. "Okay. I hope not."

Sienna winks at me. "I swear."

"We all swear," I add. "Ramona and Sienna will hold me to it. Right?"

"Absolutely," Ramona chimes from the back. "We won't let her leave our next stop without a call to you. Photographic evidence of her arrival, even."

"A call will be enough, but thank you," Papi says. "So, are you girls enjoying the trip so far?"

"Yes, we are. And let me please thank you for your incredible generosity, sir," Sienna chirps. I catch Ramona's eye in the mirror, but she looks away. Right. I get it. "We're beyond thankful for this opportunity, and we will ensure Chloe is well taken care of."

"As long as you all are safe, that's what matters to me," Papi says.

From the background, I hear Karina yell, "And have fun!"

"We'll be careful," I promise Papi. "And I'll check in with you later."

"You'll *call*," Papi reminds me.

"Yes, Papi. I'll call. Give Karina a hug for me, and remind the baby not to show up too soon. I love you."

"Love you too, mi querida." The line disconnects.

"God, Sienna. What is with that customer service voice?" I ask.

"I'm so sorry to hear you're unhappy with this voice. Is there something I can do to help brighten your day?" She gives me a plastic grin.

"Gross! Quit it," Ramona groans. "You're making my headache worse."

Sienna flops back in her seat, letting the facade fall. "At least it seemed to calm your dad down."

"And for that, I'm grateful," I admit. "I really do hope they manage not to have the baby before I get home."

Sienna takes a long sip of her coffee. "Karina can't exactly control that, you know."

"Yeah, I know. But I don't want them becoming a family without me there." I grip the steering wheel, my voice growing soft. "That would be scary."

"Well, shit, Chloe," Ramona murmurs.

"You're *already* a family, though," Sienna says gently. "I hope you know that."

"I guess, yeah, but...I still sort of feel like once the baby is born, they'll become this perfect little unit. Papi, Karina, Baby Girl. A scatterbrained older sibling away at art school doesn't exactly fit in with all that." I've kept this thought quiet for so long that saying it out loud makes my throat tighten. "Papi will get to start over with his new little girl, Karina will be the perfect mom who never abandons her family, the baby will be sickeningly adorable, and I'll have to watch from far away."

"It won't be like that," Sienna assures me. "Did you hear the love in your dad's voice just now? He's not going to turn those feelings off just because there's another little girl to love."

"My mom had five kids. Five. And she always said each one made her love the rest of us even more. It'll be the same for your parents. They adore you." Ramona reaches forward and pats my shoulder. "You can't be replaced by a dumb baby. They don't even have teeth."

And that makes me snort.

"Thanks, guys." I shake my head. "I think I've just been having a hard time because so much is about to change, you know? I'm leaving them behind, and saying goodbye to Diego, and having to become a boring adult. It's all a lot."

"I can't imagine leaving," Ramona admits. "My apprenticeship at Permanent Record will keep me in town for at least another six months, so I don't have to think about it too much yet. After that, though, who knows where I'll end up?"

"Elmwood's not so bad, if you want to stay," I offer. "Kind of wish I could."

"Emerson has a nice visual arts program, Chloe," Ramona offers. "If you would rather stay in state, I mean."

I arch an eyebrow. "Do they really? I don't think I knew that."

"I mean, it's not RISD—but it's still good. If you really didn't want to go to Rhode Island, there are tons of schools in Massachusetts. That's all." She shrugs. "Not that I care one way or the other."

I try to let that go. "Never said you did."

The car goes quiet for a few minutes, and I notice that Sienna hasn't said much. When I glance her way, she's staring out the window.

I nudge her knee with my hand. "Hey. You good?"

She turns. "Oh, sorry. Did I miss something?"

"No, but you seem like you're in another world, so I wanted to check in."

Sienna glances down at her hands in her lap. "That phone call with your dad. I don't know. I wish I had that."

"Aren't you close with your parents?" I ask, surprised.

She forces a laugh. "Um, I don't know that *close* is exactly the word I'd use. I would say we love each other, for sure. But they aren't the people I turn to when things are good or bad, you know? They're present for me, but not *there* for me, if that makes sense."

"Wow, I really had no idea," Ramona says. "It never came off that way."

"Intentionally, yeah. It's hard to explain. My parents are good to me, and they provide me with what I need. I love them. And I know they love me. But they also expect a lot from me, especially academically. They want me to be perfect. Every time I'm not, I feel like I'm disappointing them."

"That's so hard," I say softly.

"And I hate it because I feel like I disappoint them *all the time*. And that makes me wonder…how would things have been if my bio dad was around? Then I hate myself for wondering that because I know I have it good. I do."

"I don't think it makes you a bad person to wonder," I say.

We've had a version of this conversation before, but I can really feel the heaviness in Sienna this time. Her bio dad has understandably always been a sore spot for her. He and Sienna's mom were a brief thing, and he left right after her mom got pregnant, without even knowing about her existence. Despite Sienna's ongoing pleas, her mom has adamantly refused to give her any details about her bio dad—no name, no location, nothing. Her mom says it's better that way, but Sienna has said it should be up to her to decide. It's always been a point of contention for the two of them.

"Have you gotten more info about him? Since we were kids?" Ramona asks.

"Sort of…" Sienna pauses. "Does stealing my mom's credit card and buying an Ancestry.com membership so I could finally know his name count?"

I nearly choke on the sip of coffee I just took. "Oh!"

"I know. On the one hand, don't steal from your mom. On the other hand, I almost felt like I had no choice! She wouldn't budge on giving me his name and I was starting to feel desperate." She bites at one of her nails.

Ramona leans as close to the front seat as her seat belt will allow her. "So you know his name."

Sienna nods slowly. "And maybe where he lives?"

"Holy shit, dude," Ramona breathes. "Where?"

"He lives in Pagosa Springs, Colorado." She pauses for a moment. "He looks nice, actually. I have his eyes."

I pat her on the knee reassuringly because I truly don't know what else to do. "Shit. Well. I bet that brought up a lot for you."

"Like you wouldn't even imagine. It was also weirdly comforting, in a way? I don't know. I've always been the only one in my family with light eyes, and as soon as I saw his picture, it was like my own reflection staring back at me. It felt like I knew him."

Ramona pushes her phone toward Sienna. I'm still driving, so I can't look.

"What is it?" I ask.

"Pagosa Springs isn't far from where we'll be staying in Colorado," Ramona explains.

In a quiet voice, Sienna says, "Yeah. I know."

And then I get it: This is why she said yes to this trip.

A pit forms in my stomach at the realization. "Oh."

"I was going to tell you guys," she insists. "I haven't even really made up my mind yet what I'm going to do. In my head, it would be absolutely bananas to just show up on his doorstep, like, 'Hey, Dad, it's me, the kid you don't know about! Let's hang!'"

I can hear Papi in my head, screaming out all the reasons Sienna even *considering* seeing her bio dad is a terrible idea. There are a few from me I'd like to add too.

Sienna continues, "Yet there's this other part of me that is like, 'What if it goes well? And you get the dad you've always dreamed of?'"

"Or, what if the address could be wrong and it's not even the right person?" I ask. "Or what if it is the right person and he's a *murderer*? Am I the only one who thinks this is a horrible idea? I mean, maybe there's a reason your mom has kept him away from you."

"Jeez, Chloe," Ramona hisses. "A little harsh, don't you think?"

And then Sienna is crying, and it's because of me. My chest tightens.

"No, it's true," Sienna sniffles. "I am well aware of how outlandish this whole idea is. I feel totally delusional. But I also feel like I have to at least try."

"So you use my birthday road trip as an opportunity to pursue that?" I ask bitterly.

"Hey, go easy on her," Ramona warns.

"What? This sucks!"

"I get that, but let's not, okay?"

"Of *course* you side with her." I'm driving, but the urge to cross my arms like a child is so strong right now. I can feel myself tumbling back in time and becoming that girl who would get jealous whenever it felt like Ramona and Sienna were getting too close and leaving me out, and I can't even stop it. "You only agreed to come so you could get a stupid tattoo! How am I not supposed to be angry at the both of you for being so selfish?"

Ramona snorts. "Us? Are you *kidding* me? You approached us out of absolutely nowhere with your little 'we used to be besties' speech in very intrusive ways!"

"I meant everything I said! I wanted to reconnect with the both of you, and I'm seeing now how fucking stupid I was to even consider it!" I argue. "You two only had yourselves in mind when you said yes to this!"

"Let's be real: the only reason you even guilted us into going to this concert is because you can't let go of the past! You don't even know us now. Our kiddie days are ancient history, you understand that, right?"

Her words careen into me and take the air out of my lungs.

"That's how you feel?" I glance over at Sienna. "Both of you?"

Sienna wipes at her eyes. "I mean, we both agreed we were taken by surprise with the invite, but that's not—"

"So you guys were talking about me behind my back? Nice. Some friends!"

"That's just it, Chloe!" Ramona argues. "You keep trying to force this, but we aren't friends!"

The air in the car goes cold.

"Okay, time out," Sienna says. "I think we're all hungover and dealing with our own shit and we need to regroup. Can we pull over somewhere and take a break?"

A giant sign for a big-box store called Tommy's Tools & Treats stands in front of us like a flashing arrow. I put on my blinker and turn in without another word.

When I need to quiet my brain, I often go outside. I wouldn't call myself an outdoorsy girl, but being around plants does calm me. It's why I've tried so hard to foster a green thumb, even though I suck at gardening.

So, in this random store along I-90, of all places, I find myself on a bench in the Home & Garden section, surrounded by leafy plants, and the vibe is actually surprisingly nice. Oldies music—I recognize it as a Beach Boys song, I think—plays overhead. I have no idea where Ramona and Sienna went, mostly because I pretty much ran ahead of them into the store so I could have a few seconds alone.

I immediately pull out my phone and text Whit. My impulsivity right now is *strong*. I type a message to her.

Me: soooo those intonation tickets? they're ✳ yours ✳

My finger doesn't even hesitate to hit the send button. Because there is actually no one who deserves these tickets more than Whit and her family. She and her sister grew up on Intonation, and their abuela is pretty much the sweetest person in the whole world. They should be on that stage.

Whit: I'm sorry WHAT

Whit: Absolutely not!!!

Me: ummmmm YES

Me: let's trade

Whit: NO?????????

Whit: Those are LITERAL ON-THE-STAGE SEATS

Whit: You could make eye contact with Rider!!!!

Whit: Or touch Lucas's hand!!!

Me: or YOU could make eye contact with rider and lily can touch lucas's hand. i'm more of a liam girl anyway!!

Me: and your abuela can propose to henry obviously

Whit: LMAO OKAY BUT SHE WOULD

Me: i know!!!! and i live for it!

Me: but seriously, my plans for the show seem like they're falling through

Me: and tbh you deserve these tickets more than anyone i know

Me: if you're willing to trade, i will happily take floor seats and sing/ scream my face off from there.

Me: i am being serious here. nothing would make me happier than watching you and lily and abuela live it up

Whit: Gahhhhh, Chloe.

Whit: I don't even know what to say

Whit: Please don't make me say no again!

Me: okay great, then don't!! i'll transfer the tix to you now

Me: have the best freaking time!!!!!! i mean it!!!! that will make me so so so happy

Whit: Chloe.

Whit: I'm literally crying.

Whit: You have no idea. My abuela is going to sob. I am just... wow. I really don't know what to say.

Whit: You have the biggest heart of anyone I've ever met and I'm so beyond happy we became friends this year

Whit: Please please please don't ever change

The last text makes me swallow hard. Not everyone feels that way. Not even me.

Me: just make sure i get invited to abuela's wedding to henry

I sometimes feel like I have so many feelings I don't know what to do with them. But giving these tickets to someone who deserves them, and will actually enjoy and appreciate them, is the right call. I have no doubt in my mind about that.

And right now, I can't imagine going anywhere with Ramona and Sienna, let alone to the concert. How is it possible they *both* had ulterior motives when they said yes to this trip? That...hurts. They didn't have to say yes to the invitation, they didn't have to come, but they did. They used me. It makes me wonder if I really *was* delusional, assuming we could reconcile and have a fun adventure together.

If Papi were here, he'd probably tell me my feelings are valid but encourage me to try to see things from their perspective. Feelings can't be wrong, he'd say. We can all be right in how we feel, and because of that, we should try to understand how others feel too.

I take a deep breath. Fine, Papi. You win.

If I wanted to be understanding, I *guess* I'd say I could sort of see how these two people I hadn't spoken to in years might want to have some kind of backup plan to this trip, to ensure they got something out of it even if it was miserable.

Still... shit sucks.

It sucks they didn't view this whole thing the same way I did.

It sucks that my brain can sometimes be so dreamy I forget about reality.

It sucks to hear Ramona remind me the three of us aren't friends.

I text Diego.

Me: im sitting alone in a random store called tommy's tools and treats and im depressed

Diego: ur first mistake was stepping into that store at all

Diego: but go on

Me: me, ramona, and sienna got into a big argument

My screen lights up with Diego's face, and I press to accept the FaceTime call.

"Who do I need to fight?" He puts on his best death glare.

I pout. "Me, for having hopes."

Then I tell him what happened, sparing no detail. He gets angry at all the right parts, and I wish so badly that Diego were here and I could hug him. Diego would've been the best road trip partner, but instead, I'm miserable and cranky and hungover.

"Okay, so, we have a few options for dealing with this. There are some obvious ones—like everyone going home—that I'll skip because I know you won't go for it. First option: murder."

I roll my eyes. "Pass."

"Boring," Diego says with a sigh. "But fine. Second option: Leave Ramona and Sienna stranded and I fly out there to take their place."

"Better, but my dad will kill me if I leave two people he feels he's responsible for stranded in the middle of nowhere."

Diego huffs. "Oh, whatever. There's no such thing as stuck in the world of Ubers and GPS."

"Next option, please."

"Okay, but you're going to hate it. Final option is to maybe accept that it's okay if Ramona and Sienna had hopes for this trip—" I glare at him, and he holds up a hand to me. "Let me finish! It's okay if Ramona and Sienna had hopes for this trip that were different than yours. It's also okay to be hurt by how all this information was shared. What's not okay is how you all lashed out at each other. So maybe you, like, talk. Set new expectations. And try to enjoy the rest of the trip."

I make a face. "Can we go back to option one?"

"Um, always. That's my favorite option. Murder sounds exciting!" Diego jokes. "But for real. It probably wasn't the wisest for all three of you to jump in, feetfirst, without hashing some things out. Fights are bound to happen when you're cramped in the same car for a week. I'm honestly impressed it took until day two for the first explosion to happen."

I let out a long, over-the-top sigh. "I guess you're right."

Diego cups his hand around his ear. "Excuse me? What was that?"

"I said I guess you're right!"

He grins. "Feel better?"

"No, I don't." I shift in my seat on the bench, which is growing uncomfortable. I guess you can only sit on a wooden bench in the middle of Tommy's Tools & Treats for so long. "Now how was the drag show last night?"

Diego's face falls. "Venus the Flyest Trap made it into the finals."

Venus the Flyest Trap is a drag queen from two towns over who has garnered a reputation for herself in the drag world as a flake, but she makes up for it with her incredible stage makeup, charisma, and death drops. Crowds love her, even though the queens and organizers putting on shows often don't. If she wins the competition and joins the Speakeasy official performance roster, that will be a particularly cruel defeat for Diego, who I know would dedicate everything to the opportunity.

I gasp at the news. "Oh, no! We hate her!"

"Tell me about it. I was gutted."

"Sounds like you have no choice but to chew her up and spit her out."

Diego makes a face. "That's disgusting."

"I was going for, like, mean but encouraging?"

"Your pep talks could use serious work. Model yours after mine."

"I'm trying!" I argue. "Sorry we can't all be you."

"Sad, isn't it?" Then Diego tilts his head and grins. "I miss your stupidity."

"Right back atcha."

We say goodbye and hang up. I go back to ogling plants and think about how terrible I feel and how nothing's easy and how that's incredibly annoying. Just once, can't the world be perfect instead of continuing to be a hot dumpster fire?

Chapter Twenty-One

SUNDAY, DAY TWO: TOMMY'S TOOLS & TREATS ALONG I-90,
EARLY AFTERNOON

"Doritos or hot Cheetos?" When I look up from the orchid instructions I've been reading, Ramona is holding a bag of each in either hand.

I cross my arms. "Both, obviously."

She tosses the bags into the hand cart her arm is looped through. "A girl after my own heart."

"We're not here to shop. We're here because this trip was the dumbest fucking idea I've ever had."

"No one thinks that," Ramona says. She rubs a hand on the back of her neck. "I think things got heated in the car and we all said some things we regret. But you didn't expect everything to be peachy from the jump, did you?"

I shoot her a look. "It's like you don't even know me."

She chuckles. "Right. Okay, well. I saw Sienna wandering around the travel section. I think she's eyeing one of those neck pillows."

"Fine," I say with a huff. "Come on."

We find Sienna, who did indeed secure a neck pillow, and then we decide we should probably eat something, hydrate, and talk. We each add a few items to Ramona's hand cart: nuts, precut fruit and vegetables, cheese, crackers, olives, seltzer. We get enough snacks for an impromptu picnic out in the parking lot, which is the best we can swing right now. None of us want to go inside a restaurant and have this talk.

"So, that fight in the car was…intense," I begin. "Is it okay if I go first?"

Sienna nods. "Of course."

"I was hurt. I *am* hurt, actually. It really sucks to hear that I'm self-ish when I feel like I genuinely extended this invite from a good place. I feel like it was really wrong of you guys to agree to come with me if you had no interest in my friendship. But I'm also sorry if I made you feel guilted or pressured or anything like that. Truly, that wasn't my intention, and I am sorry. And, now that we're out on the road, I do want us all to get something out of this. Sienna, if that means you want to consider meeting your bio dad...okay. I recognize how important that is for you as a human being. We should figure that out and make sure we have a plan. I want you to know you have my full and complete support no matter what you decide to do."

She gives me a soft smile. "That means a lot. Thank you."

"And Ramona, I'm so sorry I called your tattoo stupid. Please know that's not how I feel at all. I actually think your idea to pay tribute to your mom is really thoughtful and beautiful."

She laughs a little. "It's really no big deal."

"It is a big deal," I insist. "You never do anything without putting tremendous thought into it, so I know you've probably been planning this tattoo for a while and that it means a lot to you. So if it means a lot to you, it means a lot to me, too. You finally have a chance to make it happen, and I'm happy for you. Really."

Her gaze meets mine. "Thank you."

"Can I hop in now?" Sienna asks, and I nod. "Just because I've been considering seeing my bio dad doesn't mean I wasn't also interested in this trip for sentimental reasons, like you, Chloe. Both of those things can be true for me, and they are."

I perk up a bit. "Really?"

"Really. If all I wanted to do was see my dad, I could've stolen my mom's credit card again and charged a flight to her," Sienna jokes. "But seriously. I've missed us all being friends. I've missed you guys. I've missed *you*, Chloe! I would never have agreed to come unless I sincerely felt that way. I swear. And I also still have a huge soft spot for Intonation."

"Um, same, on all counts," I reply. "I hoped if we got together again, we could maybe stay friends this time, you know? The three of us had so much fun together and I really miss being part of your lives. Anyway. We've been talking a lot. Ramona?"

Ramona clears her throat. "So, I'm going to go ahead and apologize, but I'm not about to get anywhere near as sappy as you two did." That makes us laugh. "Admittedly, I did say I was only here because of the tattoo. But that wasn't really true. I knew almost immediately I wanted to come along, I just didn't know if it was a good idea after...everything. So I also booked a tattoo with an artist I love in case things sucked. I'm sorry I wasn't honest about that, and Chloe, I'm sorry I said you can't let go of the past because that's not true. Obviously, we all feel some type of way about the past, or we wouldn't be here."

"Hearing we aren't friends sucked more, honestly," I admit. "I mean, I was hoping we could be again. If we wanted to be."

"Okay, and we're here. We're trying. We're doing this thing. We have a lot of ground to make up for and yet it's been okay so far, don't you think? Aside from when I got seasick."

"And the fight..."

Ramona rolls her eyes. "*Anyway.* I'm trying to say this mostly hasn't been so bad. And that I'm not using you, even if it sounded like that. Really. I'm sorry I said we weren't friends. I didn't mean it."

I tilt my head at her. "So you think we're friends?"

"Don't twist my words, now," she says, giving me a playful scowl. "I didn't say that."

Sienna grins. "And yet that's actually what we heard, isn't it, Chloe?"

I point at Ramona. "Yep. You like us!"

"I barely tolerate you," Ramona argues.

"You liiiiike us," I sing. "You think we're bessssties!"

Ramona looks over at Sienna. "Can you please shut her up before I change my mind about this entire thing?"

"On it." Sienna grabs a piece of cheese and shoves it in my mouth. "Done."

"Ooh, it's pepper jack!" I say with my mouth full. I chew and swallow. "There is one more thing I should probably share, so that everything's out in the open."

Sienna dips a pretzel into some hummus. "Don't tell us you have an ulterior motive too."

"I don't, but...I may have traded Intonation tickets with Whit Rivera? So the stage tickets are maybe not ours anymore?"

Ramona squints at me. "Fuck, we really did hurt your feelings, huh?"

I busy myself using a toothpick to retrieve an olive from the glass container. "Maybe."

"At least the tickets went to someone who really deserves them?" Sienna offers.

"She really does deserve them. She's the biggest fan I know, and she's taking her abuela and little sister Lily with her. I had already been considering trading tickets with her, so when I saw our concert plans falling apart, I sprang into action." My cheeks flush. "I can sometimes be a tad impulsive."

Ramona and Sienna both gasp loudly.

"Yooooou? Nooooooo!" Sienna insists.

"You could never," Ramona echoes.

"Okay, okay, I get it. We still have floor seats!"

"Honestly, that might be better. I was kind of stressed out thinking everyone could see my dorky dance moves onstage," Sienna says, laughing. "And we'll still get to cross the item off the BFF Bucket List."

I arch an eyebrow at her. "Are we still doing that?"

Ramona reaches into her back pocket and slams a piece of paper down on the picnic table. "I didn't bring this list all the way from Massachusetts for us not to commit. We already have two crossed off!" I glance down to see Ramona's been keeping track of our accomplishments on her copy of the bucket list—the one I'd given her and Sienna when I was trying to convince them to come on this trip with me.

"Plus, Ramona and I voted, and you get to pick the next item we cross off the list." Sienna waggles her eyebrows at me.

I scan the list in front of Ramona, noting she has carefully crossed off *Get drunk together* and *Take a road trip,* and my insides go warm. Maybe she does care. Maybe they both do, in their own ways.

"How about *See a firefly*?" I suggest. "The middle of nowhere seems like a good place to do that."

Ramona gives me a firm nod. "See a firefly it is."

Sienna snatches the list from us. "*After* we get to our next stop."

Chapter Twenty-Two

Given that we had seven hours' worth of driving to do today and about a bajillion distractions, I'm impressed we even make it to our hotel before 8 p.m.

The first thing we do is FaceTime Papi, like we promised. Sienna even makes sure we show him the hotel room, proof that we really are exactly where we're supposed to be.

At least for now.

The second we hang up, we freshen up and head back to the car.

"There's starting to be an imprint of my body in the front seat," Sienna whines. "Isn't eight hours in this thing enough?"

"You're the one who said we can't see fireflies in the city," Ramona reminds her. She puts on her best Sienna voice. " 'The firefly population is declining due to light pollution, so we'll need to go somewhere dark.' "

"Which means we're not going to have any luck around Indianapolis," Sienna points out.

"Right, but we're not going to look in Indianapolis. I have a plan," Ramona says. "And actually, you know what? Why don't you take the back seat so your seat's body imprint can take a break and I can navigate?"

"Fine, but you'll see how much hard work being a passenger princess really is."

"I think I can handle it," Ramona assures her. Then she slides into the front seat beside me. "It's not far. Promise."

"Can I choose what we listen to?" Sienna asks from the back seat. "I'm tired of Ramona's emo music."

"Oh, boohoo." But Ramona selects Sienna's phone from the Bluetooth menu. To me, Ramona says, "I'll tell you the directions as we go, all right?"

From the speakers, a woman's voice says, "And as he comes toward her with the axe, the moonlight brightens his face so she can finally see his identity. And she recognizes him, crying out—"

"Oops!" Sienna hits pause. "Didn't mean to start us in the middle of an episode."

"Well, that was dark. What the hell was that?" I ask, easing us out of the parking lot of our hotel.

"It's my murder podcast! Which we're totally gonna listen to. Not that episode, though. There's a really creepy one on the Grim Sleeper that's up next for me," Sienna explains.

"Oh, right, of course, how silly of us not to assume we'd be listening to your *murder podcast*," Ramona says, emphasizing the last two words. "That sounds very chill and relaxing."

"You'll love it," Sienna promises.

"Or what? You'll murder us?" I mutter, and Ramona stifles a laugh.

"I heard that," Sienna says. "Don't tempt me."

* * *

We find ourselves at a place called Eagle Creek Park, which is one of the city's largest.

"It's listed as one of the best places to stargaze around Indianapolis, and since lightning bugs do best in humid climates around water, I figure this is our best bet," Ramona explains. "Still might be a long shot, though. The Googling I did about fireflies was super depressing. Did you know they only live, like, three to four weeks and then they die? That's why it's harder to see them in late summer."

"A pitch-black park. Great. I'm definitely not imagining all the ways we might die thanks to Sienna's creepy podcast," I joke.

"Being paranoid is being prepared!" Sienna calls from the back.

"Here." Ramona digs into her pocket and pulls out some cash. "This will cover the entry fee."

"Oh, you don't have to—"

"I want to," she assures me. "You picked *See a firefly*. We're gonna see a damn firefly."

I smile at her. I hadn't been expecting Ramona to go out of her way to try to make this happen, but I'll admit that her commitment is sweet.

We pay our entry fee and drive inside, but not before the cranky guy at the tollbooth looks more than annoyed to see a car full of girls roll up at nine o'clock, and he reminds us three times that the park closes at nine thirty.

We park and get out of the car, Sienna immediately shining her flashlight on the ground. "Only until we get where we need to go. Then I'll turn it off for the sake of our firefly friends."

"Google says we need to find a place called the Crest," Ramona explains. "It's on the northwest side of the reservoir." She points. "That way."

The park is peaceful this time of night, so still and quiet it feels like Earth has gone to sleep.

I stay as close to Ramona and Sienna as humanly possible. "Really wishing we hadn't listened to murder podcasts the whole drive up..."

"Sorry!" Sienna says. "I forgot we were coming out into the middle of the woods."

"It's not the middle of the woods. There are park rangers and security!" Ramona assures us. "We'll be fine."

"Since when did you get so confident in nature? I seem to remember you scream-crying in my backyard once when you were being chased by a bee," Sienna teases.

Ramona whips her head around. "I thought I was allergic! You'd be running from a bee too if you thought it would bring on sudden death."

Sienna puts up both of her hands in surrender. "Oh, sure, blame it on the fake allergy."

"Suddenly I remember reading that fireflies are deterred by talking," Ramona sniffs. "So we should be really, really quiet."

We walk in silence until we come upon the Crest. If not for the moon above, the area would be near pitch-black. In the sky, stars twinkle against the dark sky, their light reflecting on the water down below.

"That alone is pretty incredible," I breathe. I don't think I've ever seen the night sky like this—so clear and vivid, shimmering gemstones on black velvet. It's impossible not to be awestruck.

"Man, we're tiny," Ramona murmurs, looking up. "Shit like the stars really remind you of that, doesn't it?"

"Totally. Especially because of the aliens," Sienna says. It catches me off guard and I let out a laugh that echoes through the trees. "What? Aliens are obviously real. You can Google it!"

"I didn't say they weren't!" I whisper.

"I'm going to signal to the aliens to come grab you both if you don't chill," Ramona warns. She scans the horizon and squints. The corners of her mouth dip down. "I'm not seeing any fireflies."

"I'm not either," Sienna says with a sigh. "What a bummer."

I glance around, as if some might magically appear if I look hard enough. When they don't, I say, "Let's wait a few more minutes. The stars are pretty good company for now."

I pull out my phone to try to take a photo of the sky, even though I know what I capture will never do justice to what I've seen in person. Sienna does the same. After a few minutes, Ramona touches the tips of her fingers to my elbow. A chill goes down my spine—from the cooling air, obviously.

"Should we head out?" she asks. "I don't want that park ranger to track us down."

I tuck my phone into my tote bag. "Yeah, we should go."

"Wait!" Sienna whispers. "Am I losing it, or could that be one?"

Ramona and I look where she's pointing. I stare for what feels like minutes but must only be seconds, until there's the tiniest flicker of light.

"Oh my gosh," I whisper, watching as a handful of dainty yellow specks begin blinking like Christmas lights. Goose bumps prickle on my arms.

Sienna's hand rests on her heart. "They look like fairy dust."

Ramona chuckles lightly. "Seriously, but pixies don't have shit on these guys."

We are quiet for a moment, and I feel my eyes get watery. Knowing how increasingly rare it is to see a firefly makes me really grateful to be here right now. "I can't believe I've always wanted to see a firefly and now here we are."

Cranky park ranger be damned, we watch for a bit longer. Then we reluctantly tear ourselves away from the shimmering bugs who have generously put on a show for us.

As we walk back to the car, I can't help but appreciate how much effort Ramona put into making this happen.

"Did you guys hear that?" Sienna whispers.

"Hear *what*?" I ask.

"I swear I heard something from over there!"

"This is why your *death podcasts* are a bad idea!" Ramona hisses. "Come on!"

We rush back to the car, not resting until we're safely locked inside. Once the doors are closed, we look at each other and burst into laughter.

"Okay, but guys, I'm actually really scared," Sienna admits. "No more horror shows. And can we sleep in the same bed tonight? Like old times?"

"We're not in middle school anymore. We'll be completely squished," Ramona says.

"Feels worth it for safety, don't you think?" I ask.

Ramona groans. "Ugh. Fine. But I refuse to be in the middle."

~ THE BFF BUCKET LIST ~

1) ~~See a firefly~~
2) Eat ice cream for dinner
3) Be in three places at once
4) Go camping
5) ~~Get drunk together~~
6) Skinny-dip
7) Stay up all night and watch the sunrise
8) Make out with someone
9) ~~Take a road trip~~
10) See Intonation together LIVE wearing feather boas like from the "Late Nights" music video and maybe have them each fall in love with us

Chapter Twenty-Three

Who has two thumbs and forgot to account for weekday traffic in the creation of her road trip itinerary?

This girl.

It doesn't help that there's construction that's shut down every lane on the highway except for one. We're basically sitting in a highway parking lot.

Sienna is less than thrilled.

"We've been stuck in the same spot for, like, ten minutes now!" she cries from the back seat. "This is torture."

"Hey now. At least we get to look at that giant billboard of a zebra that says 'Take the next exit to find your stripes at the Indy Zoo'! Now we can have great conversations like: Is a zebra closer to a horse or a donkey?" Ramona says archly.

"Not helping." Sienna takes a huge stress sip of her iced chai.

"I'm sorry! I should've taken work traffic into consideration when I was plotting everything out," I say. "This is totally my fault."

"It's fine," Ramona assures me. "We didn't think of it either."

"But we have a seven-hour drive ahead of us and we're not going anywhere soon," Sienna whines. "You *know* how much I hate getting off schedule."

Ramona shrugs. "Whether we drive seven hours this morning or later today, it really doesn't matter. The end goal is the same: end up in East Bumfuck, Missouri. I don't see what the big deal is."

It's too early for bickering, so I pull out my phone. Yes, texting and driving is illegal, but does it count as driving if we're at a full standstill here? There's a message from Diego.

Diego: sooooo are things heating up with sienna yet or what

Me: lol!

Me: definitely not

Me: altho we did share a bed last night

Diego: !!!

Diego: excuse me!

Me: now who's abusing punctuation marks?

Diego: 👆

Diego: how are u gonna share a bed and not text me IMMEDIATELY

Diego: rude

Me: omg chill, it was all three of us

Diego: u just got so much cooler

Me: NOT LIKE THAT

Me: we shared a bed bc we got spooked by one of sienna's murder podcasts and we were afraid of being killed

Me: it was very wholesome

Diego: ew, gross

Diego: still tho

Diego: sleeping in the same bed w/ your former crush isn't nothing

Before I reply, I look up to check on the traffic. Still at a standstill.

Me: weirdly?

Me: it didn't feel like anything

Me: and tbh it hasn't really since the first day of the trip. like, i was FULLY expecting to be a nervous wreck around sienna but she feels exactly like a friend?? no butterflies at all

Diego: ew im bored

Me: but

Diego: ok im intrigued again, go on

Me: ramona?? is trying to be nice??

Me: she organized this whole out-of-the-way side trip just so we could see fireflies 🥹

Me: and like

Me: idk

Me: she is very pretty?? and she touched my elbow last night and i FELT THINGS????????

Heat creeps up my neck as I type this, and I glance in the rearview mirror to check on Ramona, certain she can sense I'm talking about her. But she's popped her earbuds in and is contentedly drawing on her iPad.

Diego: omfg yes

Diego: she is so hot

Diego: u need to get her to touch more than ur elbow

Me: DONT

Me: DONTTTT

Me: can we talk about something else please before i die of embarrassment???

Diego: yes

Diego: im glad u asked

Diego: me n benny are now a thing

Diego: please clap

Me: OMG!!!!!!

Me: I'M SO HAPPY FOR YOU!!!!

Diego: ok chill

Diego: it's not that serious

Me: YES IT IS AHHHHHHH

Me: BENNY AND DIEGO UP A TREE

Diego: no

Me: UGH FINE

Me: then i will simply say

Me: congrats on the dick

Diego: thank u

Me: ok now im supposed to be driving lol bye

Me: tell benny i said hi ♥♥♥♥♥♥♥♥♥

I tuck my phone away and find my gaze falling on Ramona once more in the rearview mirror. My eyes trail over her brown skin, the beauty marks that dot her collarbone, the way one of her curls has come free from the ponytail at the top of her head and is now reaching for the tablet in her lap.

Do I feel something for Ramona, after all this time?

Or is this another one of those hyperfixations of mine, where my heart can't tell the difference between real feelings and temporary excitement?

"This traffic is killing me. Can we listen to something fun?" Sienna asks suddenly. She changes the song that has been playing, and familiar notes from Intonation's "About Last Night" flow through the speakers.

I grin. "The boys!"

We immediately start singing the opening lyrics at the top of our lungs:

"Passion ignited, emotions are high,
Caught in the moment, can't say goodbye.
The touch of your skin lingers on mine,
I'm lost in you, can't keep track of time.

"About last night, the secrets we shared,
The way we surrendered, the way we dared.
As the sun rises, and dark turns to light,
I can't stop thinking about last night!"

"God, this song still hits," I say with a laugh.

"It really does!" Sienna turns around in the seat. "Come on, Ramona. You know you want to sing along with us!"

Ramona looks up and points to her earbuds. "A little busy here."

I pout. "Aww, come on, Nightshade."

She stares at me and I can see the wheels turning in her head.

"Quick—the next verse is coming!" Sienna says.

With a huff, Ramona pulls out her earbuds. "Fine!"

And the three of us sing:

"We danced under the stars in the moon's glow,
The way you looked at me, I couldn't let you go.

Clinging to whispers, to kisses, to touch,
Any moment together feels like a rush!"

It goes like this for the rest of the song, and I know it's these small moments I've really been missing.

"Well, looks like we moved about five feet during our little concert." Sienna frowns. Then her face brightens. "You know what? Screw it."

"Screw this?" I motion toward the traffic. "Um, yeah, clearly."

"I mean, screw waiting in this mess! Let's get off at the next exit and go do something."

"Whoa, whoa, whoa. Sienna the Scheduler is endorsing a detour?" Ramona teases.

"Yep! I've had it. My anxiety can't take this anymore. And you know what the next exit is, right?" There's a twinkle in Sienna's eye.

My brows furrow. "What?"

She points at the billboard out the window, and Ramona grins. "The Indy Zoo!"

I smile, too, and put on my blinker to ease our car into the line for the next exit. "Time to find our stripes."

Chapter Twenty-Four

The Indianapolis Zoo is more expansive than I even imagined. According to the signs as we drive in, the zoo also includes an aquarium and a botanical garden called the White River Gardens. Even though it's warm, it isn't humid, so it feels like a good day for a zoo adventure.

"I'm dying to check out the garden," I say as we park. We've had a really busy last few days, and the plant section of Tommy's Tools & Treats was fine, but I could use some time to recharge in the quiet of an actual garden. Maybe I'll even be inspired to make some art. From the trunk, I retrieve the travel watercolor set Diego gifted me for my birthday and tuck it into my tote bag.

"I think it makes the most sense to make a big loop around the zoo." Sienna gazes down at her phone. "Maybe start with the gardens and conservatory, since that's up front, then swing by the Wild Encounters area—you can actually interact with animals there! We'll hit the Forests section from there, Flights of Fancy, Plains, Deserts, then do Oceans last and back through the garden."

"How the hell did you manage to plan that all out in minutes?" Ramona asks.

Sienna shrugs. "I crave efficiency."

"Maybe you should see someone about that," she teases. "Gardens first works for me. And I'd love to do the aquarium last. I find aquariums really relaxing."

I blink at her. "Do you now?"

She nods. "Something about the water is very soothing. Plus, the lighting in there always feels like a dream."

"You know, I can kind of see it," I offer, and she gives me a considering glance.

After we get our tickets, we head to the gardens, which strike me as having been plucked straight out of *Alice in Wonderland*. Sprawling trees surround the entrance, while the center path is lined with neatly trimmed shrubs that entangle to make intricate designs. It leads us to the outdoor DeHaan Tiergarten, where vibrant flowers stretch toward the sky from all around us. There's a bed filled entirely with dozens and dozens of raspberry-colored cosmos, and a winding pathway lined with flowering trees and whimsical blue-, yellow-, orange-, and pink-petaled flowers. Fountains, pieces of art, and even small ponds with lily pads pop up here and there.

"Well, this is pretty as hell," Ramona says.

"Like right out of a picture book," I muse.

Sienna squeals when she sees the conservatory decorated in giant, colorful butterfly sculptures. "Come on!" She gestures for us to hurry up and follow her.

The sticky air is what I notice first when we step inside, but I'm quickly distracted by all the towering tropical plants. The glass panes of the building cascade light onto the palm leaves and the bright blooms. A mix of monarchs, morphos, and a few other species I don't recognize flutter around inside. Abstract butterflies made from jewel-toned blown glass decorate the entrance, and there's even an incubator filled with chrysalises.

Sienna watches them in wonder. "In my next life, maybe I'll be a butterfly."

"But then how will you pester everyone about sticking to schedules?" Ramona teases, and Sienna gives her the stink eye.

I look up, slowly twirling in a circle and watching as a butterfly with velvety black wings and a bright red body flutters over to a flower. "How many butterflies do you think there are in here?"

"About a thousand," responds a butterfly keeper wearing a name tag that says LORENZO. "We'll be doing our next release in a few minutes, if you stick around."

My eyes widen and I turn to Sienna. "Can we, Mama? Please, please, please?"

Sienna rolls her eyes. "You're free to do whatever you want! But I think I'm going to head toward the Wild Encounters area. I really want to make sure I see everything."

"You guys go have fun. I'll be okay alone. I actually wouldn't mind some time to sit and relax." I reach into my tote bag and pull out my art kit. "Even brought my watercolors."

A look comes over Ramona's face that I can't quite read. "Sure?"

I nod. "I'll be fine, really. Meet back up in an hour?"

We say our goodbyes and I grab a spot by the incubator so I can watch the butterfly release. It isn't long before Lorenzo emerges with several butterflies perched on his glove, ready to join their friends. It's sweet to watch them take flight and experience the vastness of the pavilion.

But the humidity is starting to get to me. I head back into the open gardens and find myself among the raspberry-colored cosmos, where I secure a quiet space to paint. This is the first time in ages I've been struck by the urge, and I don't want to waste it.

I pull out the square watercolor sketchbook Diego packaged with the kit and open to the first page. I clip the wooden watercolor palette to the inside front cover. One side of the palette holds the paints and on the other is a space to mix them. From my tote bag, I grab my watercolor brushes and a tiny spritz bottle filled with water. It doubles as the water for this paint set and a curl refresher for my hair. Sienna would be thrilled by the efficiency.

Alone for what feels like the first time in ages, I start to layer in the background with thick, watery strokes. After the paint dries and I get the right colors for the background, I can layer richer colors and fine lines to build the foreground. I let myself drift into the process, not thinking too much about whether the blooms look perfect or whether the shadow is at exactly the correct angle. That's not the point. Making something is. That's all I want to do right now.

Especially given the revelation through my texts with Diego while we were stuck in traffic. I hadn't been expecting him to check in with me about my feelings for Sienna, and I was even more surprised to find myself admitting that I've been thinking about Ramona instead.

It takes me back to that closeness the two of us had. I always felt like we had a layer deeper than what we had with Sienna, something that felt at once comfortable yet tender. I didn't hide anything from Ramona. She was the only one aside from Diego I ever trusted with *all* my secrets and insecurities. Ramona had this way of knowing exactly when it was okay to be playful, and when she should be tough on me. She could read me like no one else.

Our friendship was sometimes hot and cold, though. We fought a lot. Mostly over Sienna. We were both eternally jealous, and the second it felt like one of us was favoring Sienna over the other, *boom*. It only got worse after Ramona realized I liked Sienna, almost like I could never get that delicate balance right. I always thought the intensity of our friendship was normal—#JustBestieThings—but now I'm spinning out, wondering if the intense range of emotions I felt around her were more than friendship feelings.

Maybe it was always meant to be something more.

Chapter Twenty-Five

"There you are!" It's Ramona's voice that finally makes me look up from the piece I've been putting the final touches on.

"Shit. What time is it?" I frantically search for my phone and see it's fifteen minutes past when we were supposed to meet up. I have a couple of texts I missed from both Ramona and Sienna asking where I am.

Ugh. One of my worst ADHD traits is time blindness. When I get into something, I can get really into it. Forget things like my phone or even eating and drinking; in those moments, it's like the world around me goes fuzzy and all I see or think about is whatever's in front of me.

"I'm so sorry. I got totally caught up. I didn't even see your texts."

I expect them to be irritated at me—this habit of mine drives Papi crazy, and I don't blame him for finding it frustrating—but they're both smiling.

"Yeah, we figured," Ramona says with a laugh. "But it's no big deal."

"Really," Sienna assures me. "How'd painting go?"

"Actually, quite well." I turn my notebook toward them.

"Wow." Ramona's eyes take in all the details, going back and forth between what I've painted and what's in front of me. "You're even better than I remembered."

"You're really talented," Sienna agrees.

My cheeks flush at the compliment. Art might be My Thing, but that doesn't mean I'm comfortable with praise for it. "Thanks, guys. I had a lot of fun. Kind of wish I'd been painting scenes from each of our stops."

"Who says you can't?" Ramona asks. "You have photos from each, right?"

"And even if you don't, I do. I've been taking tons! I'll text some to you," Sienna offers. "More importantly: I got you something."

I close my notebook and look up at her in surprise. "What?"

"Wait, that was for Chloe?" There's a sharpness to Ramona's voice. "Funny you didn't mention that."

"Yeah! Nothing crazy." Sienna hands me a bag from the gift shop. I reach inside and pull out a tiny, fluffy stuffed flamingo. "Remember that time we stayed up super late at your house and you couldn't stop crying over how sorry you felt for flamingos? 'It's so embarrassing the way they have to stand! I bet the other animals make fun of them!'" Sienna laughs. "This little lady made me think of you."

I give the flamingo a little squeeze. "Oh my gosh, she's adorable. Thank you, Sienna."

"You know, I actually saw a sign that says you can feed the flamingos," Ramona offers with a casual shrug. "If you're interested, I mean."

"Oh my God, really?!" I shove my art supplies into my tote and hop up. "Come on!"

Ramona flashes me a grin. "Awesome."

I practically skip ahead of her and Sienna. "Just so you know, if I do this, I might cry again!" I call back to them.

"We would expect nothing less," Ramona calls back.

* * *

As it turns out, feeding flamingos is equal parts fun and messy. They eat krill (the same tiny shellfish blue whales eat!), which is fed to them using a cup of water. And yeah, I did cry a little because flamingos look really silly and they don't even know it and I love them.

Then the three of us venture into the aquarium, our final stop before we get back on the highway and drive to Missouri.

The aquarium is dark and cool, and I love how it feels like we've stepped into the ocean. Ramona and I are taken by the seals, who seem to *know* they're adorable as they zip around their tank, while Sienna can't get over the cute penguins. There are coral and angelfish, eels and stingrays, seahorses and sharks.

"This is really making me have to pee," Sienna announces. "I'm going to find a bathroom. Anyone else?"

"I'm good," Ramona says.

"Me too," I agree.

"Be back soon. Don't wander off!"

Sienna waves and turns to go, leaving Ramona and me in the underwater dolphin viewing zone. It's a domed room made of glass, one that appears to immerse you in the water. It's as if you're actually swimming with the dolphins: the animals glide over your head and beside you. It's the closest I've ever felt to being a mermaid. Ramona is looking into the water with pure wonder, and I can't help but sneak a glance at her, watching her watch the dolphins.

She turns to catch my eye and motions for me to join her by the glass. "Come here. Look at the little baby." I step closer to her as she points toward a small dolphin swimming alongside its mother. But I'm distracted. Ramona and I are now standing so close I can feel the warmth from her skin, a stark contrast to the chilly air-conditioning.

Though we're surrounded by a bunch of families (plus what I assume is a day care class of babies and toddlers), it very much feels like it's only the two of us.

Or maybe that's my brain hoping for that.

"What a sweetheart," I murmur. "I see what you mean about aquariums now. They are pretty dreamy."

"Aren't they?" Ramona smiles. "You should paint this."

I take a few photos. "Now I can." Then I tuck my phone back into my bag. "I have yet to see your art, by the way."

She shrugs. "I'm not hiding it from you."

"You'll have to show me, then."

"Whenever you want," she says. Her gaze falls to her boots and she kicks the ground with her toe. "Also, um. Sorry if I was weird about the little flamingo."

I laugh. "Her name is Bubblegum, thank you very much."

"Really, though. It's sometimes still hard, to see the two of you—"

"Miss me?" Sienna's voice rings out. Ramona and I both jump.

My hand goes over my now-racing heart. "Jeez, you scared us!"

"Good," she laughs. "Ready to hit the road?"

Ramona and I look at each other once, then just as quickly look away.

"Sure," I say.

And we say goodbye to my new favorite zoo.

* * *

That night, when we finally arrive at our hotel in Missouri, we're beat.

But at least I have a new plushie flamingo named Bubblegum.

"Why am I so tired all of a sudden?" Sienna asks, flopping onto one of the beds.

I stretch my arms over my head. "I didn't realize how intense a road trip would be. It's like your whole body is so cramped from being in the same position that it basically shuts down. What is this *nonsense*?"

"Do you want one of us to take on the next shift of driving?" Ramona asks. "Your knee must be toast."

"I wish you could, but my dad only listed me as a driver on the car. Maybe we can hang out in the hotel tonight?" I suggest.

Ramona nods. "I'm all for that."

I reach for the hotel menu and scan it. "We could do room service?"

"Now that's a great idea," Sienna says.

Ramona wrings her hands together. "I don't know. It feels like we're spending a lot of your dad's money."

I smile at her. "It's okay. Meals are actually on me."

Sienna bolts up in bed. "You never told us that, you little sneak! We could've been splitting everything this whole time!"

Which earns her a well-deserved eye roll from me. "That's exactly why I didn't tell you. This whole thing was my idea, so I want to make it as painless as possible. I've been saving up."

"You still shouldn't have to cover everything," Ramona says sternly. "Let me pay for dinner tonight."

I make a face. "No way! I'm the one who suggested room service, and we all know that pricing will be astronomical."

Ramona stiffens. "I can cover it, you know."

"Of course you can. But I don't want you to."

Sienna grabs the menu from me, her eyes scanning the listings. Then a smile spreads across her face. "Wasn't one of our BFF Bucket List items to eat ice cream for dinner?"

"It was," I confirm.

"The menu lists several types of ice cream for room service. So I think it's time we cross that one off our list." Sienna arches an eyebrow. "Deal?"

"Only if I can treat," Ramona insists.

"And I get the next meal," Sienna adds.

They both look at me, determined, and my stomach is rumbling, so...

I nod. "Deal."

~ THE BFF BUCKET LIST ~

1) ~~See a firefly~~

2) ~~Eat ice cream for dinner~~

3) Be in three places at once

4) Go camping

5) ~~Get drunk together~~

6) Skinny-dip

7) Stay up all night and watch the sunrise

8) Make out with someone

9) ~~Take a road trip~~

10) See Intonation together LIVE wearing feather boas like from the "Late Nights" music video and maybe have them each fall in love with us

Chapter Twenty-Six

TUESDAY, DAY FOUR: KANSAS CITY, MO
DESTINATION: DODGE CITY, KS

To keep things super chill and not at all confusing, the next leg of our trip will take us from Kansas City, which is in Missouri, to Kansas, where Kansas City is not. I hate US geography.

We've learned our lesson about avoiding work traffic, so we leave later in the morning.

Sienna settles into the back seat with my noise-canceling headphones and a headache (she's prone to them in the summertime whenever a storm is brewing—I can't even imagine). Ramona keeps me company up front.

"Passenger princess twice in a row?" I tease. "You're getting spoiled."

"Don't get too used to it," Ramona jokes back. She reaches into her bag and pulls something out. "Do you still like these?"

I glance over to see her holding out a dulce de leche–flavored lollipop. It's a brand her older brother, Manny, used to keep stocked in his room. We would sneak in when he wasn't home and steal some, which made it taste that much sweeter. "Oh my gosh! Where'd you find that?! I look at the store all the time and can never find any!" I take the lollipop and tuck it into my tote for later.

"I still steal them from Manny when I stop by his apartment. I have no idea where he gets them, and I kind of don't want to. Better to take them when he's not looking. It's my right as his little sister," Ramona says with a soft laugh. "You'll have that to look forward to soon, you know."

I arch an eyebrow. "Having my sister steal from me?"

"Yeah! It's all part of having a sibling. I steal from Manny; Luz, Gracie, and Andres steal from me; and your little sister will steal from you. It's a rite of passage," she explains.

"Well, when you put it that way, I guess I have no choice but to look forward to it." I smile. "God, how is Manny, anyway? I haven't seen him in forever."

"Manny's good. He has an apartment downtown and he's dating a girl named Sanya. I really like her, actually. She's sweet and doesn't take any shit, which is what he needs. He's been talking about proposing soon."

"No shit?" I ask. "Isn't he only, like, twenty-two?"

"Twenty-three, yeah. I told Manny I think he's too young, but he came back from serving thinking he knows everything." She rolls her eyes. "Still. If he's going to propose to anyone, I'm glad it's Sanya. She's good with the kids, too, which is nice because Manny has them over a lot to help Mami. Andres is especially taken by her because she lets him blow bubbles in their apartment."

"You know, I feel like that might win me over too."

Ramona laughs. "Yeah, right?"

I try to mentally calculate in my head how old each of her siblings must be now. The last time she and I spoke, Ramona was fourteen, Luz eleven, Gracie six, and Andres was only two. We didn't go to her house often because there was nowhere for us to hang out without being in the way. But I liked seeing her sisters and brothers. There was always a game to play or something to do, so her house was never boring.

They were small then, though, and it's been more than four years since I last saw them, which would mean...

"Wait, is Luz in *high school* now?"

"Sure is, and she's much cooler than we were at her age."

I furrow my brows and pretend to be hurt. "Are you saying making up dances to boy band songs isn't cool? I'm offended."

"It's funny because I'm actually so glad I had that. I look at Luz now and sometimes I think she's too serious, too much on her phone. You just think you know everything at that age and you don't know shit."

"Tell me about it. I'm eighteen now and feel like I still don't know shit," I say with a sigh.

Ramona nods. "Mami tells me often that the older she gets, the less she feels like she knows. So yeah. I think it's normal."

"And how is she? Okay?"

"She's tired," Ramona admits. "The other day, I was looking at her and I noticed these wrinkles around her eyes she never had before. She's not even old, you know? But it's weird to watch your parents change. Like, usually when I look at her, I still see her as the Mami from when I was little. But that day, for some reason, I really *saw her*-saw her, and I could tell she was getting older. It freaked me out a little."

"Yeah, I know what you mean," I say. "Papi's beard is going gray now. He's only in his forties, but in my head, he's forever twenty-six, which is how old he was when I started kindergarten."

Ramona wrinkles her nose in disgust. "God, that's like if Manny had a baby in three years. Can you imagine?"

I shudder at the thought. "No way. Too weird."

We're quiet for a moment, and it's so nice that we've been able to talk like this again. I realize that in losing Ramona, I lost out on not just her, but the details of her life and everyone in it. No wonder her absence—and Sienna's—felt so big.

"Hey, promise not to tell Mami I noticed her wrinkles?" Ramona asks, holding out a pinky to me. "She'd kill me if she knew."

I laugh quietly and wrap my pinky around hers. "Only if you promise not to tell Papi I've noticed he's going silver."

* * *

For the rest of the drive, we play I Spy, which Ramona is shockingly good at; we share earbuds and listen to a podcast, which feels strangely intimate (but I tell myself I'm overreacting); and I, as always, point out a cow or a horse whenever I see one. Sienna is still in the back seat resting, though she has taken off the headphones.

"So…this is Dodge City, Kansas, huh?" Ramona asks, peering out the window as we near our hotel. "You know, I was looking up things to do here, and I saw that the phone number on the city's official website is literally 1-800-OLD-WEST."

I laugh. "You're messing with me right now."

"I couldn't make this shit up." She holds up her phone and I glance at the screen, confirming she's right. "They specialize in being a 'former bustling frontier town for cowboys.'"

"Well, *that's* concerning. Don't want to get killed in a shoot-out between the sheriff and an outlaw. Should I drive past our hotel and keep going? Denver's only another six hours," I josh.

"I know you're kidding, but part of me is like, yes, keep going. I'm not sure how I feel about three queer girls rocking up to this tiny town! I'm sure the people are nice and all, but…" She shudders. "Sienna's murder podcast has planted *bad thoughts* in my head."

From the back seat, Sienna chimes in. "My headache is only getting worse. I'm sorry. I really need to lie down somewhere quiet."

"Don't be sorry. We're almost there," I assure her.

It's raining by the time we pull up to our hotel—thankfully, a regular ol' Hampton Inn & Suites—and I check us in as Ramona helps Sienna into our room. Poor girl had to wear sunglasses inside because her migraine was making her eyes so sensitive to light.

I meet them up there, and we make sure the curtains are drawn, the air-conditioning is cranked, and Sienna is well stocked with snacks and water. Then Ramona and I slip out and leave her to rest.

I scroll on my phone, trying to figure out what we can get up to. Out loud, I read off some of the possible attractions. "So, they have a casino we're too young for, distilleries we're too young for, a water park or historic walking tour—"

"But it's raining," Ramona puts in.

"Yep. Let's see. Churches, a football stadium. Oh, here's something: 'Many artifacts from the town's past have been preserved in Boot Hill Museum, which was built on the site of the infamous Boot Hill Cemetery.'"

"Stop it right now," Ramona hisses. "We are not setting foot in that place to get haunted by racist ghosts!"

I giggle. "I know, I know. Oh, okay, a farmers' market?"

I tilt my phone to Ramona. She clicks and frowns. "Only open on Saturdays. But the movie theater is open!"

"Oh my gosh, yes. What're they showing?" I ask.

She scrolls. "Looks like . . . *The Birth of a Nation*." I give her a horrified look, and she breaks into laughter. "Now *that* was a joke."

* * *

The only thing that's playing at this movie theater is a children's film called *What the Fork?* and it's about a Claymation fork that has an existential crisis, escapes the kitchen where it lives, and explores the world. It's our only choice, so, fine.

We get snacks and drinks and settle into the plush theater seats. We're about fifteen minutes early to the showing, but we're the only ones in the theater, except for a family of four who chose to sit all the way in the front. Ramona and I opted for the back, taking seats in the middle of the row.

"The back row is always my favorite," Ramona says.

"Totally. I never understood the hype about being all the way up front. If you're too close to the screen, it starts to feel like the actors are watching *you*."

As the previews switch from one to another, Ramona leans closer to me. "Sucks about Sienna."

"Yeah, seriously. I hope she's okay."

"Me too," she agrees. "And, um. About yesterday. With the flamingo stuffed animal. Again, sorry if I was being weird."

"Oh, it's fine," I say. "You didn't do anything."

"I felt like I made it awkward or whatever, saying she should've told me she was buying you something. I already apologized to Sienna, actually." She shrugs a shoulder, and I'm sorry she's been feeling so bad about what she said when I hadn't even given it a second thought. "I guess I was feeling a little jealous. It sort of reminded me about when we were younger and we used to bicker about her all the time."

"Ha, yeah. That was a wild time I don't necessarily want to revisit."

"No, I know that. It's just—" She looks up, searching for the right words. "There have been a few little things that made me think, like... never mind."

"No, no. Made you think what?" I ask. "Say it."

"Made me think maybe you were still pining for her or whatever. And that maybe she was reciprocating those feelings a little."

I swallow. "And that would mean...?"

"I don't know."

We're quiet for a moment.

"I was never pining for Sienna," I clarify. Ramona shoots me a look. "Okay, fine. Maybe I was wondering about her and me at the start of the trip. But really, I think that crush is in the past."

"It was more than that. It was like she was your whole world."

"Okay, but you were *both* my whole world in different ways," I say, getting defensive. "And I know we both suffered when we lost her."

"Yeah...yeah. That was all really hard," Ramona replies. "On both of us, you're right."

"Yes. It almost felt like it broke me a little. Which sounds dramatic, but...I don't know. You guys were all I had. And she was my first unrequited love, fair enough. But now? No. I'm truly not interested in her like that. I mean it."

The corner of Ramona's mouth twitches up. "Oh? Cool."

"Yeah," I say casually. "Cool."

The theater goes dark, and our conversation quiets. We distract ourselves with an anthropomorphic fork with big dreams, and I try to ignore the fluttering in my chest every time we reach for popcorn at the same time and our fingers touch.

Chapter Twenty-Seven
TUESDAY, DAY FOUR: DODGE CITY, KS, EVENING

So far on this trip, my ADHD brain has been mostly fine, probably because I've been diligent with my medicine, and Sienna has been ensuring we stick to a semblance of routine. But when I get back to the hotel and try to let Ramona and me into our room, I can't find our key.

"Everything good?" Ramona asks as I search through my tote.

"Yep. Totally good. I definitely didn't misplace our hotel key."

"You mean the one hotel key we have?"

"That one, yep," I say. My searching turns a bit frantic. Because why did I have to go and lose our room key? Every time I've traveled with Papi, he's emphasized the importance of me making sure I had my key in a safe place. It showed responsibility, he said, and he always made a huge deal if ever I lost mine on a trip—so much so that, as I got older, I would keep my key cards in obvious places, like my socks, just so I wouldn't accidentally misplace them. "Remind me why we opted for only one key card again?"

Ramona smirks. "You misheard the clerk at the front desk when she asked, 'How many keys?' and said, 'I love bees!' and then you were too embarrassed to correct yourself. Remember?" Oh, right. When I don't laugh, Ramona's face goes serious. "Hey. We can get a new key. It's no big deal."

Only it *feels* like a big deal. My neck starts to get hot with embarrassment because I *hate* when I do this. It's like, one second I have the thing and it's perfectly safe and fine, and then I get distracted and forget about its existence completely and have zero memory of where it went or why. Or, worse, I can picture exactly where I left the thing and I get angry with myself for not taking two extra seconds to make sure I had it with me.

"I know I had the key. I did!" I insist.

"I know you did, but it's okay. Things happen. We're not stranded. Sienna's just inside and she can let us in." Ramona's voice is calm and soothing. She knocks on the door, but I can't let this go. While we wait for Sienna to answer, I kneel on the floor and turn my tote upside down, letting the contents spill out. "You don't have to do that, Chloe."

"I know it's here somewhere!" I hear myself sounding frantic, but it's only because I am. Where is that stupid key card?!

Then my heart sinks with realization as I remember: I put the key on the table near the door so I wouldn't forget it, but then I needed to grab my water bottle before Ramona and I left, and… "Oh. I think I left our key in the room."

Ramona gives me a sympathetic look, and I wish I didn't hate that, but I do. "That's okay. Seems like Sienna might still be asleep. How about we go down to the front desk and see if they can give us another one."

I blink back tears and start shoving things back into my bag. "Then I'll have to admit I lost it!"

Ramona kneels down beside me and puts a hand on top of mine. If I weren't freaking out right now about the key, I would be freaking out right now about her hand, and the latter freak-out would be so much better.

"You can't possibly be the first person in the history of this hotel to have misplaced their key card," she says. "It's really fine."

"It's really *not*," I say, grabbing my wallet and shoving it in the tote. "My brain is the literal worst sometimes."

"I actually kind of like your brain." Ramona takes her hand off mine and reaches for my ChapStick, which is still on the floor. She gives it to me, then tilts her chin toward the stairs. "Come on."

As we make our way downstairs, I text Diego.

Me: fun news!!

Me: i lost the ONE key we had to the hotel room

Me: and now i have to be brave and, like, beg for another from the front desk

Me: i have papi's voice in my head lecturing me about RESPON-SIBILITY and SAFETY

Me: i am the worst!!!!!

Diego: ok, rude, only i can say that about u

Diego: but it'll be fine. just go to the front desk and channel ur inner doe-eyed bird

Me: WHAT A GREAT IDEA

Diego: i know, i am gifted

Ramona nudges me with her elbow. "I'm glad something's got you smiling."

"It's just Diego. I told him I lost the key and he said I should try my—and I quote—'doe-eyed bird thing.'" Ramona raises an eyebrow questioningly, so I explain. "Diego is convinced I can use my alleged adorableness to get things I want. Like, to get out of a speeding ticket or something. He calls it my 'doe-eyed bird thing' and says I bat my eyelashes or whatever and it gets authority figures to feel bad for me."

Ramona laughs. "Oh, man. He's right. You totally *do* do that!"

"I don't!" I scoff.

"You absolutely do. I've *seen* it. You got us out of getting suspended that one time when our teacher let us have class outside and we walked to get ice cream. Don't you remember?"

The memory comes flooding back to me and I can't help but laugh. "Oh my God, that's right! I told Mr. Medina my blood sugar was low and I needed food, so we had no choice but to get ice cream, didn't I?" I pause and wrinkle my nose. "Am I evil?"

"Crafty, yes. Evil? Also yes." Ramona takes a seat on one of the lobby chairs and grabs a book. "Now work your magic."

I take a deep breath and make my eyes as big and woeful as possible as I walk to the front desk. I wish little things like this didn't feel so stressful to me, but here we are.

"Can I help you, miss?" a young man, whose name tag reads TYLER, asks from behind the desk.

"Hi. I'm so sorry to bother you, but I can't find the key to my hotel room. We only had one between me and my friends, and it was completely my fault for misplacing it. I know I had it with me, but I think I left it in our room. I checked my tote, my wallet, my pockets—I've looked everywhere," I explain quickly, another wave of shame washing over me as I speak. "I don't know what to do."

"Oh, okay," Tyler says, totally nonchalant and completely unfazed by my distress. "Name and room number?"

I give it to him, as well as my ID, and literal seconds later we have three new hotel keys, one for each of us, and I can't believe I was so stressed out for nothing?!

Once Ramona and I are inside the elevator, I turn to her in a huff. "So they just *give* you new keys if you lose them? My freakout was for nothing! I didn't even need my doe-eyed bird thing."

"Yeah, but if you had needed it, it totally would've worked," Ramona says, trying to make me feel better. "Chloe, you're not alone in losing stuff. Everyone does. You *really* don't have to beat yourself up if you do it a little more often."

"I guess," I say, crossing my arms. "Papi always made it sound like losing a key would get me banned from the hotel or something!"

Ramona lets out a sympathetic laugh. "That's like when Mami told me it cost a dollar every time one of us would flick the light switch on and off. She just didn't want to deal the lights flickering. But I believed that for a long time! I slept with the light on in my room for weeks."

We exit the elevator and make our way back to the room. "You know, it's not even really about the hotel key," I say.

Ramona gives me a sidelong glance that tells me she had probably already figured that out. But she doesn't say so. "Oh?"

"It's just that—before I found the right medication, my ADHD had me feeling so scattered over everything. My brain ran at a million miles per hour and I could barely keep up with my own thoughts. I'd see a book lying on the floor in my room and think about putting it away, which would remind me that I'd been meaning to sweep, which would then make me wonder where I'd left my broom, and I'd go looking for it but somehow end up reorganizing our pantry. When I'd inevitably come back to my room and see the book on the floor, I'd just be flooded with so much shame. Like, why couldn't I just put the book where it goes? Why is doing everything so hard?"

I'm rambling. I know that. When I feel my ADHD has gotten the better of me, I sometimes feel the need to explain myself. Or, more often, overexplain.

I continue, "I've mostly come to appreciate how I think and how my mind functions. But then, days like these—when I misplace something that was important or when my thoughts are all over the place or when I can't work up the motivation to do something I actually *want* to do—I'm reminded of how…weird my brain can be."

We've stopped walking just outside our hotel room. When I look at Ramona, I see her face has gone soft—not with pity, but with understanding. With seeing me. My chest feels warm under her gaze.

"That sounds like a lot, Chloe. I can see how losing a hotel key would seem like so much more." There is a gentleness to her voice as she speaks. "But, for the record, your brain also helps you make really dope art. And it's funny and kind and empathetic to others. Plus, it helps you come up with random ideas, like taking a road trip with your friends to see a boy band concert." I laugh at that. "What I'm saying is: I like your weird brain. You should, too."

I bite back a smile. "Oh yeah?"

She shrugs one shoulder nonchalantly, but she's smiling, too. "Yeah."

With that, I step toward our door and hold my new key against the lock. The light turns green, letting us know the door has unlatched, and all is well.

Inside the room, it's dark and Sienna is still asleep, but the light from the hallway spills inside enough so that I can see the missing key card sitting on the table by the door, right where I left it. I glare at it, as if it has personally offended me. (It has.)

I pull out my phone to text Diego.

Me: got a new key

Me: and i didn't need to grovel or be cute at all!!!!

Me: apparently it's not a big deal AT ALL

Diego: ya. hotels literally don't give a shit if u lose ur key lol

Me: WHY DIDN'T YOU TELL ME THAT

Diego: because that wouldn't have been as fun

Me: i hate you

Chapter Twenty-Eight

A loud crack of thunder wakes me the next morning. When I can't fall back asleep, I grab my tote and sneak out of our hotel room—triple-checking to make sure I have the key—to check out the complimentary breakfast in the lobby. I'm thankful I decided to sleep in an oversize T-shirt and some shorts rather than a matching pajama set, so this way it's slightly less obvious I fully just rolled out of bed.

With a cup of coffee and a bowl of fruit, I settle into a table in the corner that faces the outside so I can watch the rain fall and paint until it gets closer to a normal waking hour.

Now that I've started painting for fun again, it's all I want to do. I've made a list of the different landmarks and photos I want to re-create in watercolor to commemorate this trip: Niagara Falls, the food spread from our impromptu picnic in the Tommy's Tools & Treats parking lot, a butterfly on a flower at the Indianapolis Zoo conservatory, the movie theater last night with the old-school marquee that says WHAT THE FORK? My plan is to paint special pieces for Sienna and Ramona after our trip so they have a memento of our time together.

Having so many things to paint usually makes it really difficult for me to choose where to get started. This morning, though, I have one painting in particular in mind.

I scroll through my photos until I come across the stealthy shot I managed to take of Ramona in the Indy Zoo aquarium admiring the dolphins. I framed the photo so it looks like she's alone, her brown skin illuminated by the blue glow of the water that surrounds her. She is how I imagine a water goddess might look: strong but soft.

I put my earbuds in and get to work, drifting away from where I am and falling into the rhythm of creating watery brushstrokes juxtaposed with sharp, pigment-filled lines. At its best, painting can feel a lot like a dance. This is what creating is supposed to feel like, and my heart aches for when art felt like something that was *mine* rather than something I needed to perfect and monetize.

In my periphery, I see a familiar black shoulder bag, and I look up to see Ramona. Her eyes, like mine, still look heavy with sleep. She gives me an easy smile that elicits a flutter in my stomach. Even fresh from waking up, she manages to be beautiful. I smile back at her, pausing my music and taking out an earbud.

"Can I join you?" she asks. She's holding a black coffee in one hand and a plate of food in the other.

I motion toward the spot across the table. "Please. I couldn't sleep because of the storm and I didn't want to wake anyone else up."

Ramona pulls the chair out and slides into it. "I had trouble sleeping in this morning too." She reaches into her bag and pulls out her iPad. "And it looks like you and I both had the same idea."

I shield the piece I'm working on. "This is supposed to be a surprise, though!"

Ramona tilts her head to the side with a smirk. "A surprise?"

"Want to see?" I ask. "It's for you."

I turn what I'm working on around and push it toward her so she can get a better look. It's only about half done, but it's starting to take shape well, and you can get the gist of where I'm going with it.

She gingerly takes the paper into her hands, careful not to touch the places that are still drying. In a small voice, she asks, "Is this...me?"

Her gentleness catches me by surprise, and I suddenly feel a little embarrassed. Is it weird I snuck that photo? Is my idea to paint these for her and Sienna too over-the-top? Am I being too sentimental again, too much?

I rush to explain. "Yeah, from the aquarium. You said you felt peaceful there and I don't know—I could just see it on your face. So I took a pic. I hope that's okay. After you and Sienna let me have that time in the garden to work on my watercolors, I had this idea to make a piece for each of you guys, so you'll have something to remember the trip by. Like your own mini-postcard."

Ramona shakes her head. "No one's ever painted me before."

"Is it weird?" I wrinkle my nose. "I probably should've asked, huh?"

"No! No, it's not weird at all." She looks at me, the corners of her mouth tilted upward. "It's beautiful." Her voice is laced with emotion as she reluctantly hands the painting back to me.

I swallow. "Well…not yet. It will be when I'm done. Hopefully. Anyway! I'm glad you like it. Now show me yours!" She laughs. "Your *art,* I mean."

Ramona wakes her iPad, tapping until she gets to a particular set of drawings, and turns it around to face me. "I mostly draw random tattoo ideas that strike me. Some of them are okay, others not so much. But that's what the practice is for, to work through the good and the bad, you know? Here are some of my favorite recent designs."

I see intricate black-and-white line tattoos: an open book with pages that fade into a galaxy, an anatomical heart made from a strawberry, a knife made of sunflowers, a set of tarot cards—the star and the moon—where the women in each scene embrace in the middle, as if they might leave their cards and run away together.

"More!" I say eagerly, and she taps to pull up another page.

"These ones are silly." She motions at the designs: a hand with manicured nails holding the bony hand of a skeleton, a happy ghost surrounded by tropical flowers, a disco ball wearing combat boots, a boba cup filled with stars, a frog wearing a wizard's hat and holding a magic wand.

I knew Ramona was talented, but shit. It's been years since I've seen her work, and I'm in awe.

"I need all these," I murmur. "Seriously. Turn them into a sleeve and I'm in."

Ramona sniffs and looks away. "You couldn't afford my rate."

I laugh. "You're probably right."

"You really like them?" she asks, biting her lip.

"I *love* them. You're...incredible."

She buries her face in her hands. "Don't say nice things. I can't."

"You asked if I liked them!"

With a laugh, Ramona reaches for her iPad and opens an empty image. "Well, show-and-tell time is over because I hate compliments."

I shrug. "Too bad. Because I'm not stopping. You're amazing! You're wonderful—"

"*Anyway*," she says, interrupting. "I haven't tattooed anyone yet, but soon I can."

"Really?" I ask. "How long until then?"

"Depends, really. Each apprenticeship is different, but apprenticeships last two years in Massachusetts, so at least that long. I'm being mentored by Sasha Cartagena, who actually helped cofound Permanent Record, and she's been amazing so far. She goes back and forth between the shop in Elmwood and the one in Boston, so eventually I will too. She's tough, but also wants to make sure I gain tons of experience before I ink someone."

"That's super cool that you're mentored by the cofounder. Wow!"

She nods. "It is awesome. She was the one who dropped me off for our trip. With the motorcycle?"

"Oh, right. The one who drives like shit," I tease.

"It is possible that I told her to be extra dramatic with the entrance," Ramona says with a laugh. "But don't you dare tell that to Sienna. She'll never let me live it down."

I pretend to zip my lips. "So, okay. What does being an apprentice entail? Tell me everything."

"Honestly, it's a lot of grunt work. I keep the shop clean, first and foremost. When I come in, I make sure everything is organized, then I sanitize all the surfaces we touch, sweep and take out the trash, restock stuff, that kind of thing. But I also assist the artists throughout the day," she explains. "I'll get them paper towels or refill their inks or whatever. Sometimes I take calls."

"The worst. I have to do that for If the Shoe Fits." I roll my eyes. "Why can't people just text?"

"God, I wish," Ramona says. "In between all that, I'm drawing tattoos, getting feedback from Sasha, or watching her and the artists work. I'm learning when I observe them: how many times they dip their needle into the ink, how they position their hand and wrist while they pull a line. It's really fascinating, actually."

I smile, leaning back in my chair. I swear I could listen to people talk about what they love all day. "It sounds like it. I can tell you enjoy it."

"I do. I feel super fortunate." Ramona points at my painting. "But, I mean, you must feel like that too, right? You're going to your dream school."

I start fidgeting with the ends of my hair, making a mental note that I really need to touch up the lavender when I get home. "I've been less enthusiastic about it than I thought I'd be."

Ramona furrows her brow. "You've hinted at that. But why?"

"I don't really know." I sigh. "Ever since I committed, it feels like there's been this cloud hanging over me. I'm not actually sure if I want to make art my job." I glance around and let out a shaky laugh. "Wow, that's the first time I've said that out loud."

"Well, damn."

"Right? I'm so"—I motion with my hands—"like, all over the place, that I wish I could explore my options before committing. I love art, obviously. It's the one thing that feels very much mine. Yet I'm like...is that what I want to spend *every day* doing for my *job*? I've heard about people who lose their passion, and I'm worried that might be me." I start absentmindedly stabbing at some leftover fruit in my bowl as I speak. "But RISD is not really the place you go if you're unsure about being a professional. It seems like the students there are Artists with a capital *A,* and I'm over here, like, 'Maybe I should be an accountant?'"

Ramona's mouth quirks up. "I say this with love: You would be a terrible accountant."

I laugh. "Yeah, you're absolutely right! I don't actually want to be an accountant, but it's almost like...I want the option of being an accountant?" I let out a frustrated groan. "Nothing makes sense. My brain is dumb."

"Your brain is the furthest thing from dumb. It sounds to me like you want to understand all your possibilities, which is extremely reasonable."

"You think so?"

"Absolutely! I know it seems like RISD is a done deal for the fall, but you understand that you can always defer or transfer, right? You could go somewhere else—a state school, community college, wherever you want...Dream schools are overrated, in my opinion." She meets my gaze. "Whatever you decide will be justified, because it's a decision *you* made. And if you hate where you end up, choose something else."

"That doesn't make me flaky?" I ask.

"Not even a little bit. Trying things is how you figure yourself out." She smiles. "You can thrive anywhere. And I do mean *you*, specifically. Because you're you."

With those words, it's as if a million pounds have lifted off my shoulders. "You have no idea how much it means to hear that. Thank you."

"I've got you." Ramona reaches over to pat my hand.

I reach for her fingers with mine and squeeze. When she doesn't pull away, I silently think: *I've got you, too.*

Chapter Twenty-Nine

Thankfully, Sienna wakes up from her migraine-induced slumber feeling much better. In fact, she's downright chipper and immediately ready to go. We make quick work of packing, checkout, and then driving six freaking hours to our destination with minimal stops.

But…when we arrive in Monte Vista, the clerk at the front desk tells us our reservation has been canceled. Apparently the rain caused flooding in the hotel, and the room we had booked was among the ones affected.

Rain: 2. Us: 0.

"We're so sorry for the inconvenience, Ms. Torres. We emailed all guests late last night to alert them of the change," the desk clerk, Marc, explains.

I pull out my phone and open up Gmail. There, buried under emails from Old Navy, RISD, and my daily horoscope, is a message from the hotel. Sienna peeks over my shoulder and pinches my elbow.

"*Okay*, I get it," I hiss at her. I put on a bright smile. "I'm sorry—it looks like I missed that email. Total oversight on my part."

"It's no trouble at all, miss." Marc clacks on the keyboard and reads something on his screen. "I've just checked and confirmed that we've already initiated a refund, which should show up in three to five business days. We're also providing all guests who have been impacted by the flooding with a voucher for a complimentary overnight stay in the future. That has been sent to your email also, but if you have any trouble accessing it, please let us know."

"Thank you. Do you have any suggestions for alternative arrangements?" Sienna asks.

"Many of the nearby hotels have also been affected by the storm, so it may be difficult." He leans across the counter and lowers his voice. "If I were you, I would try Airbnb or something similar. Shit's bad right now."

"On it," Sienna says, whipping out her phone.

Then Marc stands back and straightens his posture. "However, I am happy to help make some calls to see if we can find something for you at one of our sister hotels. We have many across the state. Would you like me to list some of the nearby locations for you?" I'm impressed with how quickly he's able to drop in and out of his customer service persona.

"We appreciate the offer, but we're all set," I say. "Thank you so much, Marc."

"Is there some kind of survey we can fill out for you?" Ramona asks. "You've been very helpful."

"We are happy to accept customer feedback on our website." Marc gives us a pleasant nod, but he's a little dead behind the eyes. I'm sure dealing with angry customers all morning has been hell.

We thank him again and then head to our car.

"Okay, just gave Marc a five-star review," Ramona announces from the back.

"He deserved it. Thank you!" I lean over and try to get a glimpse at Sienna's phone. "Any luck?"

"I have no idea how, but I struck Airbnb gold." She turns the screen to face me and Ramona. "Look at this house!"

She shows us a one-story, three-bedroom bungalow with an outdoor patio and in-ground pool.

"It's perfect!" I say. "We each get our own room! But Sienna, I don't want you to pay for—"

"I'm paying for it," she says bluntly.

"What're we waiting for?" Ramona asks. "Let's book it."

"Just did. And it's only ten minutes from here." Sienna claps her hands together. "I'm so excited. This is going to be great. We can actually cook a meal instead of going out somewhere to eat!"

I pull our car out of the hotel parking lot. "Oh my God. I've missed home-cooked meals!"

"Seriously. Should we go grocery shopping?" Ramona asks. "I can start a list."

Sienna nods. "Yes! Okay, let's head to the house first since it's so close. We can make our list there and see what's nearby. Oh! The house is self-check-in, by the way. We won't have to see another soul."

I gasp. "Stop, I might tear up. You know how much I love not talking to people."

* * *

When we arrive at the house, I let Ramona and Sienna claim their rooms as I FaceTime Papi. He'll be stressed over the change in plans, so I add Karina and Diego onto the call too. They'll help soften the blow.

Papi answers from his office. "Mija, I'm about to jump into a meeting. Everything okay?"

Karina's face shows up on the screen next. "Chloe! How are you?"

And then Diego. "This better be goo— Hi, Tío! Hi, Karina!"

"So sorry to bother you all in the middle of the day, but I wanted to let you know our plans for our hotel have changed. There were some pretty serious storms last night and our hotel flooded," I explain.

Papi's eyes grow big. "I'm flying out there."

"Let the girl finish, Ito," Karina says. "You don't need him to fly out there, do you?"

I shake my head. "No, no. I'm good. We're good! We were able to find an Airbnb and I'll text you the address right after this. I very quickly wanted to show you how cute the house is!"

"Ooh, a house tour. So thrilling," Diego says with mock enthusiasm.

"This is the house." I turn my camera to face the neatly organized living room. "It's really cute. There are three rooms, a nice kitchen, and the best part…" I walk toward the patio and step outside. "Look at this pool!"

"It's actually cute," Diego remarks.

"What I wouldn't give to be floating in our pool right now," Karina says with a dreamy sigh. She's in her home office. "Maybe I will after I send this next email."

"Are all the windows locked? Is there a dead bolt on the door?" Papi asks. "Can you block the back door with a chair? Burglars could come in the back, you know. It might be best if you just stay inside tonight and keep everything closed. Are you sure you don't need me to fly out?"

I roll my eyes and laugh. "Papi, we're good, I promise. I'll take a video of me checking the windows as proof. Now, I won't keep you. You have a meeting to get to."

"Forget my meeting!" Papi argues.

"It sounds like they have this under control," Karina says. "Isn't it so *responsible* of Chloe to call you immediately when her plans changed? And how *resourceful* were she and her friends for taking care of their accommodations all on their own?"

Diego nods. "*Soooo* badass."

"Diego," I hiss.

"What? I'm helping!" he insists.

"Now we will let Chloe get back to her trip, which is going really well," Karina says firmly. "We love you. Be safe. Call us tomorrow?"

I blow them a kiss. "Love you guys. I will."

When we hang up, Diego texts me.

Diego: u interrupted my beauty sleep

Me: it's literally almost 4pm there???

Diego: i was taking a nap u wretched hamster

Me: lmao oh oopsie

Me: i'll let you get back to it!!

Diego: im assassinating u when u get home

Me: sounds fun, byeeeeee

* * *

Sienna, Ramona, and I find ourselves in a Safeway supermarket with a long list of ingredients we'll need for the meal we're preparing. And when I say we I mean Ramona. Ramona loves to cook (why do I find that kinda hot?). She's taken the lead in planning the menu, which is especially helpful since I wouldn't have a clue about what type of vegetarian recipes to make for her.

Note to self: Learn a vegetarian recipe or two.

On tonight's menu: seared-mushroom tacos with charred-corn salsa, plus some rice and grilled zucchini, yellow squash, and red bell peppers.

I'm all too happy to be bossed around by Ramona so I can be as helpful as possible. Following her instructions, I diligently put a few bell peppers into a plastic bag and weigh them.

"Grocery shopping makes me feel like an actual adult," I admit. "I've been avoiding growing up, but this isn't *terrible*, I suppose."

"I'm with you," Sienna says. "I go with my mom all the time and weirdly don't mind it at all."

Ramona reaches for some garlic. "Speak for yourself. I'm the designated grocery shopper in my house and it gets old fast. It helps my mom, though, so of course I do it." She pauses. "It's how I ended up getting into cooking, actually. I would plan elaborate dinners so that choosing the ingredients would be more entertaining. But it's still tedious. It's fun to make meals, but not to shop for them."

"Oh, wow. I didn't realize. So you cook for your family a lot?" I ask.

She nods. "You remember how much my mom works? I started cooking for my siblings a few years ago, to take it off her plate, and it stuck. Sometimes I wish it didn't because it's such a pain to find things everyone wants to eat."

I think of how I've never really had to help around the house, how many of the chores Papi assigned me were to teach me responsibility and not because our house wouldn't function without them. Even the job I took with If the Shoe Fits was for extra money so I could buy frivolous things like hair dye and art supplies and lipstick—not because I actually needed the money. It must be intense having your family rely on you to help take care of the house and to handle major chores. I feel very, very silly for never having to think about it until now.

We add some zucchini to the cart next to the other vegetables and tortillas. Sienna scans our list. "Okay, so, I think rice is next."

I push the cart and lead the way toward the correctly labeled aisle.

"Thank you guys for letting me sleep my migraine off yesterday," Sienna says. "It was a bad one."

I give her a sympathetic nod. "It seemed really brutal. Do they happen often?"

"Not often, but sometimes. Usually with huge changes in barometric pressure, like yesterday," she explains. "Normally I have some prescribed medication that I can take when I feel a migraine coming on. I forgot it at home, though."

"Jeez, that sucks. I'm so sorry," Ramona says.

"Seriously. I'm glad you're feeling better today, though."

Sienna reaches for a bag of rice and places it in the cart. "Me too. Did you two do anything fun while I was knocked out?"

Ramona clears her throat. "Um, no. Not really. Turns out Dodge City is basically a one-horse town."

"There wasn't much to explore, unless we wanted to see a wax figure of Buffalo Bill or enjoy a real-life rodeo," I agree. "Ramona and I went to see that little-kid movie about the fork."

Sienna laughs. "Solid choice. Was it any good? I thought the previews looked cute."

"You know, it kind of was," I admit. "I might actually buy a Fork stuffie when I get back home."

The three of us finish shopping and pay. When we get back to the house, Sienna and I get to work chopping vegetables while Ramona grates limes for the chipotle sauce.

Sienna offers to make us drinks using what's left of the vodka Ramona brought, so I take over as sous-chef. I watch Ramona in quiet awe as she effortlessly shifts around the kitchen, measuring ingredients, mincing garlic and herbs, and dressing the vegetables so they'll be ready for grilling.

"Can you help me carry some of this outside?" Ramona motions toward the backyard. "I'm going to start up the grill while the rice cooks."

I load a tray with the prepared vegetables and carry it outside, placing it beside the grill for Ramona. Then I search the kitchen for an apron, grabbing the first one I find.

Back outside, I hand it to Ramona to keep her clothes from getting dirty. "Here."

She slips it over her head and ties it around her waist. I can't help but notice how, when she pulls it tight, it perfectly accentuates her curves. I feel my neck flush and look away.

" 'Kiss the cook'—you trying to tell me something?" Ramona teases.

When I look down, I see I've managed to somehow grab an apron with one of the most cliché sayings of all time printed on it. It also serves as a flashing arrow for how I've been feeling lately.

"No! I grabbed whatever was there, I swear, I—"

She gives me an easy laugh. "I'm only teasing you, Oleander."

And there is such a familiarity in hearing her use my nickname again that it does the *exact opposite* of make me chill.

"I know! Totally. I think I'll, um, set the table?" I suggest, high-pitched. "Forks would be good. For dinner. To eat. Maybe some plates. Cups. You know…"

Ramona smirks, and it's like she knows she looks good, the way her shirtsleeves are pushed up her forearms and exposing her tattoos. "All of that would be great. I'll be here."

I rush inside so quickly I startle Sienna. "You scared me!" she says. "You good?"

"Totally." I nod. "Totally good. Nothing weird is happening at all."

Chapter Thirty

My nerves have calmed a bit by the time dinner is ready. I've done a pretty decent job of making the table look nice, actually. In the depths of the cupboard, I managed to find cute place mats, and the hosts had a matching set of orange dishes, cups, and cutlery. I swiped the vase of fresh flowers from one of the windowsills and added it to the center of the table.

Ramona sets the grilled vegetables on the table on separate serving trays, while Sienna helps bring over the taco ingredients: grilled tortillas and mushrooms, charred-corn salsa, and toppings.

I take a deep breath in. "Everything smells delicious."

Ramona pulls off the apron and hangs it over the back of her chair before taking a seat. "Thank you. I hope you guys like it. I know vegetarian meals aren't for everyone."

Sienna slides into one of the chairs. "It's a home-cooked meal Chloe and I didn't have to make. We're going to love it. Especially with the drinks I prepared."

I raise my glass. "Cheers?"

"Cheers!"

And the three of us clink our glasses together.

I serve myself some of the vegetables as Ramona assembles her tacos. Sienna takes some rice, then clears her throat. "So…"

Ramona puts her plate down. "That is the most loaded 'so' I've ever heard."

"I know, I know." Sienna laughs. "I think I've made a decision about my dad."

"Have you? I've been dying to ask, but I didn't want to make it weird," I admit.

She nods. "Yeah. I've been weighing everything—the good, the bad, the ugly, the fact that he could totally be an axe-killer."

I grimace. "Oh my God. I'm still so sorry I said that! Your bio dad is not a murderer!"

Sienna laughs. "No, I don't think he is, but I should consider all the possibilities, and that is one, unfortunately. There is also the possibility that he's kind and eager to know about me. That is the one that keeps me up at night, you know? That I could be missing out on this relationship because I'm too afraid to try. So, after a lot of really careful consideration, I think...I might want to go see him?" The last part comes out like a question, as if she's looking to me and Ramona for approval on her decision.

"You don't need us to say yes," Ramona assures her. "If that's what you want to do, then that's what you're going to do."

"What *we're* going to do," I correct. "Because I would love it if you'd let us be there to support you."

Sienna blinks. "What? I don't expect that. I can drive there and back myself."

I hold up my hands. "Hear me out. I looked it up, and Pagosa Springs is ninety minutes away. I doubt there are many Ubers out here, and you're not the driver on the rental. Papi would *kill me* if he found out I let you behind the wheel! So, putting on my best Sienna hat here, and thinking logistically—driving you there makes the most sense. More than that, though, Ramona and I can be there for you...just in case." I don't want to fill in the blanks of what that "just in case" might be; though I don't want to think Sienna's dad will be a monster, I do worry there is a strong possibility she might end up hurt in some way. I hope I'm wrong. But I don't want to pretend it can't happen.

When Sienna doesn't look entirely convinced, Ramona jumps in.

"I'm with Chloe. We can bring you to your dad's, make sure you get into the house okay, and then we'll wait. That way we give you your space, but we're also right there if you need us."

"And you won't need us," I assure her.

Ramona nods. "But it'll make us feel a lot better about the whole thing."

"Plus…Ramona and I voted, and you lost," I tease.

That makes Sienna smile. "Are you sure?"

"Beyond sure." I hold out a pinky to her. "Pinky swear."

Ramona laces her pinky with mine. "Get in here, Sienna."

With a laugh, Sienna loops her pinky around ours. Then she goes quiet. In a small voice, she asks, "Am I making a terrible decision?"

I reach over and grip her hand. "Not even close. You deserve answers."

"It could be good, right?" And my heart breaks a little, knowing this is Little Sienna asking us that question. I've asked myself versions of things like that millions of times about my own mom. What if? We're sometimes so desperate for answers, for connection, that our brains have this funny way of dreaming up implausibly encouraging scenarios. The soft parts of ourselves—the parts that don't know better, that yearn for love and acceptance and home—can't help but hope.

I smile at her. "It could be good."

"It could," Ramona echoes.

Sienna lets out a relieved sigh. "Thank you both."

We spend the rest of dinner hashing out the details for tomorrow, which suddenly feels really important to get right. I go through my drink quicker than I probably should, which only encourages my friends to do the same, so that once we finish dinner we're feeling giggly and silly. Sienna throws on a playlist while we clean up, and we dance as we wash and dry dishes.

"That pool is calling my name," Ramona announces once we're done. "I'm going in."

"Oooh, me too!" Sienna claps her hands together. "Night swim!"

It isn't long before all three of us have changed into our bathing suits and find ourselves splashing around in the pool. The sun is setting, the air turning from sticky to cool, the tiniest breeze rustling the leaves in the trees. We talk and laugh and share and even play a few silly rounds of Would You Rather, though the game takes a surprisingly confusing turn when Ramona asks, "Would you rather have hot dog fingers or kneecaps that squirt lotion every time you walk?" and, without missing a beat, Sienna yells, "Long live delicious hot dog fingers!"

It's not even that funny, yet we erupt into laughter that lasts way longer than it should. When we finally stop, my belly aches and my nostalgia cup is totally full. I feel so happy.

"You know, I'm kind of glad our plans got messed up," I admit, leaning against the edge of the pool. "This is way more fun than staying at another hotel."

Sienna nods. "Totally. But it would be even *more* fun if we could check another thing off our BFF Bucket List."

Ramona gives her a skeptical look. "What kind of nonsense are you up to?"

"Weeeell, I happened to consult the BFF Bucket List and realized tonight could be the perfect time for...skinny-dipping?" She waggles her eyebrows as she says this.

"Tonight," I repeat. "As in, right now?"

"I mean, why not? We have this amazing pool all to ourselves, and it's on the Bucket List! Besides, when else would we?"

Before I can argue, a blur of emerald-colored fabric sails between me and Sienna and lands with a heavy slap against the concrete patio.

"Done," Ramona announces.

My eyes go big. "Is that your top *and* your bottom? How did you do that so fast?!"

She shrugs. "It's a gift. Now, come on. Otherwise, I'm just the weird friend who got naked in a pool alone."

Sienna lets out a squeal as she pulls the string behind her neck and tosses her top to the side of the pool. I hesitate for a moment—mind swirling with body thoughts, and vulnerability, and crushes—before wiggling out of my bathing suit too.

Because life's too short, and I don't want to overthink this, and the BFF Bucket List told us so.

"Attagirl!" Sienna cheers as I toss my swimsuit aside. "We did it!"

"We did do it! We're absolutely bananas, but we did it." I laugh, a rush of adrenaline coursing through my chest.

"One step closer to finishing the Bucket List," Ramona says. Then her lips quirk up into a playful grin. "Now, who wants to play mermaids?"

~ THE BFF BUCKET LIST ~

1) ~~See a firefly~~
2) ~~Eat ice cream for dinner~~
3) Be in three places at once
4) Go camping
5) ~~Get drunk together~~
6) ~~Skinny-dip~~
7) Stay up all night and watch the sunrise
8) Make out with someone
9) ~~Take a road trip~~
10) See Intonation together LIVE wearing feather boas like from the "Late Nights" music video and maybe have them each fall in love with us

Chapter Thirty-One

The whole ride to our campsite, we complain about how much camping is going to suck.

The bugs.

The heat.

The humidity.

The lack of showers.

The bathrooms that are basically holes in the ground.

"Can someone remind me why we put *go camping* on our list?" Sienna groans. "This sounds like it's going to be awful!"

"I'm pretty sure we read a book about summer camp or something," Ramona says with a sigh. "We were very easily influenced."

Sienna frowns. "We were *idiots*."

"Totally," I agree. But I have a secret. While planning this trip, I decided rugged camping was absolutely not our vibe. But *glamping*? That we can do.

So when the car pulls up to a campsite with a silver Airstream—a travel trailer—with a fire pit and a covered patio strung with colorful twinkle lights, Sienna lets out a gasp. "Wait! This is cute. Is this where we're staying?!"

"Did you really think I was going to make us suffer in a tent?" I ask. "I'm not trying to be away from a shower for that long! There's even Wi-Fi."

Ramona is the first to hop out when the car comes to a stop, eager to explore the whimsical-looking campsite, which resembles something created in *The Sims*. The silver trailer is surrounded by red rocks and desert plants, and shaded by a juniper tree. There are hammocks, lounge chairs, a picnic table, and even a private shower and bathroom. Best of all, it gives the most serene view of the Rio Grande range—a majestic combination of luxury and nature.

It's camping at its finest, if you ask me.

"Can we check out the inside?" Ramona asks. I give her the code to enter. When she opens the door and peeks in, a grin spreads across her face. The Airstream features a large queen bed and two twin bunks, as well as a small eat-in kitchen. Plus... "It's air-conditioned!"

I grin back. "We'll be sleeping really good tonight."

"I'm going to explore," Ramona announces, taking off toward a sign that reads MORE THIS WAY.

I quickly FaceTime Papi to show him the grounds, and he warns me to stay away from coyotes, snakes, and steep cliffs, as if I have a habit of getting near any of those things. Then I join Sienna, who is staring at the view from the patio.

"You've really outdone yourself with this one," she murmurs. She puts her hands on her hips and gazes at the mountains in the distance. "This is unreal."

"When I see places like this, I have a hard time believing it's part of the same Earth we live on, you know?" I shake my head. "It's ethereal."

"Totally," she breathes.

We're quiet for a minute, taking it all in. Then, in a soft voice, I ask, "You still want to meet him, right?"

Sienna turns to me. "I do."

I give her a reassuring smile. "Let's spend the day here, then head out around four thirty. By the time we get there, he should be home from work, assuming he works typical hours. Sound good?"

She bites her nails and nods. I can't imagine how nervous she feels right now, taking such a huge leap of faith. My mom left, but at least I know what I'm missing out on (nothing). It must be torture not to know at all. Sienna has to do this, so she leaves this trip without regrets—and, if all goes well, with another parent.

In the distance, Ramona's voice rings out. "Guys! There's a mini-golf course. Come on!"

Sienna and I smile at each other.

"Coming!" I call. "You're about to get *wrecked*!"

* * *

We could easily spend the rest of our trip here at this hideaway, reading books and drawing and listening to music. The day feels like it passes too quickly, and before long, it's time to pack up and head toward Sienna's dad's house.

Sienna changes outfits four times before she settles on a plain white puff-sleeve dress and her signature dangly earrings.

Ramona lets Sienna take the front seat, and we use the ninety-minute drive to play through the best-case scenarios, like her dad is the present-day Mister Rogers and welcomes her with open arms and a hand-knitted sweater. We do this in hopes it helps calm her nerves a little, and because we know there isn't much we can do otherwise.

Eventually, we pull up to a modest log cabin–style home with a big porch and neatly trimmed yard. It's less extravagant than Sienna's house, but still beautiful. There are two cars in the driveway, which I take as a good sign.

"This is it," I say quietly, putting the Jeep in park and leaving it idling. "We can come in with you?"

Sienna shakes her head. "Thank you, but I think I need to do this on my own."

Ramona pats her on the shoulder. "You've got this."

"We'll wait here the whole time. We're not going anywhere, I promise." I give Sienna a quick hug. "Just give us some sort of sign when you get to the door that you're all right."

"And if you get inside, and things feel weird, text us right away. We'll be there in a flash," Ramona reiterates.

"Okay." Sienna takes in a deep breath and reaches for the door handle. "I love you both."

It's the first time any of us have dared to utter those words to each other since we were kids, and my insides go warm. "Love you too, Sienna."

"We love you," Ramona echoes. "We're proud of you."

Sienna gives us a confident nod, then leaves the car.

We watch as she walks up toward the house and rings the doorbell. I hold my breath, and we wait. And wait. And wait. Then, after what feels like eons, the door opens. On the other side is the near reflection of Sienna: a tall man with light hair and green eyes.

They speak for a minute, words we can't make out, and then a smile spreads across the man's face. He pulls Sienna in for a hug. She closes her eyes, leaning into the embrace.

"She did it," Ramona whispers.

Sienna motions toward the car, her dad's gaze following, and it looks like he asks if we'd like to join—but she waves us off, our signal to go. We each blow her a kiss before I pull out of the driveway.

"I can't believe how well that seemed to go," I say, feeling superstitious. I knock on the dashboard. Not wood, but it'll do.

"I'm shocked. *Good* shocked, but still," Ramona agrees. "Maybe it'll all work out?"

"Maybe it will."

Chapter Thirty-Two

THURSDAY, DAY SIX: IDLING IN A CAR DOWN THE STREET FROM SIENNA'S DAD'S HOUSE, PAGOSA SPRINGS, CO

By now, we've spent so much time in the car, it should be where I feel most comfortable.

But I don't. Because I'm in it alone with Ramona.

I thought whatever feelings for her that have bubbled up might tame themselves, but they seem to have only grown over the last few days. My heart has been all gooey for her, and I've caught myself doing things I never imagined: appreciating how sweet she looked at the aquarium, buzzing with electricity when we touched at the movie theater, admiring her while she cooked, looking for excuses to be near her, hoping for moments alone with her.

Now I've got that, and nervousness has taken hold of me.

"Chloe?" Ramona's raspy voice asks. "You there?"

I've done that thing again where I get all in my head and disappear. "Sorry, what did you say?"

"I asked if you'd mind if we turned up the air. I'm getting a little warm in here." She points toward the dial.

"Oh, yeah," I say. "Sorry. I was somewhere else."

"No worries," Ramona assures me. "Should we finally make use of that Uno deck you brought?"

I let out a laugh. "Yeah, actually." I dig the cards out of my tote and hand them to Ramona to shuffle. I don't know how, but she's great at it.

As she deals us each our hand, she says, "I hope everything's going okay in there." After circling around Pagosa Springs, which is teeny-tiny, we've come back to the street Sienna's dad lives on. We're waiting for her, for however long she needs.

I glance at the door and back. "Seriously. Mostly, I hope *she's* okay. It's a lot no matter how things go." I check my phone, which I've perched on the dashboard, ringer on, in case Sienna reaches out. There are no notifications.

"She'll tell us if she needs us," Ramona says. "Sienna isn't shy."

I smile. "That's true. Okay. But if we don't hear from her in two hours, it's an emergency."

"Good." Ramona flips over the first card from the deck. It's a red seven. She puts a red three on top. "Have you given any more thought to what you might do for school?"

I put down a yellow three, and we play cards between words. "Asks the person who wants me to *relax*."

"Yeah, I guess it's not the lightest topic. But I've been wondering."

"I have been thinking about it, actually." I bite my bottom lip. "I'm going to talk it over with my dad, but I'm thinking I may try transferring to someplace in Boston."

Ramona looks at me. "Really?"

"Yeah. You know, Rhode Island doesn't feel like 'the place' to me. I'll ride out that first semester, of course, but I think I want to stay in Massachusetts for school. I'm a true Masshole at heart."

Ramona laughs at that. "*I'm* a Masshole. You might be the furthest thing from a Masshole."

"I don't know about that," I say, laughing too. "But as soon as I told myself that was a possibility, I felt so much lighter. Like all the dread inside me shriveled up and disappeared."

"You have good instincts. If that's what your body is telling you, I'd listen," Ramona says. She pauses a moment. "You know, Permanent Record has that shop out in Boston, which I'll be transferring to soon."

I blink at her. "Seriously?"

"Seriously. It would be kind of fun to be in Boston together. If that's what you decided, I mean."

Ramona and I *both* in Boston? My mind starts doing gymnastics sorting through all the possibilities.

"Yeah. That would be really fun, actually," I say.

A silence falls between us. A playlist Ramona has selected plays quietly as we take turns in Uno.

And yet, I keep thinking it doesn't feel right to be this near Ramona without telling her I can't stop thinking about her. "Ramona..."

"Hmm?" she asks, rearranging the cards in her hands.

"I have to tell you something." I swallow. "It's important."

Ramona looks up. She studies my face for a moment, then her mouth twists and she shakes her head.

"Don't say it," she pleads. "You told me you weren't still into her."

Her words catch me by surprise. "Who?"

Her jaw clenches. "You *know* who. The person who drove us apart in the first place."

"Sienna?"

Ramona lets out a shaky breath. "I am just now finally able to love her as a friend again, after all these years, and I don't want that to change."

"Why would it?"

"Because for the longest time, I *hated* Sienna—I blamed her for abandoning us, for ripping our friendship apart. It felt like she took everything good from me. I could see how much you liked her. I even thought you were still into her on this trip! The way you leap to help her, the way she's always up in the front seat with you, both of you doing these little giggles, that stupid flamingo...But you promised you weren't."

"I'm *not*," I insist.

"You say that, but you said that then, too."

"I was a kid then. I'm an adult now. And I wouldn't lie to you."

In the quietest voice, she whispers, "But you would kiss me and then disappear."

There is a tightness at the back of my throat. "I was confused. I—I didn't know what to do." I swipe at a tear that's escaped from the corner of my eye. "I was scared."

"That's bullshit," she challenges. "What could you have been scared of?"

"Everything." And I start to cry. "I kept thinking: What if we had ruined everything by kissing? What if you *left*? And then I lost you forever? But my worst fear came true anyway—my two best friends both vanished. Just like my mom."

Ramona's face softens. "It wasn't the same."

"But it felt like it."

"You left me first. And maybe that sounds childish, and maybe I should have reached out and tried harder, but I couldn't. You *crushed* me." Her voice hitches as she speaks.

Hearing that, I feel my face crumple. "You're right," I say through tears. "I ruined our relationship. I'm so sorry, Ramona. I shouldn't have run away. I shouldn't have disappeared. I should've stayed and been scared with you and told you how I felt."

A few tears escape her eyes too, and I feel like I could scream. I did that. That's my fault. Ramona swipes at her cheeks with her sleeve. "Yeah, you should have."

"I'm so sorry. I just wasn't ready. And now it's too late."

She sniffles and narrows her eyes at me, cautious. "What do you mean?"

"I hear you when you say I've hurt you. And I know I don't deserve good things with you, not after how I treated you. But I also can't stop thinking about you. I sneak glances at you all the time. I dream about you. I want to be near you. Because I really, really like you, Ramona."

I expect her to banish me from the car, to tell me to go, to hurt me the same way I did her.

Instead, she reaches for me.

"Come here." I lean closer to her. With trembling hands, she wipes at my wet cheeks. "We were just kids."

I nod. "I know."

"What happened between us...It was a lot for people that age. Babies." She's holding me now, her breath on my ear.

"I know," I say again. She strokes my hair, and that makes me want to cry more, because I don't feel I deserve any sort of tenderness from her. "But I still fucked up."

"Yeah, you did." Ramona breaks into a soft smile. "But I did too. I didn't try at all to keep us together—I just let it go, without even *trying* to talk to you. Because I was scared too. So maybe we're both jerks. And maybe now we can be jerks together."

"Really?" I ask in a small voice.

"Really," she whispers, lacing her hand with mine.

I press my forehead to hers, our faces mere centimeters apart. My skin feels electric with possibility, with hope, with longing.

"Please," I whisper, "can I kiss you?"

Ramona closes her eyes, her long, dark lashes brushing against my cheeks, and gives the gentlest nod. I close the gap between us, flooded by the scent of her flowery rose and coconut perfume, almost the same as the one she was wearing that first time when we were fourteen. And that alone nearly breaks me.

Our lips are soft together—gentle, and forgiving, but it doesn't feel like enough.

I pull back the tiniest bit. "More?" I ask. Because I need it.

Ramona pulls me closer, pressing her body to mine, and I melt into her. Her hands cup either side of my face, lips hungry. We kiss like it's been too long, like we've missed each other, like we're saying sorry, like we're mending the past, like we hope this moment never ends.

My phone rings.

Ramona sits back first, breathless. "You have to get that."

"I know," I say, my voice coming out shaky. I bite my lip to keep the smile on my lips from taking over my entire face, because I feel incredible—like my heart is so big and light I could fly right up into the sky. I reach for my phone and see it's Sienna's name. I hit the green button. "Hey. Are you okay?"

On the other end, there's a sob. "We have to go."

Chapter Thirty-Three

Sienna rushes out of the house carrying a cardboard box in her arms and collapses into the car in tears.

"Please, drive," she croaks. Ramona climbs into the back seat and holds her, running a hand through her hair, as I pull the car away from the curb and onto the road.

"It's okay," Ramona whispers, rubbing her back. "We've got you."

I drive us back to our campsite. Sienna cries for much of the way, then goes still and stares out the window, not ready to talk. When we park, Ramona grabs blankets from the trailer and wraps Sienna in one, guiding her to one of the chairs around the fire pit while I start a fire for us. I make us tea because that's what Karina does whenever I'm really sad, and it usually helps. Ramona takes the cardboard box Sienna was carrying and, unsure of what to do with it, places it on one of the chairs. Then the three of us settle around the campfire.

"We're here whenever you're ready," I say gently. "Do you want to tell us what happened?"

I expect Sienna to refuse, but she doesn't. "My dad's a piece of shit. What more is there to say?"

"Everything," Ramona says. "We're listening."

Sienna's breath hitches, left over from the crying, and she swallows. "It seemed okay at first," she begins. "The door opened, and there he was. This man who had my face. His name's Michael Price, by the way. And he just looked so kind. So I told him, 'Hi, I know this is weird, but my mom is Paloma Aguilar, and I think I might be your daughter.' He wasn't surprised at all that I was there. He smiled, actually. That's when he hugged me and told me he'd been hoping I'd eventually come."

"That sounds nice," I say softly. "What went wrong?"

"Well, I was confused, of course. How could he have been hoping I'd come if he didn't know about me? But he invited me in and said he'd love to know more about me. We sat at the dining room table, and I asked how he knew about me because I'd been told I was a secret. He tells me to hang on and he leaves and comes back with a box." Sienna pulls her blanket tighter around her shoulders. "It wasn't even a nice box. It was a ratty old cardboard box, like it had been used to mail a package or something. It said '2001 tax documents' on the side, and I'm so confused, until he opens it. And there are just all these sealed letters from my mom. He said she'd been writing to him, but he never opened them after the first one came."

Her eyes close tight. "He's known about me this whole time. He told me he'd actually been with my mom through her whole pregnancy. He even held me! That man held me, a tiny little baby, in his fucking arms...and he still *chose* to leave."

Through sobs, she continues, "He knew where we lived! And he still left and never thought about me again! He said he opened that first letter and it seemed like my mom 'was in a really bad place' so he decided not to open any of the others. But he'd been hoping I'd visit someday so he could give them back to me because he felt guilty throwing them away—as if that *matters*. And he's saying this, and I'm looking around the house, and I see there are toys everywhere, and the mantel is lined with photos of him and a woman and three little girls that look exactly like me, and I just lost it. I grabbed the box and ran."

"*Fuck,*" Ramona mutters.

My breath shudders. "That's so, so dark. I'm sorry."

Sienna lets out a sad laugh. "How is it possible my mom actually *wasn't* the villain this whole time? She really was trying to protect me from that asshole, and I was a huge brat."

"You weren't," I argue. "How could you have known?"

"One of the greatest things about you is that you assume the good in people," Ramona says. "You can't be angry with yourself for doing that with your biological father."

"The sperm donor," Sienna corrects. "Because that man isn't my father. Fuck that guy."

"Seriously, *fuck* that guy," I echo.

"Fuck him forever," Ramona agrees.

"The worst part is, like, my mom and stepdad look like complete angels in comparison now, but they're still so difficult to live with." She sniffles. "I've spent so much time daydreaming about running away and escaping the pressure they put on me to succeed and do well, and now there's no getting away from it. They're the parents I have, and I should shut up and appreciate them." She looks over at the box and scoffs. "And now I've got this stupid fucking box of letters where my mom is probably saying the nicest things about me, like, 'Sienna learned to say *Mama* today,' and I know if I open it, it will shatter me."

I reach over to put my hand on top of Sienna's. "You don't have to open that box right now. Or ever, if you don't want to. And all these things can be true, okay? You can love your mom and your stepdad but also wish they weren't so hard on you. You can be angry at the sperm donor for failing you in every way possible, and also wish it had been different."

"Screw this whole idea that you need to be grateful for whatever you get because 'it's family.' We can love our family and still feel like we need more," Ramona says forcefully. "And though our situations aren't the same, if there's anyone who's going to get it, it's me and Chloe. Maybe it's time to resurrect the Deadbeat Parents Club."

And Sienna surprises us by laughing. "Fuck. I forgot about that."

"I think I still have my button somewhere," I offer. "You can have it when we get home."

Sienna wipes the tears away from her eyes and shakes her head. "How do you do it? How do you get over the suffocating feeling of rejection?"

"It's horrible. And I don't think you do get over it, really. Or at least I haven't," I admit. "My mom left so long ago she's little more than a fuzzy memory. But the pain doesn't go away. It just shifts. It grows with you. A parent's responsibility is to stay with you, and love you, and care for you, and keep you safe. Leaving is the ultimate betrayal. I don't ever miss my mom—she doesn't deserve that—but I miss the *idea* of her all the time. Like, sometimes, I'll get really sick and I'll think, *I want my mom*. But I don't really. I want *a* mom, you know? I'm lucky because my dad and Karina more than make up for her absence, but there's still longing. It's complicated."

Ramona nods, clearing her throat. "Yeah. I'll never understand why my dad left, and honestly, I don't want to. I don't think he deserves any of my sympathy. I don't even think he deserves my anger. What he did to my mom—leaving her with *five goddamn kids* to take care of, alone—that's just unforgivable to me. So I've tried to make him nothing to me. Not something I miss or long for or anything. There are times when I still feel sad. How can you not? But I make it through because I deserve to. I deserve to be happy and loved. And you do too."

Sienna lets out a big, long sigh. "Thank you both. I needed to hear that. And I'm sorry I made you take a detour for such a shitty, horrible reality."

"Don't," I assure her. "This is something you needed to do, and we're glad we could be here to support you."

"Plus, now you have two other people to help you throw darts at pictures of the sperm donor's face," Ramona adds lightly.

We laugh, and it feels good to let some of the pressure go in these vast mountains, like it's safe to do so here. We let Sienna lead the conversation: wondering aloud how she'll tell her mom and stepdad, imagining what life could be like if—maybe, someday—she ever connects with her half-sisters . . . and eventually we move on to less painful topics.

I'm so eager to cheer Sienna up that I offer to do my princess impressions from my If the Shoe Fits gig, and Sienna reenacts my shock from when I walked into her little cousin's birthday party. I pantomime eating cake while wearing an enormous starched gown, and then I talk loudly and awkwardly about window plants while Sienna makes pained faces. It's such a dramatic reinterpretation of my awkwardness that Ramona can't stop laughing.

Together, we make s'mores, and Sienna sets fire to a couple of marshmallows she names after her dad, which she says feels oddly therapeutic.

As darkness falls, Ramona announces she has something to show us. She disappears into the trailer and reemerges with her iPad.

"I've been saving this for when we really need it, and tonight feels like the perfect time." She stands between the chairs Sienna and I are sitting in and pulls up a drawing of three beautiful flowers surrounded by leaves.

Ramona points to the flower on the left. "Hydrangea." Then the next. "Oleander." And the final one. "Nightshade. Deadly Flora."

Sienna gasps, her hand over her mouth. "Those are our flowers?"

"They're phenomenal," I breathe. "We obviously need these as tattoos."

"I would get this tattooed on me in a heartbeat." Sienna reaches over to squeeze Ramona's arm. "Thank you for this."

I meet Ramona's gaze. "Thank you."

She shrugs, trying to be nonchalant. "I'm happy the band is back together. That's all."

But Ramona can't wipe the smile off her face as she closes her iPad, clearly pleased that we appreciated her work.

A yawn catches Sienna by surprise. "Oh! Jeez. I guess I'm a little tired."

"It's been a long day. Maybe we should head to bed?" I suggest. "We have a big day tomorrow. It's nearly four hours to the Four Corners Monument, and then somehow, we'll be reaching our last stop: Vegas, which is another seven."

Ramona nods. "Yeah, we should pack it in."

She and I douse the fire with water and sand while Sienna packs up the remnants of our s'mores. Then we head into the trailer.

"You should take the queen bed in the back," Ramona says to Sienna. "You could use a really good sleep tonight."

"Totally. We'll grab the bunks." I motion toward them. "Rock, paper, scissors for the top?"

Ramona laughs. "That's all you. I don't love heights."

We all get ready for bed. Ramona takes a shower first, and while she's away, I use the time to text Diego.

Me: i kissed ramona

My screen lights up with a FaceTime call, but I decline.

Me: cant talk, im with sienna and she doesnt know

Diego: u little whore!!

Diego: tell me everything

I do—or, as much as I feel comfortable sharing right now, when so much is unspoken and in limbo. I feel like Ramona knows I'm talking about her the second she walks in from the shower, hair still wet, a crooked grin on her face.

"What?" I ask innocently.

"Nothing," she says with a shrug. "Shower's free."

I take next up, mostly because I want to kiss Ramona again so badly I don't know if I'd have the self-control not to the moment we found ourselves alone. When I emerge from the bathroom freshly showered, Sienna is settled with a book at the dining table, and Ramona is drying her hair.

"I'm going to brush my teeth," I announce, even though no one asked.

Ramona follows me into the bathroom.

We brush our teeth together at the sink, and she bumps her hip into mine.

After leaping into friend mode to be there for Sienna, I've had zero time to process...well, everything. Sure, my mind has been fluttering back and forth between Be Serious for Sienna and OH MY GOD RAMONA, but the tiny hip bump pushes me firmly over onto one side, bringing everything rushing back all at once.

"You *liiiiiike* me," I tease, keeping my voice low.

She grins. "Try and stop me."

We finish brushing out teeth. When the two of us emerge from the tiny bathroom, Sienna wraps us both in a hug. "Thank you again. It meant so much to have you both there with me today."

"That's what friends are for," I say.

"We'll always have your back," Ramona says. "Promise."

She pads to the primary suite in the back of the trailer, pulling the door closed behind her. Then her trusty sound machine switches on.

Ramona and I lock eyes and laugh.

"What's so funny?" Ramona asks.

"Nothing!" But I giggle again anyway. "Go to bed."

We head to our bunks—top for me, bottom for her. Though it's cozy nestled beneath the blankets, I find myself buzzing. I turn, then turn again, then turn once more, trying to get comfortable enough to rest.

The trailer is dark except for the light from the moon outside, and quiet except for Sienna's sound machine and the intermittent howling of coyotes in the distance.

"Ramona?" I whisper.

"Yeah?" she whispers back.

I lean over the edge of my bed to look down at her, though she's mostly invisible in the black. "I'm suddenly afraid of heights, too. Can I come down there? With you?"

My heart thumps as I wait for her reply.

"Yes," she says softly.

I hear her body shift to make room for me.

I climb down, my arms and legs feeling shaky, like this is some kind of out-of-body experience. When did I suddenly get so bold?

Ramona pulls back the blankets to let me in, and I slip beside her into the warm bed, our bodies pressed together on the small twin mattress. Her skin is hot against mine.

I face her. "Hi."

She licks her lips. "Hi."

"About earlier..." I trace a finger along her cheek and feel the slightest shiver from her. "I have no regrets. I want you to know that. I meant what I said."

Ramona nestles her cheek against my hand. "Tell me you like me again."

"I like you," I whisper. "I like you so, so much."

"What is it about me that you like?" she asks, so quietly it's almost inaudible, as if she needs me to reassure her it's real.

"That's easy." I press my hand to her chest. "I like your heart. I like your thoughtfulness. I like that you don't let people in easily. I like how fiercely protective you get of those you love. I like your tenderness, which you only permit your favorite people to see. I like your amazing art, and your resilience, and your beautiful face. I like your tattoos. I like your style. I like your hair." I toy with one of her curls. "I like your eyes. I like your nose. I like your lips. I like that, after all these years, you still wear the perfume I bought for you."

I press my nose to hers, and she tilts my chin up.

"Because," she whispers, "it came from you, and something in me knew that it's always been you."

And that's all I need to hear.

I kiss her, our mouths crashing together, the same longing from earlier back once more. Her hands roam my body, fingertips grazing my skin and leaving tiny bolts of lightning where they've touched.

She pulls away a little, letting out a breathy laugh. "Wait. Is this too much?"

"No," I whisper. With a trembling hand, I reach for her wrist, guiding her fingers beneath the waistband of my pajama bottoms.

Her breath hitches. "Are you sure? But—Sienna?"

"I'm sure." I nod against her. "I promise I'll be quiet."

~ THE BFF BUCKET LIST ~

1) ~~See a firefly~~
2) ~~Eat ice cream for dinner~~
3) Be in three places at once
4) ~~Go camping~~

5) ~~Get drunk together~~

6) ~~Skinny-dip~~

7) Stay up all night and watch the sunrise

8) Make out with someone

9) ~~Take a road trip~~

10) See Intonation together LIVE wearing feather boas like from the "Late Nights" music video and maybe have them each fall in love with us

Chapter Thirty-Four

Ramona and I are carrying a secret, so delicate and precious we have to protect it with everything in us.

Because for now, we are not two women who spent the night together, nor two girls who found their way back to each other. We're two best friends here on a trip with their other best friend, who's putting on a brave face but nursing a broken heart.

Our shit can wait, which is why I set an alarm early and sneaked back into my own bed before Sienna woke up. When she did, she insisted we continue with our bucket list—deadbeat bio dad be damned.

So we find ourselves at Four Corners Monument, the only place in the US where four states meet: Arizona, New Mexico, Colorado, and Utah. To be honest, there isn't much *to* the landmark, which isn't even a monument but instead is a concrete slab marked with dark gray lines that lead to a granite disk in the middle. In the center of that circle is a smaller bronze circle. The surrounding four areas are labeled with each state name.

It's not really about the look of it, though: it's about being in three (four!) places at once, like our list said. Plus, this place marks the boundary between the Navajo Nation and the Ute Mountain Ute Tribe Reservation, and is lined with local Navajo and Ute artisans who sell souvenirs and food.

We get there when the monument opens right at eight o'clock (even though it meant waking up before the sun) because sometimes there are lines to take photos on the spot where the corners of the states touch.

"Little bit of an overachiever, huh, Chloe?" Sienna asks. "Our bucket list said be in three places at once, and you somehow managed to find four."

I shrug a shoulder. "What can I say? Your neuroticism is rubbing off on me."

She sticks out her tongue.

I walk beside Ramona, fighting the urge to reach for her hand and hold it. We're not the first group here, not by a long shot, but we are *among* the first. The line to the quadripoint goes quickly. We each take an individual photo over the center. It takes some creativity to actually be in all four places at once: Sienna lies down so her top half is in Arizona and New Mexico, draping her flowy skirt over Colorado and Utah; Ramona stretches into a backflip, one limb in each state; and I merely sit, because I am neither a fashionista nor a contortionist. We ask the person in line behind us to take a photo of us all together, too. He tells us there's another marker nearby that shows the actual Four Corners point (something about the original lines changing after the Civil War), so we take photos there, too, for good measure.

"That was surprisingly easy," Ramona says. "I sort of feel *better* than everyone else, now that I've mastered the art of being in four places at once."

"The arrogance looks good on you," I tease. "I can't believe we might actually complete this bucket list. Young us would be so proud!"

Sienna reaches into her bag and pulls out a piece of paper.

"Looks like we only have one, two…three left? See Intonation live together, obviously, plus stay up all night and watch the sunrise and make out with someone." She frowns. "We really gotta find some pretty girls to make out with." I catch Ramona's eye and she bites back a smile. "Anyway. Shall we shop?" Sienna puts the list away, then loops her arms through mine and Ramona's so she's in the center, leading us to the area for souvenirs.

We browse for a while, overwhelmed by all the gorgeous handcrafted Native jewelry and art. Eventually, I choose a pair of earrings for myself, plus a matching set of bracelets for Karina, me, and the baby (it's a mini version). Papi gets a hand-painted mug, and Diego gets a vibrant beaded necklace that'll look stunning on Coqui Monster.

Then we get back in the car to start our seven-hour drive to Vegas.

"Pee before we go," Sienna reminds us. And when she disappears into the restroom, Ramona grabs me and kisses me, a sensation still so joyful and unexpected it sucks the breath right out of me. When she pulls back, there's a goofy grin on my face.

"Haven't changed your mind yet, right?" she asks.

"I could never." I hold out a pinky to her. "Promise." She squeezes her pinky against mine.

"Good." Ramona pulls back from me, looking around to be sure Sienna didn't see us. "Now, that's all you get until we can sneak off somewhere private in Las Vegas."

~ THE BFF BUCKET LIST ~

1) ~~See a firefly~~
2) ~~Eat ice cream for dinner~~
3) ~~Be in three places at once~~
4) ~~Go camping~~
5) ~~Get drunk together~~
6) ~~Skinny-dip~~
7) Stay up all night and watch the sunrise
8) Make out with someone
9) ~~Take a road trip~~
10) See Intonation together LIVE wearing feather boas like from the "Late Nights" music video and maybe have them each fall in love with us

Aside from the occasional gas station, there isn't much to see along US 160, the route we're taking from Four Corners Monument to Las Vegas, so it's up to us to figure out how to entertain ourselves.

From the back seat, Sienna kicks things off by making a paper fortune teller, having us pick a color, then a number, then reading us an Intonation-related fortune. She tells Ramona that she'll be blessed by Henry Roberts (the proud religious member of the band), while Rider Morales (the bad boy) will get a tattoo in my honor. Her own fortune is that Liam Hayes (the adorable chubby gamer aka *my fave*) will use her as inspiration for a new love song.

The other fortunes she wrote include: *Alexander Sun (the sweet one) will write you a poem; Lucas Thomas (the British lead singer) will serenade you onstage; The whole band will fight over you; The band will reunite for good in your honor; and Their rival band, SINGIN*, will experience bad karma for life.*

"How did you even come up with these?" Ramona asks, laughing.

"I spent *way* too much time thinking about what middle-school-me would've been thrilled by," Sienna confesses. "But come on—I'm trying to get us hyped for the show tomorrow!"

"You want to trade fortunes, Sienna? You know I have a thing for Liam," I joke. Liam has hands-down been my favorite since I became a fan of the band. He has killer blue eyes and the best sense of humor of all of them, even though Alexander is *supposedly* the funny one.

"Happily. Rider still makes my heart sing." She lets out a dreamy sigh.

"Does anyone else find it hilarious that three queer girls fell in love with a boy band?" Ramona asks. "I mean. I couldn't be more of a lesbian, yet here I am lusting over Alexander all these years later."

"They're queer icons in their own right," I say. "I think it makes perfect sense."

"Do you guys remember when we skipped school so we could wait in line for that super-limited edition of that vinyl record?" Sienna asks.

"Oh my gosh, yes! And we couldn't tell our parents because they'd have killed us, so we had to split it with our own money," I say. "Who got custody of that thing, anyway?"

Ramona sheepishly raises a hand. "Guilty."

"Lucky," I tease. "You know, I can't remember anything from algebra, but I still have all their birthdays committed to memory."

"Favorite colors, too," she admits. "Blue for Lucas, green for Rider, orange for Henry, red for Alexander, and gray for Liam." Ramona shakes her head. "I only wish we'd thought ahead and kept their dolls sealed in the boxes. Aren't they worth a ton now on eBay?"

Sienna pulls up her phone to check. "Holy shit, yeah. We could all be rich right now."

"I feel like the experience of playing with the dolls was more important," I argue. "Liam and I had some very private moments."

Sienna playfully smacks my shoulder. "You're gross."

I feign shock. "I only meant that I brought him to bed with me as my emotional support doll, you pervert!"

All at once, we hear a loud **BOOM**, and the car suddenly jerks to the right, silencing the laughter in the air.

"Shit, shit, shit," I mutter, panic rising in my throat. I try to remember what Papi told me to do if ever a tire blows, and all I can remember is him urging me to stay calm and don't do anything out of the ordinary.

Ramona puts her hand on my leg. "It's okay, it's okay. Just grip the wheel tight." Her voice helps soothe me. She instructs me to keep the car as straight as I can and to gently press the gas pedal so I can regain control of the car. "That's good. Now step off the gas pedal nice and slowly." I do, hitting the emergency lights, and let the car come to a natural stop in the breakdown lane.

"Fuck, that was scary. Is everyone okay?" Sienna asks.

"I'm okay," Ramona assures her. She looks right at me. "You good?"

I nod, my adrenaline still pumping from the shock of what happened. Then the dread sets in. We're in the middle of nowhere, stranded on the highway.

"I've got Triple A. Let me give them a call," Sienna offers, pulling the card from her wallet and stepping out of the car.

Once she's out of earshot, Ramona leans over to give me a hug. "You did great."

"It was terrifying. My mind went totally blank." I close my eyes. "That was awful."

She rubs my back in slow, soothing circles. "It was. And you kept us safe. You should be so damn proud."

I take in a deep, steadying breath and let it out slowly. I pull back from the hug and shake out my hands to rid myself of some of the lingering jitters.

"Thank you," I say. Ramona squeezes my knee. "Where even are we?"

"I saw a sign back there that says we're in Kayenta, Arizona. Which is not the worst place to be." She taps a few times on her phone. "There's at least a semblance of civilization nearby. Can you imagine if we'd blown a tire back by the Four Corners Monument? We'd have been stuck there."

Sienna opens the door to the back seat and slips inside, a frown on her face. "They say it'll be at least an hour, maybe two, before they can get here and tow the car to a nearby mechanic. Because it's a highway, they advise us to get out of the car, too."

I groan. I had hoped to surprise Ramona and Sienna tonight with reservations for dinner to celebrate the end of the trip, but there goes that.

Between the wait for help and the need for a tire replacement, chances are slim we'll even make it to Las Vegas tonight. If we get stuck here, we'll have a *six-hour drive* to make tomorrow, the day of the concert. And that doesn't even account for getting Ramona to her tattoo appointment.

To say I'm feeling grumpy would be an understatement.

"Thanks, Sienna." I give her a weak smile.

Ramona sighs. "I hate to say it, but I think our best bet is probably to hoof it to the nearest hotel. Google Maps says it's only a fifteen-minute walk downtown."

Sienna wrinkles her nose. "In the heat of the day."

"Beats waiting around outside for the tow truck to arrive, don't you think?" Ramona starts to gather her things. "If you want, I can head to the hotel and see if they can send a car to pick you up or something."

"You're not walking there alone," I say firmly. "C'mon, Sienna."

We gather our most important items and start the long, hot walk to the hotel off the road. When the clouds cover the sun, it feels like a gift. By the time we arrive, all three of us are sweaty and overheated—but the hotel is air-conditioned *and* has a suite with two queen beds available.

Once we're in our room and drink about a gallon of water each, I FaceTime Papi. He's smiling when he answers, but when he notices my worried face, his expression changes.

"What's wrong, mija? Are you okay?"

"We blew a tire on the highway," I say, frowning. "We had to walk all the way to our hotel."

Papi stands. "What?! The rental company promised me they had done a thorough inspection of the car! I'm calling my lawyer." His voice is so loud Sienna and Ramona both shoot me a concerned look.

Ramona mouths, *Everything okay?* but I flash her a thumbs-up. She taps Sienna on the shoulder and motions toward the door to give me the room.

"Papi, no, no. We're all safe. Sienna called Triple A and they're sending someone out."

"She shouldn't have had to do that! This is the rental company's fault. I knew I should've gone with my usual, but they were all booked up, so your tío assured me this other company would be just fine." He lets out a sharp laugh. "Wait until I see him!" He starts cussing in Spanish, and I do my best to get him to focus.

"Papi. Papi! You can argue with them later. Can we figure out what to do next first, please?"

He stops angrily pacing the room and focuses back on me. "Okay, nena. I'm listening. What do you need?"

I tell him where I've booked a room, and we hash out the details of what comes next. We lose an entire, hellish afternoon to painstaking phone calls, borrowed rides courtesy of the hotel, and waiting—for Triple A, for the car diagnostics, for the local mechanic's assessment, and, finally, for the replacement tire. It feels like we ran a marathon through hell, and by the time we get the car fixed and parked in our hotel parking lot, I'm spent, and Papi is ready to burn the rental company to the ground.

"Don't get yourself in trouble. It's not worth it," I warn him. "We'll be okay. Thank you for all your help. I love you so much."

"I love you infinitely, nena," Papi says. "They'll pay."

And I can't help but give him a tired laugh, too exhausted to argue any longer. "Okay," I say. "I'll call you in the morning."

When I hang up, I flop back on my bed. What a night.

Still, I need to check on my friends, who have been gone for hours at this point. I texted them to let them know my dad and I would handle things, but where did they even go?

I text our group chat.

Me: the car's back, and we're all set for tomorrow. you guys okay?

Ramona's the first to write back.

Ramona: We're fine! Been hanging out in the coffee shop next door. ☺ We were way more worried about you

Sienna: All good here!! Thank you for taking care of everything ♥

Sienna: Has your dad calmed down? Lol

Me: barely. i think he might personally find the rental car's ceo and give him a piece of his mind

Me: at least we're all set tho. anyone else starving??

Ramona: One step ahead of you! Knock knock

There's a real knock on the hotel door. When I open it, Ramona is holding a large brown bag, while Sienna is juggling some drinks from the vending machine.

"We got delivery," Sienna says.

"Of course, the only vegetarian option was a salad." Ramona rolls her eyes. "But at least it's something!"

I take the bag from Ramona and set it on the circular table in the corner of the room. "Have I mentioned how amazing you two are?"

"Oh, we know," Sienna teases. "We planned something fun for later, too."

"Something fun? How can you think about fun when our whole plan has been blown to pieces?" I ask.

She shrugs. "I survived my bio dad. I think I can survive an unexpected change of plans. It's called growth."

"Look at you go," Ramona teases.

"I love that for you," I say, meaning it. "So…what's the fun thing you have planned for tonight?"

There's a twinkle in Ramona's eye when she turns to me. "Have you ever heard of a rage room?"

Chapter Thirty-Six
FRIDAY, DAY SEVEN: THE RAGE CAGE, KAYENTA, AZ

Honestly, I'm a little put off by the idea of spending our evening at a place called the Rage Cage, a space designed so that you can destroy everything in the room with random weapons, like baseball bats. For one, it sounds kind of terrifying, especially because I've never been a particularly rageful person. Emotional, yes. But ready to hit something with force? No thanks. As someone who prides herself on being eternally soft, going to a place where the entire business model is built on breaking things feels against my very nature.

But Sienna and Ramona convince me. It helps that I think it's sweet they planned something to take my mind off the stressful day we've had.

The Rage Cage doesn't mess around. Before we're admitted into our reserved room, we have to watch a safety video, sign a bunch of paperwork, and get into protective gear, including face shield, gloves, and coveralls. (Gotta say, I'm bringing the cutest bi-girl energy in my getup.)

The Rage Cage staffer who's working tonight double-checks to make sure we're each wearing closed-toed shoes and that our face shields are snug. Once he confirms, he gives us a thumbs-up and lets us into the room with a simple "Rage on, my dudes."

As he closes the door, Intonation starts blasting from the PA system.

"Who chose the music?" I demand with a grin.

Ramona shrugs. "Hey, I'm simply trying to grant Sienna's wish of getting us hyped for the concert."

"Who wants to go first?" Sienna asks, taking a crowbar from a weapons rack and swinging it in a circle. "I think it should be Chloe."

Ramona reaches for the sledgehammer, and I take the baseball bat.

"Go for it," Ramona says, nodding at me.

I turn to face the roomful of breakables. Sitting on a long iron table is an old television, a defunct laptop, lamps, glassware, plates, picture frames, a keyboard, and even a printer. Dramatically, I point my baseball bat at the open laptop. "You're toast."

Then I swing the bat over my head and hit it. But unexpectedly lightly? Because at the last second I feel pity for the poor, pitiful, thrown-away laptop.

Ramona and Sienna bust out laughing.

"That was the gentlest swing I've ever seen!" Sienna says between fits of giggles.

Ramona is doubled over with laughter. "Oh, that was *adorable*."

"I feel bad breaking it!" I protest.

"Do it again, but better," Sienna encourages.

"Yeah. Harder!"

"Okay! Here I go!" I swing again, this time actually cracking the screen, but it's nowhere near as violent as I'm supposed to be.

Ramona steps forward with her sledgehammer. "Like this." She swings it over her head and it slams down on one of the plates, shattering it into pieces that sail across the room. "That felt great. Go ahead, Sienna."

Sienna rolls her neck and shoulders before slicing the crowbar through the air and expertly decapitating a lamp. She hits the light bulb so hard it practically turns to dust. "*Rage on, my dudes!*" she shouts, a war cry, before she starts slamming her crowbar into the television.

I look over at Ramona, shocked by Sienna's transition from boho nerd to vengeful crusader. Though Ramona and I do some damage to the things, Sienna goes *in*—smashing glass, throwing plates on the floor, hitting things that don't break immediately over and over. She's grunting and yelling, and all at once, she starts to sob—raw, overwhelming emotion from all that happened coming to the surface.

"Okay. It's okay," I murmur, holding out a hand to get her to stop swinging. "Come here."

"Hey, we've got you." Ramona drops her sledgehammer and reaches for Sienna. She collapses into Ramona, chest heaving, and I come up from behind and wrap my arms around them. Together, we rock Sienna.

"I know. I know," I whisper. "We're here."

"*It's not fair!*" she wails.

Ramona runs a soothing hand over Sienna's hair. "It's not."

Seeing her emotional like this, I feel my own tears start to bubble up to the surface. "You deserved so much more," I choke out.

Ramona somehow catches the hitch in my voice, even over the music that's still so loud, and I see that her eyes are watering, too.

I pull the two of them tighter, and we cry—all three of us, together.

Yet when the song switches to one of Intonation's earliest—where Henry, the baby of the group, sounds like a literal child because he was only fourteen when they recorded it—we exchange looks and start to laugh. Our emotions are like powerful waves, controlling us rather than the other way around, and we can't stop.

I laugh so hard that my belly aches. I can hardly catch my breath, because *fuck*, this has been such a wild few days, and a wild life, but I'm okay because I'm here with my friends, and we found each other again.

And maybe that's what I needed all along.

We destroy every single item in that room, some twice over. When our time is up, everything is demolished, but I feel so much lighter.

After, in the darkness of the parked car, it finally feels okay for me to ask: "What happened to us?"

Sienna and Ramona are quiet for a moment.

In a small voice, Sienna says, "I don't really know."

"We drifted," Ramona offers gently. "That can happen."

I grip the steering wheel. "It wasn't supposed to happen to us."

"It wasn't my fault I had to switch schools," Sienna whispers.

"They made me. They wanted me to get better at everything: school, grades, extracurriculars, tests. I had to get an SAT tutor even though I was only in the ninth grade! And pick up an instrument, and volunteer. They didn't want me 'wasting my time'—their words—on a boy band or sleepovers anymore. When I started at the new school, I got in with some of the smartest kids there, and it made my mom so happy. I felt like, *finally*. Something I'm doing is right in her eyes."

Ramona turns in her seat to look back at her. "Oh, Sienna..."

"I didn't want to pull away from you guys. You were my best friends in the whole wide world." Her chin quivers. "I sometimes felt so guilty, like I drove you two apart by leaving."

I swallow. "It wasn't your fault. We tried to make it work without you, but...I was a rotten friend to Ramona." I look over at her. "I'm so sorry."

Ramona shakes her head. "It's no one's fault. We had growing pains."

"But I wish we had grown *together* rather than apart," I say.

Ramona puts a hand on my knee. "Then maybe we wouldn't be here today."

"God, we've been through some shit, huh?" Sienna sighs. "For what it's worth: I still think the both of you hung the moon."

"We found our way back to each other, and that's all that matters," Ramona says.

I sniffle. "Can we still start a band called Deadly Flora?"

It makes Sienna and Ramona laugh.

"Yeah," Sienna says, nodding. "But let's learn to play instruments this time."

Chapter Thirty-Seven

It's close. Really, really close. But we might *actually* be able to cram everything into our day. We get up at five o'clock to race (at a respectable, definitely-not-breaking-the-law speed) down the highway toward Las Vegas.

With minimal stops for bathroom breaks, we make it there by eleven. Since we had booked our room for the night prior, we're able to check in right away and go up to the room, where I call Papi, then we unload our bags, shower, and leave immediately. We have a tattoo appointment to catch.

We head to a place called Battle Scars, where Ramona has booked her appointment with Addy Kaur, the artist she loves.

Only, before we all go in, Ramona stops us. "I may have done something sneaky."

Sienna crosses her arms. "How sneaky?"

"Cute sneaky? I hope, anyway." Ramona reaches into her duffel to pull out her iPad. "You remember those floral designs I made for each of us? Back at the campsite?"

"Of course," I say with a nod. "They were beautiful."

She flips open her tablet cover, taps, and then turns the screen to us. The three flowers she drew—hydrangea, oleander, and nightshade—have been colored and shaded.

"After it seemed like you liked what I made, I reached out to Addy. I asked her if I could trade my spot for my big tattoo—which definitely would've made me miss the concert, by the way—for three small tattoos instead. When I explained about the road trip and how much you guys meant to me, she moved some things around so she and another artist can ink all of us today."

"Wait, what?" I shake my head. "What about the tattoo for your mom?"

"Addy was so touched by the idea of us getting matching tattoos that she says she'll hook me up next time she flies out to Boston. She sometimes does short stints at other tattoo shops," Ramona explains. "I want to make it clear that neither of you have to do this. I'm going to get my nightshade tattoo either way, so there's zero pressure."

Sienna chews on her thumbnail, thinking. "It seems like you've sacrificed something special for yourself for us."

Ramona holds up a hand. "I don't see it as a sacrifice at all. I promise."

"If you're sure, then okay. I'm in," Sienna says, beaming.

I eye Ramona, still not quite sure I believe her. "You're positive this is what you want? Matching friend tattoos?"

"You know, the more I thought about it, the more I thought Mami would actually hate it if I got a tattoo for her. I think she'd rather do something *with* me. So I'm going to figure that out instead," Ramona says contemplatively. "And I know matching friend tattoos are a little cheesy and all, but…I guess you guys have grown on me or something."

I grin. "That's all I wanted you to say. I'm in."

* * *

The tattoo hurts infinitely less than I expect it to. When all of us are through, hours later, we each have a perfect representation of our flowers. Sienna has a hydrangea on the back of her left shoulder; Ramona has a nightshade bloom, plus some nightshade berries, on her chest; and I have oleander on my forearm, so I can always see it.

The tattoo artists wrap us each up with a clear plastic wrap called Second Skin, then give us strict instructions to follow over the next two weeks so we can preserve the tattoos' vibrancy as best as possible.

When I check my phone, I see I have a bunch of missed calls and unanswered texts from Whit that came in hours ago.

Whit: Ummmm I have some AMAZING news for you

Whit: Like I'm actually CRYING

Whit: CRYING!!!

Whit: Pick up

Whit: Pick up!!!!!

Whit: OKAY YOU MUST BE BUSY BUT

Whit: FACETIME ME ASAP!!!!!!!!!!

"I have to call Whit, like, right now," I announce.

"Is she okay?" Ramona asks.

I shrug as the phone rings. "Apparently it's good news?"

Moments later, Whit's familiar smile (and those supercute dimples!) lights up my screen.

"Hey! Are you here?!" I ask, meaning Las Vegas.

"Oh, I'm here. And GUESS WHAT?!?!" she shouts into her phone.

Suddenly the phone switches perspectives until Whit's little sister, Lily, comes into view. "We're about to meet Intonation!"

"Wait, what?!" I demand. Ramona and Sienna crowd behind my phone to get in view of the screen and be part of the conversation.

"Lily!" Whit's voice hisses, then the phone switches hands again and Whit comes back into view. "Way to steal my thunder."

From off-screen, Lily says, "Sorry, but this is the most exciting thing to ever happen to us!"

Whit rolls her eyes, but smiles and turns back to the screen. "She's totally right. This is the most exciting thing to ever happen to us! We're about to meet THE GREATEST BOY BAND OF ALL TIME." She lets out a high-pitched squeal.

"Details! We need more!" I beg.

"Yeah, don't hold out on us, Whit," Sienna urges. "Spill!"

"Okay, okay, so! *Apparently* all the onstage tickets are part of this whole VIP package. Did you know this?"

"Umm, news to me..." I say slowly. I think back to my birthday party, when Papi presented me with the ticket. It was a mockup, so he'd have something physical to give me. I remember it saying something about a VIP package, but I assumed it was referring to the ticket location, not extra goodies including a meet and greet!

"That's what I figured! So, here's the thing. The VIP package comes with this whole swag bag of stuff—"

Lily shoves into frame and holds up what looks like an autographed photo. "We got signed pictures!"

"—*Plus,* we got these wristbands to attend Intonation's freaking sound check and get a picture with the boys!" Whit holds up her wrist to show off a neon-pink bracelet. "We're in line now!"

My eyes widen. "Holy shit! That's amazing!"

"Kind of regretting you giving away those tickets now..." Sienna murmurs, and Ramona elbows her to hush.

"Here's the best part. Are you ready?" Whit asks, and her excitement is so infectious I can't stop smiling.

"I'm ready!"

"We got these passes that offer admission to the after-party where fans get to hang out with the band!" Whit dangles three lanyards in front of the camera. "They're for you!"

Sienna lunges forward, as if she can grab the passes through the phone. "Excuse me?!"

"I tried to get in touch with you as soon as I found out because I thought this had to be a mistake. I wanted to give these tickets back to you, but when you didn't answer, I needed to make a call. Anyone who wanted to get into the sound check had to go through security, so I figured you'd rather have *someone* go than have the passes go to waste." Whit's words spill out of her mouth so fast she sounds like someone has put her on fast forward. "But since you called, I can hop out of line and explain the situation and beg for mercy and you guys can come to the sound check?"

"Now hold on a minute..." I hear Lily say from off-screen.

"Absolutely not!" I argue. "You made the right call. You, Lily, and your grandma deserve to go to the sound check. We're *not* taking the tickets back. We wouldn't make it in time, anyway!"

"You're the best," Whit says, grinning. "So let's meet up after this and I'll give you your after-party passes, at least! And maybe scream our heads off because oh my God!"

"I know! Text me after the sound check? Then we can also get a few pictures together before the show starts."

Whit nods enthusiastically. "Of course! We'll find you." Then her eyes dart off-screen and she—and maybe everyone else in the room with her, based on the volume—lets out an earsplitting scream. *"They're here!"*

Whit quickly switches us over to the back camera on her phone and sure enough...

Lucas Thomas, the lead singer with the sexiest British accent; Rider Morales, the tattooed bad boy; Henry Roberts, the wholesome baby of the group; Alexander Sun, the prankster with a laugh like a melody; and William "Liam" Hayes, the artsy gamer, are laughing and joking together on the stage.

This is the moment where I find out that I, too, scream at the sight of Intonation. I'm a tween again, and I grab Sienna and Ramona and we let out a collective shriek. (Ramona's hand slaps over her mouth, as if she can't believe herself.)

"I feel like I just saw God," Sienna whispers.

I squeeze her arm. "I might pass out."

"Hey," Whit's voice shakily says. "I gotta go. I'll text you as soon as I can."

I reach for the screen, like I might be able to touch Intonation from here. "Goodbye, sweet angels."

Sienna blows them a kiss. "We'll see you soon, babies."

Chapter Thirty-Eight

Maybe I've died and gone to heaven and right now, I'm not actually taking an elevator up to our hotel room; I'm merely floating upward on my little ghost legs.

That's what it feels like, anyway.

Because I just saw Intonation, live, for real, through Whit Rivera's phone, and my whole body is trembling from the rush.

"I can't believe I screamed," Ramona grumbles for what must be the tenth time since we hung up with Whit. "I don't scream!"

"Apparently you do. And for *boys*. Some lesbian," I tease.

"I can't stop sweating," Sienna says, fanning herself. "How am I going to survive the after-party?"

"By wearing something revealing," I say with a shrug. "And making them fall in love with us. That *is* on the BFF Bucket List, isn't it?"

Ramona shoots me a look. She points to me and mouths, *Mine,* and now I'm feeling electric for a whole other reason. Why is being claimed so hot?

"I need another shower," Sienna announces.

"Try not to get your tattoo too wet," Ramona reminds her.

"And make it quick," I add. "You take the longest to get ready!"

Sienna flips me the bird before disappearing into the bathroom. When I hear the door lock behind her, I saunter over to Ramona. "So...those boys really did it for you, hmm?" I run a finger over her shoulder. "You going to leave me for them or something?"

"Maybe I will." She places a hand on either side of my hips and pulls me to her. "If you can't play nice."

"But I'm always nice." I kiss her on the nose. "See?"

"Hmm..." Ramona taps a finger on her chin. "I'm not convinced."

I smile and tilt my head, gently pressing my lips to hers. She takes the opportunity to deepen the kiss, our hands roaming each other's bodies. I kiss down her neck, and across the beauty marks on her collarbone, and she lets out a tiny moan. To quiet herself, she kisses me again, hard. Our chests are heaving when we pull apart.

"How was that?" I ask quietly.

"You win. You're nice." Ramona laughs, leaning her forehead against mine. "Promise me this thing we're doing won't be over after this trip."

Her question catches me off guard. "Us?" She nods. "You don't want us to be over after this trip?"

I feel her shake her head.

I place my hand over her heart, the same way I did a few nights ago. "Then I'm all in with you."

The shower turns off, our cue to pull apart.

From behind the bathroom door, Sienna calls, "I don't hear you getting ready! And you say I take forever."

We laugh and listen to our friend. We help each other with hair and makeup when needed, and when we're done, we even have time for pictures.

For my outfit, I've chosen a pastel-pink sequined bustier and pencil skirt, which pays tribute to Intonation's iconic *Bubblegum* era. Sparkly pink-framed glasses complete the look. Sienna has gone all in on the *Teal* album, rocking a sequined teal halter crop top, teal heart-shaped sunglasses, and teal flare jeans. Even Ramona has committed, with a sleeveless white bodysuit (that shows off her tattoos and incredible curves, not that I'm looking, except that I totally am) under a black mesh skirt peppered with holographic stars, in honor of Intonation's album *Under the Stars*. I can practically hear Diego telling us we look incredible (if incredibly cheesy).

"One more thing," Ramona says.

Sienna's face brightens. "Is it time?"

"It's time. Close your eyes," Ramona instructs.

I do as I'm told. "Is this going to be like the time where you sprinkled me with glitter and tried to convince me fairies were real? Because you know I'm gullible and that almost worked."

"Not this time," Sienna says. "Okay. Open!"

When I open my eyes, Ramona and Chloe are both wrapped in feather boas: black for Ramona, teal for Sienna. A pink feather boa lies on the bed behind them.

"You guuuuuys!" I hold my hands over my heart. "You brought boas?!"

Ramona laughs. "I wish I could take credit, but it was all Sienna."

"I don't like to half-ass anything, and it was on the list," she says with a grin. "Now I think we look perfect."

I text Whit to let her know where to meet us, then we take the elevator down to the Planet Hollywood venue two dozen floors below. Together, we take tons of photos of ourselves: outside, in front of the marquee, with some of the concert's promotional materials, with the cardboard cutout of the band that they have outside the box office. Then Whit joins us and we grab photos with her, Lily, and even Abuela.

Abuela takes my hands in hers. "Bless you for gifting us these tickets. Because of you, I met my Henry tonight!"

"There is no one who deserved it more," I tell her, meaning it.

The six of us crowd into the souvenir line. Ramona, Sienna, and I show off our new tattoos. Whit, Lily, and Abuela show off the secret pictures they snapped during the sound check. (Their VIP photos won't be available for a few days.) We buy merch we don't need that's covered in Intonation's logo and faces. And then we head inside, just in time for the opening act.

Whit, Lily, and Abuela are ushered to their seats onstage. From our floor seats, I can see Whit practically hyperventilating at how close they are, and I can't help but giggle. I'm seated in the middle, Ramona on one side, Sienna on the other.

"This is going to be the best night ever," Sienna says with a dreamy sigh. "I'm so happy I get to spend it with the two of you."

"You're so soppy," Ramona teases.

"But we love it and agree. Now, another selfie?" I ask. "We look so damn good."

The three of us pose just as the lights shut off. The place erupts into screams, and my stomach does a cartwheel. It's time.

Chapter Thirty-Nine
SATURDAY, DAY EIGHT: INTONATION CONCERT

Though the opening act is good and all, we all know who we're here for. My body is practically humming from the excitement.

As we wait for Intonation to take the stage, someone starts a chant of the band's name—*In. To. Na. Tion. In! To! Na! Tion!*—and then, giddy when it catches on, someone else gets each section to do the wave.

When the DJ plays an old-school Intonation song, we all sing at the top of our lungs. Somehow, well before the band has even taken the stage, the crowd has made it clear that we're here to have a good time together.

As the venue suddenly goes dark for the second time, I leap to my feet and scream. All around me, girls who have loved this band scream too. They yell "I love you!" and "Woooooooo!" and "Marry me, Lucas!" and a million other things all at once, the sound so deafening I'm certain people on the street can not only hear us, but *feel* us too.

The first few notes of Intonation's infectious dance-pop single "Best Night Ever" cascade through the venue as five silhouettes float down on platforms from above the stage. The music cuts, giving the crowd a moment to scream—and then all at once the notes swell and the song comes back to life.

A spotlight shines on Lucas, and he sings the opening verse:

"Feels like the city's alive tonight
Moving and shaking, oh, what a sight

The night is young, we're ready to go
With friends by our side, they can't tell us no…"

Sienna, Ramona, and I scream-sing along as the lights illuminate Rider next.

"The streets are calling, we're gonna have a blast
No holding back, we're breaking free at last
The stars aligning, destiny on our side
We're gonna make this night our wild ride…"

Fire erupts from either side of the stage and all five boys are bathed in a bright yellow glow as they launch into the chorus.

"It's gonna be the best night ever
We'll dance until the morning light
Together, we'll make memories we'll treasure
We'll live like there's no end in sight!"

We watch as the platforms lower, the fans going absolutely wild when the band members hop onto the stage and shift into synchronized steps. As they finish that song, the music seamlessly shifts into "Bubblegum," a bouncy pop hit that sat at number one for so long the choreography caught on beyond the boy-band world. I can't wipe the smile from my face.

One of my favorite ballads, "Easy," comes next. I watch in awe as Whit grabs her sister's and grandma's hands and they sway together onstage. All around us, there are families like them, spanning generations: mothers and daughters, grandmothers and granddaughters, aunts and nieces, fathers and sons, and it's impossible not to feel something.

I look over at Ramona, watching the flashing lights from the stage dance across her face. She looks beautiful. I lean close to her ear. "Can I hold your hand?"

She looks surprised and motions toward Sienna. "Are you sure?"
But how can I not?
Intonation is singing this song for us:

"Sweatpants, messy bun,
I know I'm not the only one
Who sees how beautiful you are.
Yet somehow it's me you chose,
And my love for you, it grows,
Loving you (yeah), loving you is easy."

I smile and nod eagerly. She holds out her hand and I lace my fingers through hers.

It takes a moment, then Sienna tugs on my wrist. She motions toward my and Ramona's intertwined hands. "What is this?!"

Ramona grins. "It's a thing."

"What kind of thing?" Sienna demands. "Are you guys together?!"

I laugh. "We *may* have kissed a few nights ago…"

"And maybe a few times since then?" Ramona bites at the corner of her lip, failing to hide her smile.

"Oh my GOSH!" Sienna grabs us both and shakes us. "*Finally!* I've been shipping you two for years!"

"You have *not*," Ramona insists.

"Have too. I'm president of the Ramona/Chloe shippers. We call ourselves Ramonies. We write fanfic!" Sienna throws her arms around us. "I love you guys. And I love you guys together." Then she stands up straight and pouts. "Also, no fair because you got to cross *make out* off your list and I didn't!"

We both laugh. "There's still time!" I promise. "We'll find you someone cute!"

"You better," Sienna warns. She turns back to the stage but keeps sneaking glances over at me and Ramona for the rest of "Easy." It's deliciously corny, this moment, and my heart feels lighter than a feather.

If Ramona weren't anchoring me to the floor, I might just vanish up into the sky.

I'm only grounded again when the song shifts and Intonation disappears for a costume change. On the giant wide-screen digital displays we see a video of the band celebrating their triumphs throughout the years.

As images from their first tour, early television appearances, interviews, and behind-the-scenes photo shoots flash across the screen, Lucas's voice says, "It's weird, you know? To think that if any one thing hadn't happened exactly right, we might not be here today, as a band, performing together after all these years. It makes me feel grateful for everything. Even the difficult moments. Because without them, we wouldn't be us."

The crowd cheers and the video cuts into a bunch of clips of the band through the years as an instrumental version of their song "Moments" plays.

And I'm such a softie that I tear up. Music montages always get me.

Ramona nudges me. "You know, for a boy band member, what Lucas said was pretty insightful."

I roll my eyes. "Oh, stop it. You love this."

And she grins big. "I really, really do."

It's hard to put into words how much just a few hours at a concert can mean to a fan.

Not everyone gets it, but those who do know that nights like these can feel life-altering—the way the music, the dancing, the singing, and the memories old and new all come together to make you feel *so alive*. It's thrilling and vulnerable, to be in public singing your heart out with people who understand; to tear up together when the band lets the crowd finish the lyrics; to re-embody the version of yourself from when you first heard these songs you love so much; to appreciate how that one flicker of sadness when the show is halfway through pulls you into the present so you can really be *here, now*.

That this crowd is almost exclusively made up of women isn't lost on me. Girls have quietly been carrying the weight of the music industry on their backs for lifetimes, and there is something about the collective fangirl experience that's transformative. It's where we find belonging, where we forge new friendships, and where we discover who we are.

Here, under the colorful lights, the flashing lasers, and the confetti that rains down on us all, we sing and shout and stomp and dance and laugh and feel, and if that isn't one of the most beautiful things in the world, I don't know what is.

Here, with my best friends, I feel whole.

Dozens of Intonation songs later, I can feel the concert careening to an end. Every part of me wishes we could stay here all night, that the band would play every single song they've ever recorded and then some, that this weren't one night only. But I know all I have to do is listen to this music whenever I want, and I'll conjure these feelings up again like magic.

Intonation officially closes the show with "Hope," their charity single, and that feels perfectly fitting.

But I know it isn't the end, not even when the band disappears offstage. I reach for Ramona's hand, as well as Sienna's, and squeeze them both.

"One more song," I whisper.

We wait, and we cheer, and we wait, and we cheer.

Then the band reappears right as the familiar upbeat opening chords of "Girl Be Mine"—their most popular single to date—pour from the speakers. The crowd loses it.

Because there is *nothing* more perfect than listening to your favorite band sing your favorite song on your favorite night with your favorite people.

Tonight is, without a doubt, the best night ever.

~ THE BFF BUCKET LIST ~

1) ~~See a firefly~~
2) ~~Eat ice cream for dinner~~
3) ~~Be in three places at once~~
4) ~~Go camping~~
5) ~~Get drunk together~~
6) ~~Skinny-dip~~
7) Stay up all night and watch the sunrise
8) ~~Make out with someone~~
9) ~~Take a road trip~~
10) ~~See Intonation together LIVE wearing feather boas like from the "Late Nights" music video and maybe have them each fall in love with us~~

Chapter Forty

The promise that we'd get to "party with the boys of Intonation" may have been a biiiit of a marketing ploy, but Sienna, Ramona, and I are riding such a high from the concert, we don't care.

We wait in line to be admitted to the 18+ nightclub called La Fête, where Intonation's VIP after-party is being hosted, and see that the band is up on an elevated stage at the center of the club rather than mingling with the crowd. But it makes sense. I wouldn't exactly want to be groped by my fans either.

Ramona, Sienna, and I don't get flashy gold wristbands upon entrance because we're not old enough to drink, but who cares?

We're at the club with Intonation!!!

The five guys have changed out of their stage outfits and into street clothes. Lucas grabs the mic. "We can't thank you all enough for an incredible show tonight. When we decided to reunite for a charity concert, we never imagined the overwhelming support you would all show us." He puts his hand over his heart. "Thank you, all of you, for being here with us."

He passes the mic to Liam. "So here's how this is gonna go. We're going to start by posing for pictures over there." He motions toward a corner of the nightclub where there's a professional camera setup in front of a black sequined backdrop. "Then each of us is going to DJ a set for you so we can dance. We're going to drink."

Henry leans over to the mic to add, "Those of us who are of age."

Alexander lifts his golden wristband into the air, and people cheer.

Liam continues, "Then we're going to perform a few songs for you—ones you *didn't* get to hear at the show..."

More cheering from the crowd. I grab Ramona. "If they perform 'Booked and Busy' I'm going to lose my mind."

Without hesitation, she shouts through the noise, " 'Booked and Busy'!"

Alexander points toward her. "That might be one of them!"

She turns to me, eyes wide. "Holy shit. Did *Alexander Sun* just speak to me?"

"You're fangirling right now, babe. And I love it."

"Lastly," Liam finishes, "we're all going to do the limbo. Winner gets bragging rights, and all of us in their bedroom—"

The club erupts in screams.

"—courtesy of this really dope trophy made in our likeness."

There's laughter as Rider proudly holds up the trophy for all to see. It's a huge three-tiered golden trophy with miniature golden statues of each Intonation member. Rider steals the mic from Liam and shouts, "Now, let's keep this party going!"

As the boys hop off the stage, Sienna, Ramona, and I make a beeline for the photo check-in area. There are already dozens of people ahead of us, but whatever. We're not leaving without a photo. Fans pile behind us in groups of two, three, and four.

I get a text from Diego.

Diego: guess who's officially been added to the drag queen roster at speakeasy

I turn to Ramona and Sienna. "My cousin Diego won the Speakeasy drag competition!"

Ramona's face breaks into a grin. "That's amazing!"

"I need pictures! Immediately!" Sienna says.

"I'll get them, I promise. I need to call him first!" I FaceTime Diego immediately. He answers in full drag, and he looks drop-dead gorgeous.

The grin on his face tells me how proud he is of himself without him even saying a word. "Holy shit! You did it! Congratulations!"

Sienna and Ramona crowd around the phone to share their congrats too.

"Thank you, thank you." He leans in close to the phone. "I demolished Venus the Flyest Trap. Fill you in on those juicy details later. But first..." He takes his phone and pans the video so I can see who's with him, and my heart nearly bursts. Titi Rosa, Tío Gabriel, Papi, and Karina are all with him. "Look who came to cheer me on!"

"Oh my God! Hi!"

"Hi, mija!" Papi yells over the Speakeasy music. "Why didn't you tell us your cousin is so talented?"

Diego comes back into view. "Yeah! Why didn't you tell them?"

"I was sworn to secrecy! But I'm so happy we all know. Can we celebrate somehow once I'm home?"

"Obviously," Diego says. "It's what I deserve."

"I'm so happy for you!" I'm beaming at him, and I know it. "And I'm so, so proud of you, Diego. You're incredible."

He shrugs. "I know."

There's lots of noise behind him, and I spot Benny and a few of his friends, so I know I should cut Diego loose so he can focus on the night ahead.

"I'm going to let you go, but I have a lot to fill you in on too. See you tomorrow?"

He nods. "With bells on."

I blow him a kiss—which is normally not our thing, but I miss him so much, I can't help it—and he actually pretends to catch it before we hang up.

I return my attention to the line, which is moving faster than we thought thanks to the handlers who are keeping photos churning. While we wait, we become fast friends with the girls in line behind us, sharing our favorite Intonation memories from tonight and years past. Before long, we're up next for our photo with Intonation.

"Go get 'em!" one of our new friends cheers.

"Ohmygosh I can't breathe," I say, feeling like I very much might hyperventilate. "They're *right there*."

Ramona stares at them. "How is their skin so flawless in real life? Unreal."

Sienna's face goes pale. "It's our turn! I'm gonna pass out."

Ramona bravely takes the first step toward Intonation, the boy band the three of us have loved with our whole hearts since middle school. Sienna follows, and I bring up the rear.

"Hello, hello!" Liam is the first to greet us.

"Loving these outfits, ladies," Lucas says brightly, and I nearly melt into a puddle.

"Don't be shy." Alexander motions for us to get closer to them. "Come on in!"

He reaches for a hug from Ramona first, and we each start to go down the line, saying hello to and getting hugs from each band member. That I get to *hug* my *favorite band of all time* is the most out-of-body experience I think I've ever had.

"Did you enjoy the show tonight?" Henry asks.

"It was perfect," I gush.

"*Beyond*, really," Sienna adds.

"No other concert will ever compare," Ramona says seriously.

Alexander laughs. "You're going to give us all big heads. Now, get in here!"

The handler directs us all to squeeze in tight, then counts down, and the photographer snaps two photos of us all smiling.

"And a silly one!" Liam calls out.

I cross my eyes and stick out my tongue until I hear two more clicks. Then we say thank you and we're ushered out of the photo area to make room for the next in line.

"Did that really happen?" Sienna asks dreamily. "Pinch me."

"They were so nice!" Ramona says. "And I normally hate everyone!"

I let out a happy sigh. "They're perfect."

A moment later, the girls we'd befriended round the corner to where we're standing. When they see us, we all squeal excitedly.

"We just met Intonation!" each one of us shouts.

"And now, we celebrate!" Sienna calls. "Let's dance!"

The DJ has put together the perfect mix of Intonation-era songs for us to dance to, so, with nonalcoholic drinks in hand, we do. We dance through each of the boys' DJ sets, and for their performance of rare songs (including "Booked and Busy"!!!), but by the time the limbo rolls around, we're tired and hot and thirsty.

So, hearts full, the three of us leave, grab some fast food, and head back to our hotel room so we can watch the sunrise on our balcony while eating greasy French fries and burgers. Is there any better way?

Sienna heaves a sigh. "Tonight was perfect. But I didn't get to make out with someone."

"But you *have* made out with someone before," I point out. "When we wrote that list, none of us had. So technically you get to cross it off."

Ramona makes a *gimme* gesture. "List, please."

Sienna digs into her bag to hand it over.

"Pen?" Ramona asks.

Sienna offers that too.

We watch as, beside the item *Make out with someone,* Ramona adds, *OR get a kiss on the cheek from my best friends.*

"Wait, that's adorable," Sienna says. She puts a pointer finger on either side of her face. "Kiss, please!"

Ramona leans in to give Sienna a kiss on one cheek, and I take the other.

She grins. "I feel so loved."

"As you should," I say.

We settle into our chairs and finish eating, patiently waiting for the sun.

The instant it peeks up from the horizon, the three of us—now beyond exhausted and loopy—share a hug.

"We did it," I whisper. "Thank you both."

"Love you guys," Sienna whispers back.

"Love you back," Ramona says. "Now let's go to bed."

~ THE BFF BUCKET LIST ~

1) ~~See a firefly~~

2) ~~Eat ice cream for dinner~~

3) ~~Be in three places at once~~

4) ~~Go camping~~

5) ~~Get drunk together~~

6) ~~Skinny-dip~~

7) ~~Stay up all night and watch the sunrise~~

8) ~~Make out with someone~~

9) ~~Take a road trip~~

10) ~~See Intonation together LIVE wearing feather boas like from the "Late Nights" music video and maybe have them each fall in love with us~~

Just like that, it's over.

As we sit in our terminal in Harry Reid International Airport, I have this overwhelming sense of loss.

Sure, we made it through TSA totally fine. We checked our bags. We even had enough time to get coffee before we had to board our flight.

But waiting for our flight back to the East Coast signals the end, and I don't want it to.

I lean my head against Ramona's shoulder. "I can't believe how much time we wasted not being friends and now we're all about to go our separate ways."

Ramona and Sienna look up at me from the game of Uno they've been playing.

"Well, that's the most depressing thing I've heard all week," Sienna says. "And I met a dad who didn't want me!"

I give her a weak attempt at a smile. "It's not fair because I just got you two back."

"Hey," Ramona says, reaching to take my hand. "Neither of us is going anywhere."

"But that's not true. In one week, Sienna is going to Baltimore—"

"As if I won't fly back at every possible opportunity!" she argues.

"And I'm packing up and moving to Providence—"

"Which is only ninety minutes from Elmwood." Ramona gives me a sheepish smile. "I looked it up."

"You did?" I put my hand over my heart. "That's so romantic."

"The point we're trying to make here is this friend group?" Sienna motions between all three of us. "It's not going anywhere, even if we're not physically in the same location."

"I was probably the most skeptical of us all before this trip, and even I know that. But I feel like we're leaving this experience stronger than ever," Ramona says. She puts a finger under my chin to lift my face. "You're magic—you know that, right? You brought us all back together."

"Seriously. Look at us." Sienna holds up her Uno cards. "We're playing Uno!"

"Well, *I'm* playing Uno. Based on how many cards you're holding right now, I'm not so sure about you," Ramona says dryly.

Sienna rolls her eyes. "Anyway. You got the band back together! *Our* band! Now there's no getting rid of us."

Ramona holds up our clasped hands. "*And* we're doing *this*."

"If you think I'm afraid of being a third wheel, think again. I have no shame whatsoever," Sienna says with a laugh.

"You guys," I sniffle. "I love you."

"Duh," Sienna says.

Ramona gives me a kiss on the forehead. "Of course you do."

Their commitment to our friendship fills my heart right up. All I've wanted this whole time was to have my best friends back. I wanted to reunite with the people who make me laugh until it feels like my insides might burst, who are there to lean on when everything in the world goes wrong, who can make the most mundane tasks feel like a joyous escape from reality, who are equally okay reminiscing about the past as they are creating brand-new memories, who don't just get me, but who appreciate me—terrible sense of direction and all.

"Isn't it kind of funny that we drove all the way to Las Vegas, yet barely saw a thing while we were there?" Sienna muses.

"We met Intonation. Do we need anything more?" I joke.

"Good point," Sienna says. "Do you think they fell in love with us?"

"I don't know about you two, but I know Alexander fell in love with me, for sure," Ramona announces.

"And doesn't that make it all worth it?" I laugh. "Besides, maybe Intonation will do another reunion tour in, like, twenty years, and we can go back to Las Vegas to see them again."

"Oooor I could come back out to Vegas to visit Addy and get a tattoo at some point," Ramona says. "And I guess you guys could come with me."

Sienna squeals. "Road trip!"

I gasp. "We could do it next summer!"

"So, we're in, then? Next summer?" Ramona asks.

Sienna nods so vigorously her dangly earrings chime. "Definitely. But let's also make sure we see each other again way, way sooner than that."

* * *

By the time our plane lands at Bradley Airport, the trip already feels a little like a fever dream. How is it possible we crammed so much into only seven days?

After we grab our bags from baggage claim, the three of us wait outside in the passenger pickup area for our rides.

"This feels weird," Ramona admits.

"Seriously bizarre. That sadness Chloe was feeling earlier just hit me like a ton of bricks." Sienna frowns as a silver BMW pulls up next to us. "And that's my mom! Oh, no!"

I grab Sienna and wrap her in a tight hug, rocking her back and forth. "Thank you for coming."

"Thank you for using your impulsivity to plan an entire road trip for us. You're bananas, and I love you so much."

I squeeze her. "Love you more."

"All right, my turn," Ramona says as Sienna and I pull apart. The two of them hug, and Ramona whispers something in Sienna's ear.

When they separate, Sienna lets out a breath. "So, we're all meeting up later tonight, right?"

Ramona shrugs at me. "We have to. Sienna and I voted and you lost, so you have to say yes."

The grin that spreads across my face nearly breaks my cheeks. "Speakeasy at eight. See you both then."

With one last look, Sienna slips into her mom's car, and they drive away.

I look over at Ramona, suddenly feeling a little shy. "And then there were two..."

"God, you look beautiful," Ramona murmurs.

My cheeks heat up under her gaze. I motion down at myself, trying to deflect. "This messy bun and leggings are really doing it for you, huh?"

"Don't forget the plane grime." She holds out a hand for me to take. "It's just that this is the first time we're not sneaking around, and I'm looking at you like, wow. Chloe Torres is gorgeous."

I lace my fingers with hers and realize she's right; we're not hiding. We're both right here.

I spent so much of the trip sneaking glances and trying to bury how I felt, but here? Now? I can study her like a painting: the way her long lashes accent her dark eyes, the way her baby hairs curl at the nape of her neck, how her sleeve tattoos come to life when she moves, her soft chin, those full lips I want to kiss over and over again. Ramona and I can finally settle into each other and be together.

It's terrifying and exhilarating all at once.

She pulls me closer to her and I nestle into the crook of her neck. "If anyone is gorgeous, it's you. Why do you think I hid behind the counter at Speakeasy when I first saw you? My heart couldn't handle it. And now, I can barely believe we have each other."

"That's okay," Ramona whispers. "I'll believe it extra for the both of us."

She gingerly lifts my chin and leans down to kiss me, softly and sweetly. I wrap my arms around her, thinking about how I could maybe stay here forever.

"Excuse me! No lewd behavior in public," a voice scolds. I get ready to tell whoever it is to fuck off, only to realize it's Diego, driving my car. He slips into the passenger seat so he can shake his fist at us dramatically out the window. "Kids these days!"

I look up at Ramona and laugh. "You remember Diego, I'm sure."

"These days I know him mostly as Coqui, but yes. He's definitely not the type of person you forget." She holds up a hand to wave. "Hi, Coqui!"

Diego waggles his fingers. "Always great to meet a fan."

"Shut up, idiot," I call to him. Then I turn back to Ramona and swallow hard, not quite sure if I'm ready to drive home. "I can wait here with you until your ride comes. Or, better yet, you can come with me."

Ramona lets out an easy laugh. "It's okay. Manny's coming to get me. He says he's right down the road."

"Oh, okay," I say, even though that's not the answer I wanted to hear. I press my forehead to hers. "I don't know why this feels like the end of something."

Ramona tucks a piece of my hair behind my ear. "That's because it is. But it's the beginning of something even better." She leans down to kiss me on the nose. "I'll see you tonight."

I kiss her once more and put on my bravest face. "See you tonight."

With a final wave, I climb into my car, buckle my seat belt, and pull away. In the rearview mirror, I watch as Ramona gets smaller and smaller, and I feel sad and giddy and nostalgic and hopeful.

"Um, okay, wench. You think you can be making out with hot-ass Ramona when I pull up and not spill every detail?" Diego scoffs. "You have some serious explaining to do."

I laugh. "I really missed you, too, Diego."

* * *

The whole car ride home, Diego grills me about Ramona. Then he fills me in on the drag competition. *Apparently* Venus the Flyest Trap tried to sabotage Diego's performance by secretly changing out his music. But Diego embraced it and absolutely demolished Venus anyway, making his win all the more gratifying.

Papi and Karina greet me at the door after I drop Diego off and get home.

"Welcome home, mija," Papi says, enveloping me in a bear hug.

"We missed ya, kid." Karina kisses the top of my head. "I know it's only been a week, but you look older somehow."

I smile at them. "I *feel* older."

"Come, sit. Tell us all about your trip." Papi motions toward the dining room, where freshly baked cookies and three steaming-hot cups of coffee (decaf for Karina, of course) are waiting for us. "I printed out the itinerary so you can go through everything, stop by stop."

His eagerness makes me laugh. We pass around cookies and take sips of our coffee as I fill them in on all the highlights from the trip. I pass out the souvenirs I bought for them, and we coo over the teeny Niagara Falls onesie for the baby. I recall the Intonation concert and meet-and-greet for them in excruciating detail. They pass around my phone to look at photos, gasping at the views of Niagara Falls and the mountains in Colorado, though Papi frowns when he sees a picture from the Rage Cage.

"What's this? Why are you wearing all this stuff?" he asks.

"We went to something called a rage room," I explain. "It was so much fun! You basically pay to break a bunch of things with baseball bats and stuff."

Papi frowns. "You didn't tell me about that. That sounds dangerous!"

"And yet I survived." I hold up my chin triumphantly. "Told you I would be okay on my own."

There is a gleam in his eyes as he nods, taking this in. All at once, he looks both proud and maybe a little sad. He pats my hand gently with his. "Yes. And you were right."

"I'm sure you're tired. Why don't we let you rest for a bit?" Karina suggests. "We actually have a few errands to run anyway."

"We're going to the grocery store. What can we make you for dinner?" Papi doesn't wait for me to answer before continuing. "Actually, we know what you like. We'll make all your favorites."

"That sounds great, Papi. I'm glad I'm home."

Karina squeezes my shoulder. "We're glad you're home too."

I lug my belongings into my room. Everything about it looks the same: the vibrantly colored walls, the succulent in the window, the unfinished art projects on my desk, my Princess Julieta costume rumpled on top of a pile of clothes on my chair, the framed photos of me and Diego; me, Papi, and Karina; me, Ramona, and Sienna when we were kids.

In spite of all the sameness, the feeling is different. Or maybe it's me who's different. I left for this road trip feeling like a girl afraid to exist outside these four walls. I came home a young woman with a deeper understanding of herself, of what she wants in her life. I saw parts of the country I never imagined I'd explore, and I realized the world isn't so scary if you have the right people by your side.

Am I still scared of change? Yeah. But I know now that it can sometimes be okay—and even when it doesn't *feel* okay, I believe that I'm strong enough to weather the hardships change brings my way.

I see now that I can create a life on my own terms, and that there isn't one right way to be or do or exist. It's okay if I keep the past close to my heart, and it's okay to keep doing the things I love. It's also okay if parts of me shift and bloom. If I allow myself to grow in my own way, the future looks way less scary.

I'll always be just fine.

Chapter Forty-Two
JANUARY: RAMONA'S APARTMENT, BOSTON, MA

"*She'll be here any second.* Are you ready yet?" I ask, fluffing my now-blue hair in the mirror and ensuring my highlighter looks okay.

"Okay, okay. I'm ready." Ramona emerges from the bathroom, wearing black jeans, a white sweater, and a leather jacket, with her curls wrapped into two space buns.

I reach for her, pulling on the jacket to bring her close to me. "You look hot, babe."

"I thought so too," she jokes. "This skirt, though." She runs her hands down either side of my waist and kisses my neck. For a moment, it makes me consider forgoing tonight's plans entirely.

The doorbell rings.

"That's her!" I yell, racing to the door.

Sienna hasn't changed a bit in the weeks since we last saw her, except she's traded her long hair for a choppy, shoulder-length wolf cut. "You're here!" I squeal.

"And your hair!" she squeals back, reaching for a strand. "I love the blue on you so much."

"Matches the glasses." I point at my frames. "And I love this short length on you. Do a twirl!"

Sienna spins in a dramatic circle, holding her hands up to frame her face and hair.

"Looks great on you," Ramona says, pulling Sienna in for a hug. She pulls back and her eyes widen. "Did you get a septum piercing?!"

Ramona tilts her chin up to show it off proudly. "Queer rite of passage."

"Doesn't it look amazing on her?" I ask.

"It's perfect," Sienna agrees.

"Can I take your coat?" Ramona offers as she closes the door to her apartment. Sienna hands it over and Ramona adds it to the coatrack by the door. "Let me show you around. We'll be quick." I follow as she leads Sienna around her place, even though I've been here so much over the last couple of weeks, it almost feels part mine. Now that Ramona is officially a licensed tattoo artist, she snagged a spot as a full-time artist at Permanent Record's Boston shop—which is perfect, because I've transferred from RISD to Emerson, right down the road.

It's not all rainbows and sparkles: Boston is wildly expensive, Ramona shares her apartment with three (!) other people, and I am very often homesick for Elmwood. But I feel so hopeful for what's to come, especially now that Papi, Karina, and my baby sister, Elodie, can grab a train out to the city for visits.

"And that's the kitchen," Ramona says. "It's not much, but it works."

"You have your own place. That's huge!" Sienna smiles at her. "Look at you go."

Ramona gives her the stink face. "Don't get all sappy on me now."

"Can I help that I've missed you?" Sienna drapes an arm around my shoulder. "Both of you."

"We've missed you, too. How has Johns Hopkins been?" I ask. "Still going okay?"

She nods. "Actually, yeah. I'm liking it way more than I thought I would, but being out from under my mom's thumb is the real saving grace—which I realized the second I came back for winter break." Sienna rolls her eyes. "They don't tell you how impossible it can feel to taste freedom and then head back home to a mom who's like, 'Can you give me the log-in for your online grading system so I can check on you throughout the semester?'"

I grimace. "Oh, yikes."

"It's whatever. I gave her the wrong password." Sienna grins. "And my therapist is helping me set real, meaningful boundaries."

"That's huge, Sienna," I say. "I'm so proud of you."

Her voice goes soft. "Thank you. That means a lot."

Ramona checks her phone. "Should we get going? This one's been after me all night about how we absolutely cannot be late."

I swat at her forearm playfully. "You're so dramatic."

"You guys sound like an old married couple." Sienna slips back into her coat. "Also, I am so not used to how cold it is up here anymore. Baltimore spoiled me."

"Oh, perfect, I've been waiting for a chance to be one of those annoying New Englanders." I pull my own coat on and clear my throat. "'You don't even know what cold is! I walk around in shorts and a tank top unless it hits negative ten degrees!' How was that?"

Ramona pulls open the door to let me and Sienna step out. "Surprisingly obnoxious. Good job, babe."

"I've been practicing being obnoxious my whole life," I say. "It's a Masshole specialty."

We walk down the slushy streets of Boston, wet from a recent January snowfall that's already starting to melt because #climatechange. I lead the way.

"Are you going to tell us where we're going?" Ramona asks.

"And how much farther?" Sienna adds. "Remember. I'm a Baltimore girlie now."

"Not much." I take quicker strides until I see the sign I've been looking for. "There!"

A bright neon sign that reads THE STRAWBERRY JAM glows in the distance.

"The Strawberry Jam," Sienna reads. "Are you taking us out for toast?"

"As much as I love toast, I'd like to think this is even better." I turn around and waggle my eyebrows dramatically. "You guys ready for a Deadly Flora reunion?"

"Wait, is this that karaoke bar you mentioned?" Ramona asks.

"Sure is! And I've been practicing," I say.

"How did karaoke never make it on the original BFF Bucket List?" Sienna asks.

Ramona nods. "What a missed opportunity."

I grin at them. "Don't worry. I added it to the new one for our road trip this summer."

Sienna shimmies her shoulders. "Ooh, new list! Exciting!"

Ramona pokes me in the side. "What else is on this new list you've told me nothing about?"

I kiss her. "Guess you'll have to wait and see. Now, come on. Deadly Flora reunion in five minutes!"

"Fine, but I'm not dancing," Ramona says with a huff.

"We'll see about that, twinkletoes," Sienna teases. "Because Chloe and I voted and you lost."

I laugh, sure that the joy I'm feeling is radiating off me.

If I can share even a fraction of the sunshine I feel inside my chest when I'm with my two friends, the world may never have a cloudy day again.

Acknowledgments

When I was in middle school, I discovered boy band fanfiction through an AOL chat room. There, I met a group of girls who loved the Backstreet Boys as much as I did and, together, we wrote and shared stories through emails called zines. We built a community together, writing and chatting and giggling and obsessing, and I loved it. I felt like I belonged. I made wonderful friends (some of whom I am still friends with today) who taught me the importance of being myself and loving what I loved unapologetically. This book is for them and for anyone who has ever loved anything with their whole heart.

Get Real, Chloe Torres could not have been possible without an incredible community of people, and I'm so appreciative for all their support.

I am grateful for the wonderful team at Holiday House, who have always welcomed me with open arms: Mora Couch; Sara DiSalvo; Terry Borzumato-Greenberg; Michelle Montague; Mary Joyce Perry; Mary Cash; Alison Tarnofsky; Melissa See; Alex Aceves; Derek Stordahl; Miriam Miller; Erin Mathis; Elyse Vincenty; Kayla Phillips; and all of the talented folks who made this book a book!

Thank you, always, to my brilliant agent, Tamar Rydzinski. Your support from day one has meant the world, and I am so happy we get to work together. Thank you to the lovely Monica Rodriguez for the most creative and fun marketing brainstorming calls.

Thank you to illustrator and artist Saniyyah Zahid (@peach.pod) for perfectly capturing Chloe, Ramona, and Sienna and sharing your talents to create this gorgeous cover, and thank you Chelsea Hunter, who handled the brilliant jacket design.

Thank you to Jason June, Christen Randall, and Racquel Marie for generously lending their time to read this book and provide lovely, clever, and thoughtful blurbs that made me smile from ear to ear.

To the students who take the time to read my stories when they could be doing anything else, thank you. You keep me writing, and hearing from you is my greatest joy!

Thank you to all of the incredible, kind, thoughtful, and creative Bookstagrammers, BookTokers, booksellers, readers, librarians, and educators who make space for my stories. Your endless love is beyond appreciated, and I feel so lucky.

To my amazing family and friends, I love you so much. Special thank you to Writers Row, the Nasties, Barbie Parts, and my lovely community of author friends.

Thank you to Obi for being the greatest little snuggler for nearly thirteen years. We miss you every day, sweet boy. I hope you are resting well.

Thank you to my sweet girl, Maya, for making every day so much fun. You are the smartest cookie and I love you 100 hearts.

Lastly, and most importantly, thank you, Bubby. You have always been my strongest supporter, and it's because of you I have been brave enough to chase my dreams and do hard things. Every love story I write is inspired by our own, yet still doesn't compare to the real thing. I love you.